A NIGHT TO REMEMBER

At first Thunder thought he was dreaming. He shook his head. No. He wasn't dreaming . . . the little fool was still there.

He'd been lounging in the cool water when he'd first glimpsed Brandy. She'd stopped in the small alcove, then reached up, and slipped the straps from her shoulders. Her gown slid slowly to the ground and puddled around her feet. He probably should have made his presence known but something stopped him.

He watched as she waded into the water, her body bathed in moonlight, her glorious, long hair resting on her breasts. He hadn't realized he'd been holding his breath until she dove into the water.

That's when his anger mixed with his desire. Damn fool. It was dangerous to wander away from the wagons alone. And more so when you were completely naked. There could have been other Indians out here besides himself.

When she surfaced and floated on her back all his eyes saw were creamy white breasts and hard nipples extending above the water line.

That's when all his sanity left him.

Brandy had just pushed him too far. This time she was going to have to deal with him.

BOOK YOUR PLACE ON OUR WEBSITE AND MAKE THE READING CONNECTION!

We've created a customized website just for our very special readers, where you can get the inside scoop on everything that's going on with Zebra, Pinnacle and Kensington books.

When you come online, you'll have the exciting opportunity to:

- View covers of upcoming books

- Read sample chapters

- Learn about our future publishing schedule (listed by publication month *and author*)

- Find out when your favorite authors will be visiting a city near you

- Search for and order backlist books from our online catalog

- Check out author bios and background information

- Send e-mail to your favorite authors

- Meet the Kensington staff online

- Join us in weekly chats with authors, readers and other guests

- Get writing guidelines

- AND MUCH MORE!

**Visit our website at
http://www.kensingtonbooks.com**

DANCE
ON THE
WIND

Brenda K. Jernigan

ZEBRA BOOKS
Kensington Publishing Corp.
http://www.kensingtonbooks.com

This book is dedicated to
my son, Scott Alex,
who has always brought joy to my life. If a mother
could have a perfect son, I was blessed with such
a child. I couldn't be prouder of the man you have
become. You dared to dream—and look how
successful you have become!
Now Mom will have to follow in your footsteps.
I love you.

and in memory of
my mother, Bonnie Dittman, who died much too
young of breast cancer. A portion of all the
proceeds from this book will be donated to
HOSPICE, so they can help those who
can't help themselves.

also in memory of
F. Derek Wood, my favorite
Englishman,
with whom I had the privilege to work for years.
I wish you were still here to answer all my
questions about England.

Special Thanks

To my critique partners: Bonnie Gardner, Cindy Procter-King, Kathy Williams, and Diane Tobin. You are always there to correct me and provide good feedback.

I especially want to thank Bonnie, who found out she had breast cancer this past Christmas. She went through surgery and when she had to start taking chemo, she faced it with courage and determination. When she started losing her hair there were no tears—she simply shaved her head. And all through this, she was editing my manuscript.

I am proud of you, Bonnie!

By the time this book is released, Bonnie will be cancer-free. She won her battle.

PROLOGUE

Visions of death.

Father Brown shook his head. He couldn't get the dream out of his head. Sometimes death was the end . . . it could also mean a beginning . . . so just what meaning did his dream hold?

Once again, a loud knock echoed in the hallway of Saint Charles Parsonage, bringing his thoughts back to reality.

"Patience, my child, patience," Father Brown mumbled, more or less to himself, because whoever was knocking couldn't possibly hear him through the eight-inch thick oak doors. The ten-foot doors had provided good protection for those who resided within. If his visitor had not rung the bell first, he might not have heard the knock at all.

Just as he reached the front, the knocking stopped.

Had he been mistaken? He frowned, knowing that was impossible, but he opened the peephole anyway to see who stood on the other side.

"Who's there?" he shouted. Receiving no response, he rose on tiptoes and looked as far as the small hole would allow. Strange—he couldn't see anyone. Perhaps his visitor had grown impatient and left. He shook his head and started to shut the peephole, when he heard a faint cry. Or was it merely the whisper of the wind?

"Mama," a child's voice wailed.

Father Brown's bushy, gray brows drew together in a frown. He could have sworn there was no one there. Unlocking one side of the double, wooden doors, he listened as it creaked and groaned much like his old bones. A small child stood on the porch, clutching a tattered, dirty blanket. She raised huge violet eyes as she sniffed and wiped her tear-streaked cheeks. Her face was framed with the rarest, chestnut-colored hair that hung to her waist. One small hand rested on a huge wooden trunk at her side.

He lowered himself to one knee and hauled a handkerchief out of his vestments to wipe her face. He smiled, hoping to gain her confidence.

Shyly, she studied him with haunting eyes. At that very moment, he lost his heart to the child. She could be no more than five years old and she was all alone. Even for one so young, she possessed uncommon beauty like none he'd ever seen before. She appeared lost and forlorn. He wanted to scoop her up in his arms and comfort her.

"Why do you cry, my child?"

"Because I'm frightened," she responded in a quiet voice.

"Where is your mother?"

"She's gone." The child answered as her gaze shifted to her feet.

"Why didn't she take you with her?"

"Mother said I couldn't go because it wouldn't be safe. She told me to stay here with you until she comes back for me. W-will you keep me safe, Father?"

He smiled at the child in front of him. "Yes, God

and I will protect you, my child. But protect you from what?"

She shrugged her tiny shoulders. "From the men who killed my father."

"Killed your father!" Father Brown jerked back, astonished at how matter-of-fact she seemed about her father's death. The child had to be in shock.

"Did you see it happen?"

New tears sprang to her violet eyes. She bobbed her head and lowered the blanket she'd clutched to her chest. For the first time he noticed that splattered blood streaked her once-beautiful silk dress.

"Oh, my Lord!" What had this youngster been through? What had she witnessed? Unable to help himself, he gathered her in his arms and hugged her to him. Had this been the death that he'd glimpsed in his dream? "Everything will be fine now," he said in what he hoped was a soothing voice. "Come inside, my child." He patted her tiny back and gave her a push through the door before dragging in the heavy chest that had been left on the stoop. Turning, he closed the great wooden doors and barred them.

"Let's get you cleaned up." He took her hand and led her across the courtyard. "What's your name?"

"Brandy."

"What is your last name, Brandy?"

"I don't know, Father. I've always been called Brandy."

"That's an odd name, child."

"Mother said it was because my hair was the color of fine brandy. She said no one else has hair like mine."

"Your mother was right."

At that very moment, Father Brown made a silent

vow that no harm would ever come to this child as long as he kept her behind the parsonage doors.

She was truly a blessing.

And he knew that his dream had told of a new beginning for Brandy.

ONE

It was over.

Father Brown was dead.

Brandy stood at the gravesite and centered her attention on the children now in her charge. Father Brown had never intended to run an orphanage, but somehow the stray children just seemed to find him.

He had made Brandy promise to take care of them after his death, but how she would manage, she didn't know.

She found it easier to concentrate on the children rather than the words Marshal Pete was speaking.

This day, another in a month-long string of hot, humid days, brought a thin line of moisture to her brow and caused the dark dress to cling to her chest. How she longed to wear something lighter in color, maybe something open and airy, so it wouldn't be so hot.

The only relief from the heat came from the spreading arms of the shady live oak tree, which they had picked for Father Brown's final resting place. She glanced up at the green leaves and thought about how sturdy the tree appeared—much like Father Brown.

He'd been her pillar of strength over the years, and now he'd left her—as had everyone else in her life.

Soon the marshal's words became a hum in her ears as he droned on with the service.

Tears gathered in Brandy's eyes at the mention of Father Brown's name. She forced her attention back on the children—anything to keep from weeping. She had to be strong, so she concentrated on the children and tried to block out the hurt, but the pain in her chest threatened to suffocate her.

Billy West, the oldest of the children, stood across from her. At fourteen, his stance was defiant, rebellion showing in his chocolate-brown eyes. He held his hat in front of him, his head slightly bowed. However, aside from that gesture of respect, he seemed unaffected by the proceedings. His shoulder-length brown hair was curly and matched his eyes perfectly. Father Brown had taken Billy in when the men he lived with were in a gunfight and fled town, one step ahead of the law, leaving Billy behind.

He'd been a lackey for the gunslingers, running errands, cooking, and cleaning their guns. But when the men had been liquored up and in need of money, Billy had to take to the streets to beg for them. The townsfolk whispered that he'd been beaten from time to time.

Brandy could remember when Father Brown first brought Billy home. He'd had a black eye and a split lip, and he was much too thin. She had felt sorry for him, and tried to help clean him up, but he didn't want her pity, and for the next six months he had been a holy terror, striking out at anyone who tried to be good to him. Her pity soon faded, leaving in its wake a strong dislike. She had even asked Father Brown if they could send Billy away. Of course, Father had frowned and told her he would forget she'd said such a thing, and he'd pray God would forgive her, too. It was the same way that their conversations usually ended when they spoke of the children. She saw them as brats, whereas Father Brown had seen them as a challenge.

So she hadn't been very nice, but it had been how she'd felt at the time. Now, she and Billy tolerated each other, neither giving an inch. True, he had mellowed a little since then, except the pranks he liked to play. She never found them very funny, especially the time she found a snake in her bed. Yes, Billy would be a handful. She groaned inwardly and looked toward heaven; she would definitely need help.

Brandy glanced at the girls. Mary Costner, thirteen, and Ellen White, eleven, had come to the parsonage at the same time.

Mary's mother had run a house of ill repute, and Mary was the direct result of one of her mother's good times. Mary hadn't had life easy, growing up in a brothel, and had spent most of her time staying out of everyone's way. She had been rescued by some of the good ladies of Kansas City when they'd suspected Mary's mother was getting ready to put her daughter into the business. At the young age of ten, she'd arrived at Father Brown's.

Mary was pretty with long, blond hair curling in ringlets about her shoulders. Her eyes were as blue as the sky, but her rebellious nature was worse than any of the rest of the children. Last year, Mary had taken a pair of scissors and cut up Brandy's favorite dress. Brandy had prayed for patience, and she'd been rewarded.

Father Brown had pointed out that Mary's disregard was her way of protecting herself and that Brandy should remember how it was not to have any parents.

Indians had killed Ellen's parents. She had escaped by hiding in the cellar. She wasn't as pretty as Mary, but she was attractive. Her brown hair just touched her shoulders, but her lackluster hazel eyes always seemed sad.

Though she and Mary were friends, Ellen didn't possess the same evil disposition. Instead, she had a sweet nature and always strived to do anything she could to please. She was so fond of children that she had taken charge of Amy, the baby, as soon as she'd arrived, which had been a big help because a three-year-old could be very active. So maybe Ellen wasn't a brat, Brandy decided, but the girl usually sided with Mary and Billy.

Then there was Scott, the seven-year-old. He had been energetic from the start. Of all the children, Brandy liked him best. He had black hair cut in a bob and his brownish-green eyes bubbled with personality. The child must have been born talking, because he talked constantly. Even now, he whispered to Ellen and Brandy glanced at him to make him hush. She was surprised he'd been quiet as long as he had during the service.

Brandy dreaded the next few months until the new priest arrived. She had no idea how she was going to handle this unusual family. A few rules would have to be set down, that much she was sure of. Perhaps she should send a note to the bishop and ask him to please hurry.

"Ashes to ashes . . . dust to dust," the marshal said

as he motioned for Brandy to come over and throw the first handful of dirt into the grave.

She couldn't do this.

She just couldn't!

Her steps faltered. Her vision blurred.

Grief filled Brandy, choking off her breath as she reluctantly approached the gaping black hole in the ground.

The finality of death slammed into her, gripping her heart with a deadly fist. Everything was much too quiet. Even the wind had stilled. She stooped and gathered a handful of gray Missouri dirt.

Staring down at the rough wooden casket, she knew it was finally time to say goodbye. Brandy inhaled deeply, then held her breath and bit her lip so she wouldn't sob. But doing so didn't prevent the tears from trickling down her cheeks. No longer could she hold them back. Today, she had lost her very best friend. "I love you, Father," she whispered as the grains of dirt slipped through her fingers.

Suddenly, the branches of the tree above them began to creak, rustling the leaves overhead. The slight breeze caressed her face as if a gentle hand had reached out and touched her cheek. Somehow, she felt Father Brown's spirit all around her while she watched the dry dirt scatter in the wind. Then she heard his words:

Always remember . . . even though you'll not see my body anymore . . . I will be with each and every one of you in spirit. Every step you take, I will take with you. When you fall down, I'll be there to pick you up.

Turning to the children, she motioned for them to come forward and throw a handful of soil in the hole.

Many of the nearby townspeople had turned out to say their final farewells. Brandy had seen all of these people at one time or another when they'd come to the parsonage, but she didn't really know any of them. The baby started to whimper, rubbing her eyes with a tiny fist. Brandy took her from Ellen, and Amy gave up her sleepy fight once Brandy had her.

All the children formed a straight line while they shook the many hands shoved toward them.

Finally everyone was gone. Brandy moved back to the gravesite one last time before they went home. Amy had fallen asleep on her shoulder, and Brandy had to switch her to the other arm to ease the weight. "Goodbye, Father," she whispered, then added, "Promises are sometimes hard to keep, but I'll try."

Before turning to leave, she glanced up at a nearby hill. There, seated on a large horse, sat a powerfully built man. Animal and rider stood perfectly still while long, black hair blew around his square jaw. Brandy couldn't make out the rest of his features but something about the man impressed her.

Fascinated, she stared boldly at the stranger. Who was he? And why did he stay in the background instead of coming closer?

"Come on, Brandy," Mary called.

Though Brandy would rather have looked at the stranger just a little longer, she knew it was time to leave.

Before stepping up onto the buckboard, she turned and looked back toward the hill, but the stranger had disappeared. It was as if he'd vanished into thin air.

A wave of disappointment washed over her. She didn't understand this odd reaction to someone she didn't know and would probably never meet.

But for just a moment, she'd felt an odd excitement as if she were dancing on the wind.

Brandy smiled for the first time in days.

TWO

The jingle of harnesses and the creaking of wagons drew Thunder's attention. He mounted his Appaloosa and rode to the top of the hill to see what was happening. There, gathered below him, twenty to thirty people dressed in black stood around a grave. He started to leave and give them their privacy, but a young woman holding a small child caught his attention.

Something about her intrigued him as he watched the sun reflect off her chestnut hair. She stood proud, like a warrior. Yet, he sensed a sadness from her bent head. A breeze blew a wisp of hair around her face.

Many gathered around her, yet she appeared very much alone and spoke only when spoken to. He watched as she left the crowd to return to the grave. Her sorrow touched his heart, and for some inexplicable reason he longed to comfort her.

Quickly, he shook the crazy notion from his head. Had not the beautiful Elaina taught him that he wasn't good enough for a white woman?

Unfortunately, his head told him one thing and his heart another as his gaze lingered on the woman below. Finally, she looked in his direction. Her gaze locked with his, and he again felt an unexplainable pull . . . more like an unspoken destiny.

He'd probably never know who she'd just buried, though he assumed it was a husband since she held a child in her arms. All his instincts told him their paths would one day cross again, but this time he hoped he was wrong.

Thunder was heading away from the white man's world, and he wanted no part of any other white woman . . . They were trouble.

He wheeled his stallion away and returned to his camp.

Later that night, Thunder stretched out his long legs and crossed them at the ankles as he rested against his saddle flung under a tree. He had ridden hard trying to put distance between himself and the world he'd lived in for the past few years. Seeing land that started to look like home brought him some comfort, and he decided tomorrow would be soon enough to venture into Independence. He shut his eyes and reflected over the last few years. A small smile touched his lips as he recalled the horror on his grandmother's face when he'd first arrived in Boston. . . .

Thunder had been only twenty when he'd arrived in buckskins, stood on his grandparents' doorstep, and proudly announced that he was the grandson they knew nothing about. His grandmother's reaction had been immediate—she'd fainted dead away. Thunder's grandfather had taken control of the situation, motioning for Thunder to help carry her to the couch.

Ross Bradley waved smelling salts under Judith Bradley's nose, all the while assuring his wife she wouldn't be scalped, though he still looked at Thunder doubtfully.

Evidently his grandmother wasn't thrilled to have a grandson, Thunder thought. "It was my mother's wish that I be educated as a white man, so that I might learn about both worlds," Thunder told them as they stared at him.

"Then Helen is alive?" Ross Bradley asked.

"H-Helen?" Thunder said the strange name. "My mother is well," he assured him with a nod. "She sends her love and this." Thunder reached into the waistband of his buckskins and produced a letter his mother had written and handed it to his grandfather.

Ross Bradley cleared his throat before speaking. "Son, you must realize what a shock this is. We thought our Helen was dead. We were told she'd been killed by the Cheyenne, not taken captive." Ross rose and stumbled over to the liquor table where he poured himself a drink, took a generous swallow, then turned back to Thunder. "Do you have any idea what it's like to have this kind of news sprung upon us? To learn that Helen is alive, well, and a part of the people we've come to hate?"

Thunder frowned. "I understand how you feel. But should you condemn my people when you know nothing about them?"

"We thought they'd killed our daughter," Ross reminded him. Ross saw defiance in the young man— and also something of Helen. "I will wager you were not happy about making this trip or learning from my people," Ross said, his eyebrows drawn together.

Surprise registered in Thunder's eyes. "You speak with wisdom, Grandfather."

Finally, the coldness began to slip from Thunder as he began telling his grandparents about his mother and what had happened to her over the years.

Though his grandparents had not been happy to see

him at first, they changed as the weeks grew into months.

Thunder had spent the next four years in the best schools, absorbing the culture of Boston, so vastly different from his own. Gone were the open plains, replaced by tall buildings and many houses. How these people could bear the confinement was something he'd never fully understand.

No longer did he look the savage. He was known as Thomas Bradley. He wore the white man's clothes, ate their food, and learned their ways. He studied to become a lawyer. And he soon learned to love his new grandparents, something he never dreamed would have happened.

Expecting to hate everything about his white ancestors, Thunder found he'd been wrong. Yet, he never felt that he belonged.

The memories of his youth seemed so long ago—as far away as Boston, Thunder thought as he opened his eyes to see the sun had started to set. He stood and stretched his legs.

After he gathered wood, he built a fire to cook his evening meal. How long had it been since he'd had time to sit and think? Breathing in the fresh air, he marveled at the stars that had begun to pop out like tiny specks across the charcoal-gray sky. Where had they been while he lived with his grandparents?

If felt good to be going home. Returning to his people. Back to the beautiful land that knew no buildings and back to the buffalo, deer, and elk, which ran wild and provided the food he would need. He longed to hear a babbling brook in the early morning and smell the crispness of the mountain air. All the things he'd missed while being away.

He settled down beside the fire. Using a sharp stick, he skewered the rabbit he'd killed earlier and placed the meat over the flames to cook.

Watching the fire, his mind swept back over the years, to the white man's war. . . .

The War Between the States had changed the once-peaceful community of Boston, and Thunder had become a Union Soldier.

He had been no stranger to battles, but this war had been different. There never seemed to be an end to the skirmishes. Even the killing had been different. It wasn't done with bows and arrows, but with guns and cannons that ripped arms and legs from good pony soldiers. The cannons crippled men in seconds, leaving them mangled if they survived at all.

During his assignment to the 19th Massachusetts under the command of Colonel Devereaux, Thunder had relied on his Indian training to save his hide more than once.

The Battle of Gettysburg had been the confrontation which had turned his stomach. He would have felt differently if he'd been fighting for his family or his home, but this *wasn't* his war. He didn't care who won. When he'd been left for dead and no one had bothered to come back for him, Thunder had managed to bind his own wound, and he'd not returned to the battle. The Union army had already deserted him.

Gettysburg still haunted his dreams. The Northern and Southern soldiers collided, and man against man, they struggled until no one could move for the mass of wounded and dead men beneath their feet. Mutilated bodies, black with powder and red with blood, stretched as far as the eye could see.

It seemed like yesterday.

Thunder shuddered.

He blinked several times and finally took a sip of hot coffee. The memories produced the same cold sweat that drenched his body every time his mind drifted back to that time.

Thunder had learned his lessons, and he'd learned them well. No longer was he the naive brave who had left home. He'd become bitter and withdrawn.

He wasn't sure who he was anymore. Red man? White man? Brave? Soldier?

Perhaps, he didn't belong anywhere. But maybe, when he returned home, he'd find the peace he sought.

Why did she have to get up this morning?

Facing five children who expected her to be the adult in charge wasn't much of a reason. Brandy groaned. Her languid limbs protested any movement, and all she really wanted to do was linger behind the closed door, shutting out the rest of the world and avoiding the decisions that would have to be made.

Before today, all the decisions had been made by Father Brown. Brandy's responsibility had been to instruct the children with their lessons and do her few chores.

When she had come to the parsonage, Father Brown had never intended to take in children, and he hadn't for a long time, he told her. He had a full staff back then, so he had Brandy concentrate on her studies so that she could be a teacher one day. She could remember how proud he was that she took to learning so quickly. Then the staff seemed to dwindle as the children increased.

Now it seemed as if the whole world rested on her

slender shoulders, and she had a good case of feeling sorry for herself. A stab of guilt lay buried in her breast, which she tried hard to ignore. But the truth was she was scared.

She tossed and turned, trying to go back to sleep and forget all her new obligations, but they wouldn't let her rest. With another anguished sigh, she rolled out of bed and began to prepare for the day.

Looking through her simple wardrobe, she chose a plain black dress to continue her mourning. She didn't have beautiful clothes like some of the women she'd seen in town, and the ones she did have were plain. Her brightest dress, one of forest green, had been given to her by one of the ladies from town.

Clothes were not a big concern as long as they lived behind the tall brown walls. Father Brown had always told them that God would provide what they needed.

After brushing her hair, she swept the sides up with combs and looked at the results in the mirror with a frown. She definitely was plain. Pinching her cheeks, she smiled at the color they turned. Why couldn't she have been pretty like the other girls she saw in town from time to time?

She was fair, too tall, and her hair was straight and extremely unmanageable, which was the reason she kept it pulled back with combs. "I give up," she told her reflection and turned away, disgusted with herself. It was a good thing she didn't want to get married because no man would want her.

Funny, her plans had never gone any further than teaching children and helping Father Brown. What could she do now? She stared out the window at the large live oak. Could she stay on and help the new priest? But what if he thought she was too old to stay at the orphanage? What would she do then?

She had the eerie feeling that nothing would be the same from now on.

Now, for the next problem, she thought as she turned from the window. Or, should she say, the next four problems? They were probably eating breakfast. The one bright thing left in their life was Rosa, the cook who made every meal a treat.

Brandy's stomach rumbled. Speaking of breakfast, she was starved.

The parsonage was a sprawling complex. The courtyard had a fountain in the middle, and out behind the cookhouse was a small yard where they kept a cow and a few chickens. A large water oak spread its branches and provided shady relief from the hot noonday sun.

Crossing the courtyard to the back of the compound, Brandy could already smell the heavenly aroma of bacon. Her stomach rumbled again, and she realized she'd eaten very little this past week. Most of her time had been spent caring for Father Brown.

"Something smells wonderful," Brandy announced as she entered through the door.

"It's hotcakes," Scott said, his mouth full.

Brandy glanced around. "Where is Rosa?"

"She went outside for a few minutes."

Stacking her plate with several flapjacks and strips of bacon, Brandy poured thick syrup over them, then carried her plate to the table where the children sat. She took her seat at the end and, without hesitation, cut into the hotcakes, savoring the first succulent bite.

After she'd satisfied her hunger, she placed the fork down on the plate and looked around her. Brandy noticed how each child's head was bent, eyes downcast. They looked at their plates and completely ignored her as they ate. "Good morning, children," she said firmly.

"What's so good about it?" Billy answered gruffly, shoving his plate away from him.

"I see we're our usual charming self this morning," Brandy answered, undaunted by his rudeness.

"How would you like it if you were left all alone?" Mary grumbled. Apparently, she decided she hadn't said enough and pointed her finger at Brandy. "And only had someone like *you* in charge?"

Brandy breathed deeply to remain calm. She wouldn't let the children rile her this morning. After all, she had to show how responsible she could be. She had to set an example. She frowned at the thought.

Lord, she was beginning to sound like Father Brown already. She could hear him now. *Always remain calm, my child, and you can work out any situation. Remember, patience is a virtue.*

"Well, Mary, I was left alone . . . and with *me* in charge . . . and I can tell you that I don't like this situation any better than you do," Brandy answered quickly, then leaned forward and looked at Mary. Waving her fork in Mary's direction, Brandy said, "But it sure is better than sleeping in the streets which, I'd like to point out, is where we'd all be if not for Father Brown."

Rosa chose that moment to enter the kitchen, removing her white apron as she walked across the room. "I'll be leaving this afternoon, *señorita*," she said stiffly, her voice empty of its usual warmth.

Brandy took her last bite of hotcakes and laid her

fork down on her plate. "We'll see you in the morning,
then," she said.

"No, *señorita.*" Rosa shook her head. "I'll be leaving and not coming back."

Brandy didn't understand. "Where are you going?"

Rosa hung her apron up beside the door before turning back to Brandy. "I'm afraid that I have taken another job," she replied in a quiet voice. Something flickered far back in her eyes as she glanced from one child to the next.

Brandy gasped. The blood drained from her face. Rosa couldn't desert them. She'd always done the cooking. "You can't leave us . . . you have always worked here!" Brandy wailed, clutching the edge of the table with a deathgrip.

"You are one of us."

Shutting her eyes for a moment, Brandy prayed. *Father, I need some strength here.*

Rosa had tears in her eyes as she cupped Scott's face and pressed him to her motherly breast. "I will miss all of you, but I have a family of my own to think of. Yes, I have helped Father Brown for as long as I can remember, but my family cannot eat promises."

"I don't understand," Brandy whispered, desperation growing at an alarming rate. She wrung her hands under the table as she tried to remain in control.

Rosa let out a long, tired breath. "Father Brown has not paid me for the last three months. He always told me the money was coming, but it never did. I cannot wait any longer. My family must eat."

"I'll get your wages, Rosa," Brandy said, her voice revealing none of the panic she felt. "Surely there is some money in Father Brown's office."

"I do not think so, Brandy. If there had been, Father would have paid me. Besides, I have already taken another job." Rosa took Brandy's hand. "I am so sorry."

"But who will do the cooking?" Ellen asked in a horrified voice.

Rosa moved toward the door. "You and Brandy will do just fine," she said as she opened the door.

"But I can't cook!" Brandy all but shouted as she lost her composure.

"Then I suggest you learn." Rosa's last words lingered in the air as she shut the door, leaving an open-mouthed Brandy staring after her with horror crawling through her.

My God, they would all starve!

THREE

Dumbfounded, Brandy could do nothing but stare at the closed door. It seemed like forever before she managed to shut her mouth and sink slowly onto the hard wooden chair.

How was she going to handle this new problem?

She didn't have the slightest idea.

In the background the children complained about starving to death and demanded to know what Brandy planned to do about their present situation.

Before she could answer them, Mary reached over and slapped Scott for turning over his milk. In turn, Scott started to scream, and Ellen complained that Mary shouldn't have hit Scott.

"Be quiet," Brandy roared. She stood so fast that the chair scraped across the floor and fell over backwards. Immediate silence ensued as her chin lifted, and her gaze shot sparks at the ragtag family sitting in front of her.

"You might not like this situation any more than I do, but we have to stick together. All this sniveling and fighting will accomplish nothing." She tempered her anger and tried to remain calm. "Everyone will have to learn to take on a few more responsibilities around here. And that begins today!" Again she realized she sounded like Father Brown. She would have laughed if she didn't have four pairs of eyes watching her, wondering what she would do next.

If only she knew!

"Until the new bishop gets here, we will have to do the best we can to keep things in order. Mary and Ellen, you are now responsible for cleaning up the kitchen and washing the dishes."

"Why do we have to do it?" Mary complained.

"Because dishes don't get done by themselves!"

"What about the boys?" Ellen asked.

"They will have to tend the garden, milk the cow, and make repairs around here."

"And just what are you going to do?" Mary challenged before turning to the other children. "I'm not about to take orders from Miss High-and-Mighty while she does nothing. It's not fair."

Brandy felt Mary's resentment now as she always had. According to Mary, Brandy had been Father Brown's favorite, and he had always jumped to do whatever she wanted. Mary's jealousy had never let her see that Brandy had been with Father Brown years before the others had arrived. Mary didn't understand that they'd had only each other until the children arrived.

Brandy sighed. How many times had she'd heard that "it's-not-fair" speech? She stared at Mary's belligerent smirk. How Brandy would like to slap it off the girl's face! Instead, she counted to ten and took a deep breath.

Brandy heard Father's Brown voice.

Blessed are the patient, for they shall endure.

She would really like to give Miss Mary a piece of her mind, but she was trying to avoid further arguments and establish some kind of control over the brat. She stopped herself from the uncharitable thought.

"I'm going to Father Brown's study and look over his ledgers and see how much money we have to live on. If we're lucky, we might be able to purchase supplies when we need them. And seeing as the rest of you don't read that well, there would be little you could do there."

"I still don't see why I have to do the dishes." Mary stood up and folded her arms.

"Because I am now in charge, and I'm making the rules! If you don't do the dishes, you don't eat. It's just that simple!" Brandy fixed her unwavering gaze on Mary. "Perhaps you would like to turn the compost heap instead," Brandy suggested sweetly. Mary did not accept the alternate assignment, but her lower lip was still stuck out.

Billy rose, too. "I don't take kindly to being bossed around, either. But in this case, Brandy is right. We have to take care of ourselves."

"At least, until the new bishop comes," Ellen said timidly.

Brandy could have hugged them, but before she could do so, Scott interrupted. "Who's going to cook?" he wailed, worried about his stomach. He'd always been particularly fond of food.

"I am," Brandy replied as she turned to Scott, wondering how she'd ever pull off the job. She'd never cooked a day in her life, but she had watched Rosa at work. Maybe she'd learned something.

Scott curled his lip, making a terrible face. His stricken expression indicated that he figured he'd surely starve now. Brandy hated to tell the child he might be right.

She walked over to the door and then turned. "We are all in this together, like it or not. And you had best pray that I find some money."

The murmur of grumbling followed Brandy out the door, but at least the children seemed to be doing as she asked.

This time.

One battle down and how many more to go? She shook her head as she left the kitchen and hurried to the parsonage office.

Pushing open the study door, Brandy glanced about the room. It appeared as if Father Brown had merely stepped out for a few minutes and would be back shortly. His old brown desk was still cluttered with papers. His chair was pushed back and his glasses rested in the middle of a letter he'd been writing. She sat down behind the big, mahogany desk. Carefully, she moved his spectacles to the corner of the desk before picking up the letter.

Dear Mr. Jackson,
   It's possible that I have information on your granddaughter. Could you please give me a description of the child

The letter had never been finished. She looked around the blotter on the desktop, but there wasn't an address or a letter that he seemed to be answering. Now she wondered if Father Brown could have been talking about one of the girls or maybe herself. Brandy thought for a moment. It had to be one of the other girls. It had been much too long for anyone to be looking for her.

Not having any answers, she returned to her original

task. She marveled at the papers scattered over the desktop . . . there were so many!

Uncertain where to start, she decided to place everything into two piles: one for general correspondence and the other for bills. Half an hour later, she'd made progress, but the stack for bills was twice as high as the correspondence.

Things didn't look good. Why were there so many bills? What was she going to do?

She started at the beginning, reading each statement. It appeared the parsonage owed everybody in town. When had the situation become so bad? And why hadn't Father Brown told her how desperate their circumstances were? Maybe this is the reason the staff had started to thin out.

On the right-hand corner of the desk lay a faded green ledger, which she grasped and pulled to her, sending pieces of paper flying off the desk. She opened the heavy cover and started to scan the contents.

There hadn't been any entries for incoming money for the past two months. Of course, Father had been ill. Brandy rubbed her temples as she felt a headache coming on. She thought that they received money every month from the bishop . . . So, where had the money gone? And was this the reason he hadn't let her help with the ledgers over the last several months?

Still puzzled, Brandy reached for the mail. On the bottom of the stack was an official-looking document from the bishop. Good. Maybe this letter would tell them when the money they normally received to run the parsonage would arrive.

Brandy read the letter not once but twice before shaking her head at the dire circumstances described before her in black and white. Void of all emotion, she stared blindly at the wall as she realized the significance of the letter.

There it was, in dark, bold script. They wouldn't be getting a new priest.

There would be no money!

Father Brown had been instructed to find homes for the children. The bishop had decided the church should be closed.

As she eased back in the chair, tears welled in her eyes and cold fear spread over her. She wanted someone to wake her from this nightmare.

Now what? Brandy wondered. How could Father Brown have died and left her with all these problems?

"He's always taken care of everything," she said aloud. If she hadn't made that promise, she would only have herself to worry about, and that was bad enough.

But now she had five more problems . . . five *big* problems.

One way or the other, she would have to find money to support the children. If the people of the community had wanted them, they'd have taken the children already. So she had to find some money. But where?

Without warning, the door opened and Billy materialized in the doorway. "So you're sittin' here doin' nothin' while the rest of us are workin' our butts off."

Brandy glanced at him and, in a strangled voice, said, "Shut the door, Billy, and sit down. We have a problem." She sighed. "We've got a *big* problem."

Billy closed the door, but refused to sit. Instead, he leaned against the wall, his arms folded across his chest, and looked at her like the man he'd someday become. There was a suspicious line at the corner of his mouth.

For the next ten minutes, she explained their present situation, leaving nothing out. She watched Billy's scowl grow deeper, and a look of despair began to spread over his face. Finally, she'd laid it all out for him.

"So what are you going to do?" Billy asked.

"What do you mean?" Her voice rose in surprise. "What am *I* going to do?" Exasperation gathered in her chest, and it was all she could do to keep from screaming. "There is only one thing to do. You and I will start looking for jobs as soon as possible."

Billy snorted. "What can you do?" he challenged her. "At least I can muck out stalls. Your lily-white hands have never done a day's work."

Her blood pounded as her face grew hot. What Billy said was true, but it still stung. "I don't know," she answered in earnest, "but surely there must be something. We'll start looking tomorrow."

Billy pushed away from the wall and reached for the door. "Reckon we'll have to do somethin' or starve." He yanked the door open and stepped outside. "So far, you ain't doin' too good a job as our leader," he called over his shoulder. Glancing back, he ducked, barely missing the book Brandy hurled at him.

Brandy remained in the chair, thinking about her lack of skills. Thankfully, she had been well educated. Father Brown had seen to that. She had taught the children, and was fairly good at that, but Independence already had a teacher, so that job was out. Brandy shook her head. She had always assumed she would stay at the parsonage with Father Brown and teach until she got married and had a husband to take care of her.

Now she was expected to support a family, and she

hadn't the slightest idea how. Billy was right. So far she hadn't done a good job. She didn't want to disappoint Father Brown, but she was completely unprepared for the task he'd left to her.

Her head throbbed, but she didn't have time to coddle herself. She had to think of something. She had to come up with a plan.

Drawing in a deep breath, she rose from behind the desk; staring at Father Brown's records wouldn't change a thing, she thought as she left the office. Perhaps if she kept things as normal as possible, an idea would come to her. She had to try.

As the day went on, nothing improved. If anything, things became worse.

The children were in no mood to cooperate. All they did was bicker. She tried to hold classes for them, but finally gave up when she couldn't keep their attention. She could not remember this much fighting when Father Brown was alive.

Later that night, dinner was a far cry from Rosa's delicious breakfast. The meat was charred and the gravy, a thick brown paste, lacked appeal. The children stared at their plates a long while before picking up their forks. Brandy took a bite and realized it looked much better than it tasted.

"I'm sorry," Brandy said, the lump of meat she'd just swallowed sitting heavy in her stomach. "This isn't very good. I'll try to do better next time," she said. "I guess cooking is harder than I thought."

Scott looked at his food, then at her. "Could you try not making everything so black?"

"It's not black," Brandy assured him. "It's brown."

"It's black. I know my colors!" Scott informed her.

Brandy looked at her plate and shoved a stray lock

of hair out of her face. Scott was right. Everything was black. There was nothing to do but laugh, and laugh she did until tears flooded her cheeks and her sides ached. She glanced up to see the children's stares. They, evidently, thought she'd lost her sanity, and Brandy wasn't too sure she hadn't. She laughed harder, wiping the tears from her eyes.

Her laughter became infectious, and soon the children were laughing, too. Before long, the tension seemed to evaporate and they all tried to choke down dinner.

Brandy knew that her cooking had to get better. It certainly couldn't get much worse.

The next morning, the gray, sun-washed buildings stood in stark contrast to the vivid blue sky. Billy and Brandy marched across the street. Their heels kicked up little puffs of dust as they crossed Main Street, barely avoiding a horse and rider. Billy, who had been a step behind Brandy, grabbed her arm and jerked her back just as the horse galloped down the street.

"Dang it! If you don't watch where you're goin', we could be burying you right next to Father Brown," Billy said as he released her arm.

"I wasn't paying attention," Brandy told him, her heart beating furiously as they continued on.

"No shit," Billy muttered from beside her.

They moved carefully among several wagons. Independence, Missouri, had become the starting point for many wagon trains heading west. Two trails left Independence, the Oregon and the Santa Fe, so wagons were a common sight in town, as well as strangers from all over the East Coast and the world.

The folks they passed turned to look at them, and Brandy figured it was because of her high-necked black dress. She had known the day would be much too hot for such tight clothing, but she had little choice. This was the best dress she owned.

As they stepped up on the boardwalk, Billy turned to Brandy. "I think we'd do better if we split up," he said. "Will you be all right by yourself?"

Touched that he'd thought of her safety, Brandy managed not to show how she felt. Instead she said, "Of course. What in the world could happen to me?"

Billy chuckled and shook his head. "Maybe it's better that I not scare you with all the things that *could* happen to a young woman alone. Just make sure you stay on Main Street. Don't wander off onto the side streets."

She recognized a heavy dose of sarcasm in his voice. "I'm perfectly capable of taking care of myself," she quickly pointed out. "I am older than you!"

"Yea, but wiser could be debated. Hell, you were practically raised in a convent." A flash of humor crossed his face. Then he sauntered off, leaving Brandy completely dumbfounded.

After two hours of going in and out of shops, the dry goods store, and the emporium, Brandy was hot and tired and discouraged. Her puffy feet felt two sizes larger than her shoes, and her face hurt after smiling and putting on a good front. Seeing a long, wooden bench in front of the emporium, she made her way to it and sat down to rest her weary feet.

A stray lock of hair fell over her eyes and clung to her damp face. She brushed it away and secured it back into the severe bun that she'd twisted her hair into this morning.

"It's so hot!" Brandy muttered, pulling at the clinging neck of her woolen dress. That didn't provide much relief, so she unbuttoned the top two buttons and started to fan herself with the open flaps.

Every day brought new surprises. When she thought about how her day had gone, she wanted to shriek. No, she wanted to weep. Though everyone had been sympathetic to her plight, no one was willing to help her out by giving her a job. Brandy closed her eyes and thought about her last two hours.

She had entered Mr. Gardner's dry goods store, where everyone in town bought their food supplies, hoping her luck would change. But it hadn't, she thought, as she recalled the conversation. . . .

"What can I do for you today, Miss Brandy?" Mr. Gardner took off his spectacles and wiped them with a cloth. He propped his elbows on the counter and watched her.

"I would like to apply for a job."

His brows arched. He put his spectacles back on and carefully looked her over. "Now what can a pretty little lady like you do?"

"I could stock shelves or help keep your books. I'm very good at figures, Mr. Gardner," she said confidently. "I used to help Father Brown."

"That does sound appealing," Mr. Gardner agreed. He rubbed his jaw while he thought.

Just when Brandy thought Mr. Gardner might offer something, Mrs. Gardner came out of the stockroom. "I overheard what you said, and I just don't think you'd be suitable working here," she said primly and pursed her lips. "We have all the help we need."

"Suitable?" Brandy mimicked the woman's words as she sat on the bench fanning herself. What had she done to the woman to be treated so rudely? When it had been clear that Mrs. Gardner wasn't going to say anything else, Brandy had forced a polite smile, then left the store.

Unfortunately, she'd confirmed what the ledger had shown her: Father Brown owed everybody in town. And she had no earthly idea how she was going to pay any of them if she didn't have a job. Finally, she drew a deep breath for courage, then opened her eyes. Maybe Billy had had better luck.

After sitting for half an hour, Brandy grew tired of waiting. The bench had grown hard, so she got up, stretched, and strolled over to a billboard where notices and WANTED posters were tacked up.

Bounty hunter? Now that was an idea! She laughed. Her sense of humor was the only thing keeping her together at the moment. She scanned the board. There were several posters of bank robbers. And then she saw it . . .

In the right-hand corner of the board, Brandy spotted a small notice torn from a newspaper.

Wanted—*one woman who is pretty, sweet, and a good cook! For marriage to me, Sam Owens. I'm a decent, hard-working man. I will pay expenses for moving to Wyoming and all past bills. Please write and tell me something about yourself.*

Brandy read the note again: pretty, sweet, and a good cook. Well she had one of the three: She was sweet. Her mouth curved into an unconscious smile.

She'd simply lie about the rest. After all, beauty was in the eye of the beholder and maybe she'd learn how to cook by the time she met him.

She tapped her chin as she thought. "I wonder how Sam will feel about five children?" she mused. "No, better keep that to myself."

Walking back over to the bench, she knew that this could be a way out of their current dilemma and solve the question of where to go when they were told to leave the parsonage.

But marriage to a man she didn't know? *Marriage?* She'd never given the subject much thought. She often thought that marriage would be far off in the future. She had read books that mentioned love, but what was love? Did it only exist in books?

She folded her arms and leaned back on the bench. What would it be like to be kissed? Would it be like the kisses she'd given Father Brown on the cheek? They were not so bad. And she had loved him. Maybe marriage would be something like that.

Realizing she'd already made her decision, she stood and hurried down the sidewalk before she could change her mind.

Entering the post office, she went to the big window where letters were mailed, and asked the clerk for a few sheets of paper and a pen. When she explained to the clerk what she was about to do, he agreed to mail the letter. She could pay him later.

Now for the letter.

Upon returning to the faded gray bench, she started writing, carefully choosing her words, describing her features, and peppering them up slightly. What was the harm in a little lie? She told Sam Owens what a wonderful cook she was—*"Forgive me, Father,"*

Brandy whispered, looking heavenward at yet another lie. She also didn't bother to mention the five children she would be bringing along. Hopefully, Sam would be an understanding man. And if he wasn't . . . no, she didn't want to think of that. She could only deal with one problem at a time.

There. It was done. She folded the letter and looked up just in time to see Billy coming toward her.

"Did you have any luck?" Billy asked as he plopped on the bench beside her.

"Well, yes and no. I looked all over town, but no one would hire me. So, I sat down here, and that's when I found the answer to our problems."

"What? Did some divine voice speak to you?"

She ignored him. "I'm going to get married."

"You're what?" Billy jerked around and gaped at her. "You've been out in the dang sun too long." He felt her forehead to see if she was hot or maybe delirious.

"No, I haven't." Brandy laughed and swatted his hand away. She pointed. "See that notice on the board over there?"

Billy walked over and looked at it. "Wanted, dead or alive?"

"Not that one. Look in the corner."

Billy frowned. "What's it say?"

"If you had paid more attention to your lessons, you would be able to read the note for yourself," Brandy chided.

"I don't need no lecture," he said, scowling. "Just tell me what it says."

"A man by the name of Sam Owens is looking for a wife. He lives near Fort Laramie, and he'll pay all past debts. So you see, that will take care of our money predicament." She held up the letter she'd just finished, waving it in the air. "The answer to all our problems is right here." She stood and sauntered back into the post office to mail her response.

Billy couldn't believe the crazy girl was thinking about marriage. Loco, that's what she was. She had never even kept company with a man, much less kissed one. Now, she had some fool notion she was going to get married! He stood there, too shocked to move. Finally, Brandy returned from the post office.

"What's wrong?" she asked.

"If this man does answer your letter, which is hardly likely, you're just goin' to go off and abandon us?" Billy placed his hands on his hips. "You have some nerve, waltzin' off and leavin' the children," he stated flatly. "You made a promise."

"I know I made a promise. I'm taking all of you with me." Brandy frowned. "And what do you mean *if* he answers my letter?"

Billy ignored her question. "Take us with you? Have you ever thought about asking us first? What if we don't want to go?"

"You forget, Billy, that I'm in charge. You have little choice. Besides, what do you have here?" Brandy asked, her hands on her hips, too. "We won't have anywhere to live before long."

He thought for a moment, then frowned. "Reckon you're right."

Brandy's eyebrows formed into a frown. "What did you mean a while ago when you said 'if' he answers my letter?"

"There are probably a bunch of women that's written to the poor man already." Billy's mouth twitched with amusement. "Did you think you'd be the only one?"

Brandy stared at him, frowned, then hurried over to the board and snatched the note off.

"Whatcha do that for?"

"Just a little precaution to make sure nobody else gets the same idea." She folded the note and slipped it into her pocket.

"You're crazy," Billy said, shaking his head. "Let's go home."

They both stood and started down the sidewalk. "Did you find a job?" Brandy asked.

"Yeah, but it ain't much. Might help a little, though. I was hoping to land somethin' better, but I don't have much experience. And everyone said I was still too young. I get mighty sick of hearin' that."

Brandy nudged him. "So are you going to make me guess?"

"I'll be sweepin' out The Golden Lady Saloon," Billy mumbled. "Like I said, it ain't much."

"Well, at least you got a job. That's wonderful," Brandy praised him, trying to make him feel a little better. She sensed his disappointment. "I don't know if I like the idea of you in a saloon, though," she said as she walked into the street and in front of a horse and rider she didn't see until too late.

The horse reared and whinnied, the rider swore, and Brandy gasped at her close call, but she didn't bother to stop. She didn't feel like hearing another lecture, so she scurried out of the way with Billy tagging at her heels.

"That was a dang stupid thing to do," Billy yelled. "You never pay attention to where you're goin'. Twice in one day! Don't you ever learn?"

She slowed down, but her heart still pounded frantically in her chest. "I didn't see him." She didn't have time to act like a scared goose. She took a deep breath and pretended nothing was wrong. "Now, as I was saying, we need money, remember?" She looked at Billy, and he nodded. "At least your job will help until Sam sends money."

"Who's Sam?"

"My future husband, of course." Brandy laughed, the idea of home and marriage warming her.

"You mean your future husband, *you hope*," Billy teased. "It's good he doesn't know what you look like."

She eyed him with a calculating expression. "Why do you say that?"

"Oh, nothin'." Billy shrugged. "You're just ugly, that's all." His brown eyes danced with mischief.

Brandy punched him in the arm, then started for home without him. She liked this new relationship she and Billy were developing. She only hoped it would last.

Three brats were better than four, any day.

FOUR

"What the hell!" Thunder swore and jerked back on his horse's reins to avoid the woman who had darted into his path. She had merely paused, tilted her face up at him, blinked several times, and then hastened farther down the street, a young boy chasing after her.

Turning in his saddle, Thunder watched her, his attention focused on her manner of dress. As hot as it was, she was clothed in drab black, much too hot for a day like this. Her hair, or at least the few strands that blew in the wind, appeared to be the only color she wore. The severe bun on top of her head looked much like that of a Boston matron, not the young woman she apparently was. Evidently, she sought to hide her beauty, but the sun reflecting off her chestnut hair gave it a rich color that made him want to touch it.

There was something familiar about her. Where had he seen her before? Then it came to him! She was the woman from the graveyard. Of course. She'd been the one who'd stirred his curiosity. Then a more terrifying realization washed over him. How long had it been since any woman had aroused him?

However, if she didn't watch were she was going, she wouldn't live long in this town, or any other.

Thunder nudged his horse forward. If their paths crossing was to be as brief as this, he could handle never seeing her again. She was much too enticing.

Hammering from the blacksmiths' shop drew Thunder's attention as he rode by. A smithy placed a finished wheel in a huge stack, a sure indication that a wagon train was pulling out soon. The busy streets were filled with men, horses, and mules all hurrying to their destinations.

It felt good to be in Independence. It was just one step closer to his homeland and one step farther from his past. No more would he think about the war. The corner of his mouth lifted in a sardonic smile as he said, "And they call Indians savages."

Before returning home, Thunder decided he wanted to say goodbye to Ward Singer, a friend who was preparing a wagon train to move west.

Thunder had first met Ward in Boston when Thunder had been fool enough to fall in love with Ward's beautiful niece, Elaina. She was a chapter of his life he wanted to bury permanently, but he thought of Ward fondly. Ward had been one of the few bright spots in Thunder's eastern experience.

Ward had always been an adventurer and loved the challenge of taking wagon trains out west. He'd been in Boston to see his family and ended up staying for a couple of years, and, of course, he'd wanted to do his part in the war. Though Thunder had met him through Elaina, their friendship hadn't developed until they became irrevocably bound when Thunder took a bullet meant for Ward by running in front of him. After he was wounded in yet another skirmish and considered useless by the Union army,

Ward returned to his former love: guiding wagons out west.

Finding Ward would be easy. All Thunder had to do was look for the largest group of canvas-covered wagons. Sure enough, that's where he'd find his friend, right in the middle of it all.

He saw Ward towering over the crowd as his mount cantered toward the camp. With dark blond hair and a bushy mustache, Ward was tall and burly with wide shoulders straining his brown homespun shirt. Bent over to work on a wagon wheel, he apparently hadn't noticed Thunder's approach.

From the rear it appeared Ward hadn't changed much. His middle had thickened, probably the direct result of his fondness for food and spirits.

Thunder wondered if Ward would think he'd changed. The last time Thunder had seen his friend, he'd been a clean-cut Union soldier. Now he wore faded blue Union trousers streaked with dirt and sweat and a loose blue chambray shirt. His hair was considerably longer.

Thunder slid soundlessly off his horse and landed in the soft dirt. Like a feather on the wind, he approached Ward from behind and wrapped his arms around Ward's neck. "You should watch your back, old friend. I'll not always be around to protect you," Thunder whispered in Ward's ear.

"Bullshit!" Ward bellowed as he stood up, taking Thunder with him.

Thunder loosened his grip so Ward could turn and face him. "Somebody else could be after more than just rehashing old times," Thunder said with a smile.

"Thunder!" Ward shouted. "God knows, son, it's been a long time," he said as he grabbed Thunder's arm and slapped him on the back. "Let me take a look at you."

Ward smiled with pleasure. Slowly his gaze traveled over Thunder, noticing the change in his comrade's coal-black hair, which had grown long. Even the man's skin had darkened under the summer sun. "Damn if you haven't turned savage on me, boy."

"As you well know, I *am* half savage," Thunder replied. "And I could get a hankering for a scalp real soon." He grinned. "I'd be careful if I were you."

Ward laughed. "There's not much left to scalp," Ward said, removing his hat and rubbing his thinning hair. "How about giving me a hand with this here wagon wheel?"

Thunder held the wheel, his muscles straining beneath his shirt, while Ward made the adjustments.

"So what brings you to Independence?" Ward asked.

"I'm heading home. Figured you'd be here, so I stopped by so you could buy me a steak."

Ward straightened and wiped his hand on a rag. "Well, old friend, how about dinner . . . and a job?"

"Job?"

"I've been praying for a miracle, son . . ." Ward paused and grinned before adding, "And you showed up. I think it's a sign, don't you?"

Thunder took a couple of steps backwards. "Whoa. What the hell are you talking about?"

Ward gave a brief nod toward the white canvas. "See these wagons?"

"I cannot help but see them."

"Well, we're just about ready to head west, and my scout got himself killed in a bar fight. It's already the end of June, which is much later than I normally take a train out. So, I just happen to be in need of a good scout. Seeing as you're heading that way anyway, and you're the best damn scout there is . . . you could help me out."

"What makes you think I want the job?"

"I'm hoping you'll give me a hand because I'm your friend, and a friend in desperate need." Ward smiled at the frown he received. "Let's get some grub, and we'll talk about my proposition. Things will look better after you've sunk your teeth into a good, juicy steak."

"In that case, the steak better be *damned* good."

That night over dinner, with a lot of friendly persuasion, Ward talked Thunder into accepting the assignment, but only after assuring him that his only responsibility would be scouting. Ward promised he'd take care of everything else, and Thunder wouldn't have to get involved with any of his fellow travelers.

The weeks passed slowly as Brandy waited for the letter that would be their salvation. So far, they had managed to survive one day at a time. Every day, Brandy expected a letter to arrive, either from Sam asking her to marry him, or the dreaded letter telling them they would have to leave the parsonage.

This morning she had awakened with another headache, and it had lingered all day. Brandy rubbed her temples to alleviate the pounding. She seemed to have headaches frequently these days from the stress of trying to keep her unhappy family fed and warding off fights between them. Coping with her charges had become increasingly difficult. Why couldn't they just do as they were told without questioning everything?

Brandy was sure of one thing: She didn't ever want children of her own. They were too much trouble.

Her stomach churned when she thought of selling the few gold items left in the chapel, but she had to pay the bills. They used the little money that Billy made to buy food. The only item left was a gold cross that she refused to part with. It was her only remembrance of Father Brown.

She prayed for a miracle. The sooner it happened, the better.

Unfortunately, her cooking hadn't shown much improvement. Mary had proved to be a natural cook and had taken over. Of course, Mary never failed to point out just how useless Brandy was.

Billy had settled down. His new responsibilities seemed to agree with him. He liked his job at the saloon. Often he would come home with exciting tales of what happened at the bar and especially the fights. The children would gather around him eagerly, listening to every word as Billy spun his tales over supper. Even Brandy admitted she enjoyed the stories, though she wondered sometimes if they were appropriate for the children's ears.

On one such night, Brandy protested. "Perhaps you should quit, Billy. That place sounds much too dangerous. You could get hurt or, worse, killed."

Billy's eyebrows shot up. "You mean you'd care? You seem to forget that I'm the only one makin' any money around here. We do have to eat. Maybe you've got a better way to make money?"

Brandy thought for a moment before offering a weak, "No."

"I didn't think so." Billy grinned, exuberant in the fact that, this time, he was right. "Besides, when the guns come out of their holsters, you can bet your boots, I don't hang 'round. I might be many things, but a fool ain't one of them."

They were down to their last loaf of bread and a few eggs when the letter finally arrived from Sam Owens. Brandy took the letter to Father Brown's office and placed it in front of her, unread. For a moment, she was afraid to open it. What if it was a refusal? What would she do?

No, Brandy didn't even want to think of that possibility. Convincing herself she'd written a good letter describing her glorious attributes, she carefully opened the envelope with shaking hands. She whispered a quick prayer, then began to read.

Dear Brandy,
    I found your letter very interesting. You sound like just the woman I've been looking for. I love to eat, and I look forward to enjoying many meals with you.

Brandy couldn't help but snicker. They might have many meals together, but how wonderful they were would be very doubtful.

    I never spoke of children, but we can decide that after you're here. I look forward to seeing you and hope you'll book passage on the next wagon train. I trust you'll not be bored traveling alone. I'm sending enough money so you can hire someone to handle the wagon. The money will be wired to your bank tomorrow so that you may

pay past debts and arrange for your trip. Until
we meet—take care.

Your future husband,
Sam Owens

Brandy wiped the tears of relief from her cheeks
as she laid the letter down in her lap. It wouldn't do
for the children to see her crying; they would think
she was weak. But the strain of holding their ragtag
group together was soon to be over.

She thought of the money, money to pay the bills.
What a relief! At long last, she had seen her salvation.
Remorse did nag at her for thinking about the money
when she should be thinking of her fiancé. However,
she didn't know Sam yet, and she did know *all* the
creditors.

She wondered if the wire had reached the bank yet.
She checked the date on Sam's letter. Two weeks ago.
Surely the money would have arrived by now.

Brandy felt great gratitude toward Sam, but
couldn't help wishing she were marrying someone she
loved. Or at least knew! On the other hand, she wasn't
sure there was anyone out there she could love.

This might be the only way she'd ever get a husband. After all, she was very plain. Billy had pointed
it out often enough. Come to think about it, no one
but Father Brown had ever told her she was pretty,
and he was probably being nice.

Brandy was excited and scared at the same time.
Having chosen her course, there would be no backing
out. She was going to a strange land to meet a man
she didn't know.

Did that mean she was crazy?

Or just desperate?

Probably both, she thought. She began jotting down a list of things that needed to be done. First, she'd have to talk to the wagon master and book passage. She'd heard there was a small wagon train heading west, and it was booking up fast. First thing tomorrow that small matter would be taken care of. But tonight, she'd get a peaceful night's sleep, knowing their bills would soon be paid, and all their problems solved.

Early the next morning found Brandy twisting her hair into its usual knot. Quickly, she fastened it with hairpins.

"There." She peered into the cracked mirror, approving the older look of a chignon. She had to collect the money from the bank, then convince the wagon master she was serious about traveling west and wasn't some silly female who had no idea what she was doing.

On the way out, she bumped into Mary.

"Where are you going?" Mary asked, raising her chin defiantly.

"I have to run an errand," Brandy called over her shoulder without bothering to stop. "I won't be long."

Mary didn't question her any further, but Brandy could feel the girl's watchful eyes as she left the parsonage.

She headed straight for the bank and found Sam had been true to his word and wired the money. That was a good start to their relationship, she couldn't help thinking.

She paid her creditors first, relieved to be free of the burden. There was even a spring in her step as she set off on foot to book passage on the wagon train. The long walk took her to the far edge of town.

The fluffy white canvas of each prairie schooner contrasted starkly against a clear, azure-blue sky as Brandy approached the camp made up of at least twenty wagons. She weaved in and out of the wagons in search of the wagon master, but found no sign of a man who appeared in charge. She asked several travelers who kept saying, "He's around here somewhere." Finally, she found a woman who pointed to the man she needed.

The wagon master stood almost six feet tall and possessed the powerful build of a bull. He wore trousers of coarse homespun with a gun strapped down to his leg. He appeared older than she'd thought he would be, but his face suggested a kindness of heart. The man watched her approach, and Brandy prayed her observation was correct. There was no question in her mind . . . this man was in charge.

"Hello," she said. "My name is Brandy—" She paused, then quickly added, "Brown." She really didn't know what her last name was, but since Father Brown had raised her, she'd take his name.

"Nice to meet you, Mrs. Brown." Ward nodded. "I'm Ward Singer. What can I do for you?"

She raised her hand to shade her eyes from the sun. "I'd like to book passage on your wagon train."

"I do have room for one more wagon," he informed her as he stepped politely to the side to block the sun from her face. "Where's your husband, Mrs. Brown?"

Brandy lowered her hand. "It's Miss. I'm not married."

Mr. Singer gave her a leery glance. "Then the answer is no." He stared at her. A suggestion of annoyance hovered in his eyes.

Icy fear twisted around her heart. "But I must go west."

"Lady, you're crazy if you think you can make the trip alone!" His voice had gotten louder. "What do you hope you'll find there?" Ward shook his head at her. "I can tell you . . . it's trouble."

"Please, mister, you have to listen," Brandy pleaded, grabbing his arm. She'd never dreamed he'd turn her down, and she had no more pride. If she had to get on her knees, she would. She tried to think of some way to convince him. Then she remembered Sam's letter. "Look at this." She handed him the letter.

"The name's Ward," he said as he read the letter and then looked at her for a long moment before handing it back to her.

He shoved his hands into his pockets and cocked a gray eyebrow as he stared down at her. "You want to travel on my train . . . alone. Little lady, you don't look crazy, but no one in their right mind would let a woman travel unaccompanied by a man."

"But, I have money. I can pay my own way," she rushed to tell him, hoping the money would change his mind. She fought a wave of dizziness as she stood a little taller, preparing to argue further.

"That's not the issue." He kept his eyes focused on her. "Do you even have a wagon?"

"Well . . . no," Brandy admitted with a frown. "But I can get one. Just tell me where." She was frantic to convince Ward to take her because their choices were now at an end. The second letter had arrived this morning from the bishop. Next month she and the children would be out on the street, and then what was she to do? She had thought money would be her only difficulty. But now she had money and still her problems persisted.

Ward shook his head. "Lady, you're wastin' my time. I've other things to do," he informed her with a vague hint of disapproval. "You can't travel alone on my wagon train! This is not a pleasure journey, Miss," he informed her. "It's a hard, tough, demanding trip, and it'll take every ounce of strength a man has. And you, my dear woman, are no man!"

Ward looked at the petite young woman in front of him. Despite the fact she'd tried to look older with the severe hairstyle, she couldn't hide her beauty or her youth. Her strong chin and high cheekbones gave her a stately appearance. And her eyes were rare flowers indeed. He'd never seen eyes the color of violets, and unfortunately for her, beauty was another disadvantage to her chances of booking passage on this train.

"I'll not be traveling alone," Brandy persisted, determined not to give up.

Ward gave a long sigh. "As long as you have a man who can handle your wagon, then your problems are solved."

"I have Billy. He's fourteen," she told him excitedly.

Ward frowned. "Fourteen? That's a bit young, and who is this Billy?"

"He is—is my brother. You see, I'm from an orphanage." Brandy sighed before pouring out all the problems she'd kept bottled up for so long.

"It started when Father Brown died, and he made me promise to take care of the children. But I found out we didn't have any money, and we were going to lose our home." Once Brandy began to ramble she couldn't stop. She had to make Ward understand just how desperate her situation had become. "I had to do something, so I answered the ad for a bride." She grabbed Ward's arm. "I have to get to Wyoming! I have to marry Sam! Don't you understand? *We* have no place to go," she said the last in a whisper as a tear slipped down her cheek. Shame washed over her for telling her troubles to an outsider. No matter how kind he appeared, he was still a stranger.

Ward pulled her into his arms, and though she tried to resist, the need to be comforted overwhelmed her. She finally collapsed, comforted to once again be able to lean on someone else.

"We?" Ward asked.

"I'm taking care of five br—, children."

Ward rubbed Brandy's back in a fatherly manner. She was much too young to have all these responsibilities thrust upon her. "Don't cry, child. I really do sympathize with you, but I'm in charge of twenty wagons. Each one will demand my attention, and there would be resentment if I showed you any partiality."

"I know." She sniffed into his shirt. "It's really not your problem."

"Perhaps you can find a man who will take charge of your crew, and can help you out," Ward suggested, wondering just where that man would come from. Out of the corner of his eyes, he spotted Thunder standing by a wagon. Now there was the perfect man. Ward grinned. It probably wouldn't work, but it was worth a try.

"I have an idea." Ward held Brandy away from him. "See that big fellow over there? The one with the jet black hair?"

Brandy glanced in the direction where Ward pointed.

"His name is Thunder. He's my scout. Perhaps you can persuade him to keep an eye out for your wagon, but I warn you, he can be difficult."

Brandy wiped away her tears with the heel of her hand. "Thank you, Ward." She gave him a weak smile. "You're a very nice man."

Ward became captivated by her dazzling smile and heart-breaking eyes. He would look forward to Brandy's company on the trail west—that is, if she could convince Thunder. And that just might be the most arduous task she'd ever attempted. It would probably make all her other troubles seem simple. Ward smiled again, knowing it might make this trip a little more interesting.

Taking deep breaths, Brandy walked toward Thunder. On top of the heat and everything else, she had developed hiccups. "Ex—excuse me, sir." Brandy's voice broke as she hiccuped again. She felt her face flush red as she stood behind the man called Thunder, staring at his broad back. The first thing she noticed was that his glossy black hair touched the top of his shoulders. It was beautiful. If this man was an Indian, he was dressed just like everybody else. Not at all what she pictured an Indian to be.

When he swung around, Brandy's astonishment cause her hiccups to vanish instantly as she jumped back.

She stared open-mouthed at this giant of a man who stood a good foot and a half taller than she. He was, without a doubt, the most attractive fellow she'd ever laid eyes on. His deeply tanned skin flattered his handsome features. A slight scar on his left temple kept him from looking too perfect. A square jaw gave him an authoritative air, and his chiseled nose added to his rugged appeal. Everything about him spoke of raw, untamed strength. A strong urge to run swept over her like wildfire. She willed herself to stay put.

Thunder could do nothing but stare. He'd expected to find an older woman, just like all the others he'd given directions to today. He was totally unprepared for the delightful surprise that greeted him. The others had wanted to know where the wagon master was located, and what they needed to do. It seemed he was always directing somebody over to Ward.

All this waiting around had been extremely irritating when all Thunder wanted to do was move down the road.

It was the lady from the graveyard. He was actually face-to-face with the woman he'd seen twice before. The one, though he hated to admit it, who'd haunted his dreams. But in his dreams he hadn't been able to picture her face because he'd only caught a glimpse of her until now. Maybe it would have been better if she'd remained faceless.

Because the lovely creature standing before him with sparkling eyes would be hard to forget.

Mesmerized by the rich hue of her eyes, Thunder remembered many a sunrise at home when he would sneak from his teepee to watch the beginning of a new day. Just as the sun perched on the crest of the hill and teased the sky with purple and orange color, chasing away the dark blue night, Thunder remembered that for a brief moment the awakening sky had been the exact color of her violet eyes. As he stared into them, he felt a stab of homesickness which didn't improve his mood.

Brandy didn't know what to say. He stared at her so intently, she grew uneasy. A breeze caught his slate-black hair, giving him a carefree look; however, his piercing silver eyes showed no emotion. Brandy felt he went to great lengths to mask his feelings. The rush of adrenaline that surged through her scared her even more than the man himself. Without knowing why, she took another step backwards. Her heart pounded in her ears. Still feeling much too close, she moved again so she could see him better and put some distance between them.

"You don't have to keep backing up, ma'am. I promise I'll not touch you." Thunder's gaze turned much colder than before. Dangerous—that's how the man looked . . . like danger. "If you seek the wagon master, he is over there," Thunder snapped, motioning her away from him.

"I know," she admitted, wondering why he appeared so angry. "But, I'm looking for you."

"Me?" His dark eyebrows drew together with a look of surprise, followed by the same guarded expression he'd had moments ago. "Why?"

She held her breath and clasped her trembling hands together. "I'd like to see if you'd help me."

"Why should I want to help someone I don't know?"

She tilted her head. He was going to be difficult, she could feel it. "Haven't you ever helped a stranger?"

"No," he stated flatly. "What do you want, lady?" he inquired, blunt and to the point. Evidently he wanted to get this conversation over quickly.

His flat, unyielding tone and uncompromising manner left Brandy inwardly reeling, and again the urge to flee struck her. He wasn't the least bit obliging, but the urge to run died once his deep-set, silver gaze came to rest on her, rooting her to the spot. She couldn't run if her life depended on it.

"I-I must book passage on th-this wagon train, and I need to hire you to help me."

What kind of woman would ask a perfect stranger for help, especially a breed? "Why me?"

"Why not? I need a man, and you're as good as any."

"Thank you for the compliment, ma'am." Thunder felt like laughing at the insult. "You're traveling alone?"

"The wagon master recommended you. And no, I have five children who'll be traveling with me."

He lost control and started to laugh. This woman was definitely crazy. "Lady, aren't you a little young to have five children?"

His insulting laughter drew Brandy's anger. She didn't appreciate him mocking her. It was embarrassing enough having to ask for help without being made fun of. She folded her arms. Her back grew rigid. "How dare you laugh at me! The children are my brothers and sisters. I don't have a husband—yet!"

"Yet?" Thunder chuckled. "But you anticipate finding one? Maybe you should get married first and then you'll have your problem solved."

"My future husband lives at Fort Laramie, and will pay you handsomely to take me there."

"I bet he will. He'd be foolish not to want you near him," Thunder said in a serious tone. He'd not meant for his thoughts to slip out so easily.

"Does that mean you'll take the job?"

"Why would I want the responsibility of a woman

and five children?" He shook his head. "I don't need that kind of trouble."

"We are very self-sufficient. And we wouldn't be any trouble," Brandy argued persistently.

Without warning, Thunder reached out and grabbed Brandy's hand. He turned her palm up, then rubbed the tips of his fingers across her hand. It was as smooth as a baby's face.

"Just as I thought. Your hands are soft. You've never done a day's work in your life, Miss . . . Miss . . ."

Brandy held her breath. She felt the strength of his fingers as they slid across her palm. Awakening desire blossomed within her. A new emotion that excited, yet scared her, all at the same time. Her name came out in a breathless whisper. "Brandy."

When she said her name, Thunder's gaze automatically focused on her pink lips. He saw the way she bit her bottom lip, and he felt a tightening in his lower body. "What is your last name, Brandy?"

"I don't have one. I'm an orphan."

The remark stung Thunder. He'd figured she was like the women he'd met in Boston. Spoiled. Maybe this lady had a little more spunk than he gave her credit for. She was all alone, just like himself, and he sympathized with her, but still—. He'd have to be crazy to take on the responsibility of a family that wasn't his. And he definitely wasn't in the market for a family.

"Miss Brandy, find yourself someone else!" he snapped before be let go of her hand abruptly, turned on his heel, and walked away. He needed desperately to put some space between them. He hadn't been prepared for the sudden attraction he felt for the little lady with the huge purple eyes. Hell, he'd have to be insane to take on such an obligation.

Yet, he did feel a stab of guilt. Just like before when he'd seen her from the hill, he felt like she was very much alone. And now he knew she was alone. He gritted his teeth . . . she wasn't his problem.

For several minutes, Brandy remained motionless. Then, completely unaware of her actions, she rubbed the palm of her hand against her dress, trying to rid herself of the feel of the bronze man's touch. She had never been touched like that before, and even though he had only held her hand, her whole arm felt like fire, and a sudden disappointment that she couldn't explain filled her.

This had definitely been a trying day, and nothing had been accomplished except for paying her bills. However, if she didn't get a guide they would be no better off than when they started. They had to have a home.

What was she going to do? An idea struck her so fast it scared her. She must act quickly before she could change her mind. She had to find the wagon master.

"Ward," she said softly, touching his arm.

He turned with a frown, but his eyes softened upon seeing she was back. "Did he agree?"

"As a matter of fact, he did, thank you." Brandy smiled brightly, never flinching at her falsehood. "Now, can I book passage with your wagons?"

"Sure can. It's three hundred dollars," Ward said as he rubbed his chin. Surprise was clearly stamped on his face. "Perhaps Thunder has mellowed over the years," Ward mumbled.

Brandy handed a small, brown leather pouch to

Ward. "I believe you'll find the correct amount in here."

"Thank you, ma'am. I hope we'll all have a pleasant and safe journey. We'll be leaving next week," he informed her.

"We'll be ready," Brandy said, then left, saying to herself, "I hope."

She felt Ward watching her walk away. So it was a small lie, she convinced herself on her way back to the parsonage. However, the lies were adding up quickly. Father Brown would have to intercede and ask God to forgive her.

Brandy needed a plan. She refused to give up on the man with the silver eyes. Surely there was some kind of sympathy in him. He was going to help them one way or the other. She would give Thunder a little time to think about her offer, and then she'd simply ask him again. And if bad came to worse, she'd beg.

He'd see the wisdom of helping her and the children. He just had to!

FIVE

Later that night, Brandy was quiet during dinner, wondering how she was going to present the upcoming trip to the children. Many things needed to be done as they prepared for the journey and she would need everyone's cooperation. But what could she say?

Direct and to the point, she thought. That had to be the answer.

She stared at the food on her plate, not seeing what was there. What if they all refused to go? How could she care for them and keep her promise to Father Brown?

She couldn't put it off any longer. She laid down her fork, then blurted out, "We're going to Fort Laramie."

"Oh, boy!" Scott squealed, jumping up and clapping his hands. Suddenly he looked at her with questioning eyes. "What's Fort Laramie?"

Brandy laughed, realizing Scott would be excited over anything. He was easy to please, but the others . . . they had yet to speak. Their typical negative response, she thought as she saw all the frowns.

"It's a beautiful place that has plains as far as the eye can see, Scott. There will be wild ponies, streams for fishing, and fresh air. Nothing like this dusty old place."

"I don't want to go anyplace, especially a fort!" Mary said curtly, her foul mood clearly showing on her face.

"I'm afraid we don't have a choice."

"Why can't I just stay here?" Mary stormed. "I don't need the rest of you."

"Is that right?" Brandy questioned.

"Yes. The new priest will be here soon and I can help him," Mary informed Brandy. "And I'll be rid of you."

Brandy stood slowly, counting to ten and resisting the urge to strangle Mary. "I probably should have told everyone earlier, but I didn't want to upset you before I had an answer to our problems. There will be no priest. After next month we won't have a home, and I, for one, don't want to sleep in the street," Brandy admitted as she looked at her brothers and sisters.

"I don't believe you!" Mary's tone hardened, then she retorted tartly, "Where did you get the money when you've been preaching about how poor we are?"

"It's true, Mary." Billy prevented Brandy from explaining. "Father Brown just hadn't told us they were doing away with the orphanage. Even if he'd lived, we would still have to leave. Plus we owed money to near everybody in town."

"What are we going to do when we get to this fort?" Ellen finally spoke. "Where will we live?"

"I'll be marrying a gentleman by the name of Sam Owens, who has sent enough money to pay off our debts and purchase a wagon and supplies," Brandy explained.

Married. The word still sounded foreign to Brandy. Marriage was something other people did, not her, but fate seemed to be changing all their lives. "He will provide us with a good home."

"Married," Mary spat. "You've never kissed a man, and you're going to get married!" She laughed. An inexplicable look of withdrawal slid over her face. Evidently, Mary thought the whole idea was absurd, and Brandy really couldn't disagree.

Brandy shrugged. "Let's just say it's a marriage of convenience."

Mary pushed her chair back and stood. Apparently, she wasn't going to give up. "Why? And where did you meet him?"

Brandy sighed and looked to heaven. *Father, give me strength.*

She began a lengthy explanation of their situation, beginning with when they'd first discovered the orphanage was going to close.

Mary slumped down onto the chair and crossed her arms, still in a huff, but kept her mouth shut.

"Thank you," Brandy murmured as she glanced up to heaven again.

"I'm afraid," Ellen admitted in a timid voice.

Glancing at Ellen, Brandy asked, "Of what?"

"There are Indians out there." Ellen's voice cracked. She burst into tears. "I've heard they scalp people."

Brandy placed her arm around Ellen, who leaned her head against Brandy. "There are Indians here, too," Brandy said softly. "But, to ease your fear, we'll be traveling with twenty wagons. And—" Brandy paused and lifted Ellen's face up with her finger "—I've hired a big, strong man to take care of us in case there's any trouble. Believe me, he'd scare off anyone who would threaten us."

Amy toddled over and pulled on Brandy's skirt. "I'm sleepy, Bran."

"All right." Brandy let go of Ellen, then bent down and picked Amy up. "Say good night."

" 'Nite," Amy muttered.

"Good night, Amy," the children told her.

Brandy looked at all their faces. Each mirrored a different emotion as they watched her. She could see they were scared and unsure. A flicker of compassion for her charges stirred within her, but she dismissed the feeling as fatigue. Her job was to take care of them . . . and that's what she was trying to do.

If only Father Brown were here. She could talk to him and make sure she was doing the right thing. She could certainly use someone to lean on, but there wasn't anyone. She had to be the strong one. With a little help from above, she and her little group would somehow survive.

"Be thinking about what you want to take on this trip. Remember, there won't be much room, so you can't take much," Brandy told them as she shifted Amy higher on her hip. Complete silence filled the room as she turned and left.

The walk to the little girl's room seemed longer than usual, Brandy thought once she reached the door. Brandy sighed and tucked Amy into her bed. The day had started off so well, but was sliding slowly downhill. Hopefully, every day wasn't going to be as difficult as this one. Sitting on the side of the bed, she told Amy a bedtime story and waited for her to fall asleep.

Finally, Amy drifted off, and Brandy tiptoed away from the bed. She closed the door behind her and slipped outside to the porch. Billy stood, his shoulder propped against a rough wooden beam, waiting for her.

"So we're really going?" he said, chewing on a straw and waiting for her response.

"Yes," she answered, though she was still uncertain of her decision. "I don't see that we have a choice."

Billy sat down in one of the two chairs on the porch. "You are plumb crazy. You ain't got no idea what you're doin'," Billy told her, then propped his feet up on the rail and leaned back in the chair.

"No," Brandy admitted as she looked up at the star-filled night and leaned against the post. "You're probably right . . . I am crazy, but at the moment, I don't see another way."

Both grew quiet, lost in their own thoughts, until Billy broke the silence. "Who is this man you've hired?"

"Well . . ." Brandy muttered uneasily, and tried not to appear as sheepish as she felt. "I haven't actually gotten him to say yes," she admitted. "But he will," she added with false confidence.

Billy watched her with one eyebrow cocked. "Yeah? What makes you so sure?"

"He has a good heart," she said with a conviction she felt, not knowing why. Memories of Thunder were vivid in her mind. She could remember his doubting, silver eyes, and she prayed he did have a heart . . . somewhere in that huge, menacing body.

Billy threw his arms up in the air before letting them fall by his side. "You ain't got a lick of sense. A good heart? The man sounds like a real dandy. How's he goin' to protect us?"

Brandy smiled, slowly. "I wouldn't call him a dandy. Far from that." She could picture Thunder clearly now. "He's tall and muscular, and something about him is frightening. He reminds me of a sleek cat, like the ones I've read about in books. I believe they're called panthers. They're fierce, agile, and attack without provocation." Brandy smiled briefly at her description. No wonder her hands had shaken when she'd met him. "H—He's different. I think he could be very dangerous if crossed."

"And you want someone like that to take us out west? Sounds like a real nice fellow." Billy's sarcasm showed in the tone of his voice. "What's his name?"

"The wagon master called him Thunder. I thought it was a strange name, but it fits him perfectly. He's a scout for the wagon train."

Billy straightened. "Does he have silver-blue eyes?"

Brandy looked up, startled by Billy's description. "Yes, he does," she replied. "I don't think I've ever seen eyes like his. Do you know him?"

"Yep, comes in the saloon every day 'round noon. He's quiet. Usually don't talk much unless Ward's around. Your description fits perfect," Billy said as he rubbed his chin. "Must admit, I admire the way Thunder carries himself. Looks more white than Indian to me," he commented. "I liked him, though. I'm like you—there is a threatenin' power that seems to come from him. Must be 'cause he's part Cheyenne."

Brandy shoved away from the post and propped against the porch railing, facing Billy. She thought of Indians in war paint and feathers. "Strange. He doesn't look like one."

"He's a half-breed, but I wouldn't dare say that to his face," Billy said as he lowered the front legs of the chair to the porch.

Brandy looked at him sharply. "Do you think you could talk to him about helping us with the wagon?"

"I don't know. I'll try," Billy reluctantly agreed.

She looked up at the sky again. Maybe Billy could pull off a miracle. "Billy, do you know how to drive a wagon?"

"No."

Brandy started down the steps. "Then you'd better learn," she said and looked back over her shoulder. "Tomorrow we're going to buy our own wagon." She chuckled over Billy's dumbfounded expression as she walked back to her room. For once she'd had the last word.

Billy shook his head while he watched Brandy's back, and wondered if the woman was a little loco, taking on an adventure like this. No, maybe *he* was plumb crazy for going along with her. One thing for sure—they would soon find out.

"You're a traitor, Billy West." Mary stepped out of the shadows, where she'd obviously been eavesdropping.

Billy turned, then stretched his arms out to the side. "What makes you think that?"

"It's always Brandy you're with," Mary complained. "I never get to see you."

"That's not true. I'm here with you now," Billy said softly.

"But it seems we never get to talk anymore," Mary pouted. "You're always gone or with *her.*"

"Things aren't the way they used to be. I have to work, remember," Billy reminded her. He knew Mary had missed him since he'd started to work. They had been constant cohorts in torturing Brandy. He'd always understood Mary's rebellious nature, for it was much like his own. "Brandy needs some help around here, which she never gets from you."

"Now you're even taking up for her! That's just great!" Mary tapped her foot angrily. "I don't like her bossing me around."

Billy smiled. "Aren't you bein' a little unfair?"

"No! I am not." Mary's voice was cold and lashing. "Must I remind you that you used to think the same thing not too long ago?" Her angry gaze swung over him. "What happened to you, Billy?"

"Guess I did some growin' up." He turned and placed his hands on Mary's arms. "Maybe you should try to do the same," he suggested, then left Mary to think upon his words.

When Mary was alone, a sadness settled upon her. She didn't like Billy taking up for Brandy. He was changing, and Mary didn't know what to do. She missed his company and knew, in her heart, that she cared a great deal for him. She had always found strength in Billy, and had thought he liked her, too; that is, until Brandy had bewitched him. The only good news Mary had had lately was that Brandy was getting married.

"The sooner the better," Mary mumbled as she slipped back inside.

"Wait for me! I want to go . . . I want to go!" Scott came flying lickety-split across the courtyard just as Brandy and Billy were leaving.

Brandy turned back to see Scott running toward them. "I don't know." She frowned at the bouncing ball of energy. "We'll be busy today, and it won't be much fun," Brandy told him in a gentle tone.

"I want to go see our new wagon!"

"How did you know where we're going?" Brandy hadn't told anyone except Billy.

"Mary told me."

Brandy looked to Billy for help, but he just smiled and shrugged his shoulders. "You're the boss. But reckon he needs to know about wagons, too."

"Thanks for the help," Brandy muttered. She looked down at Scott's upturned face, where hazel eyes peeked out from under bowl-cut bangs. It was hard not to smile. He really was adorable and difficult to resist.

"P—please, Brandy."

"All right. You can come, but you must be quiet and speak only when spoken to."

Scott grabbed her hand and pulled her out the door. "Thanks, Brandy. I'll be quiet. I promise. Guess what?"

"What?"

"You won't even know I'm here. Where are we going? Where do wagons come from?" He held Brandy's hand, but danced impatiently at her side as they trudged down the dusty road.

"There is a man who makes wagons on the south side of town," Billy said.

"Where's the south side of town?" Scott asked and tugged on Brandy's hand when he didn't get a response. "How far is it? Are we going to get a big wagon? Can I drive it?"

Brandy's gaze met Billy's and they both tried to hide their smiles. "I thought you were going to be quiet," she said to Scott.

"Oh, I forgot." Scott giggled, then continued his chatter. "Are we getting close?"

"I'll let you know when we get there." Brandy should have remembered how far they had to walk. She'd worn a completely inappropriate outfit. She was already quite warm in her black dress, and now realized she needed to get some practical clothing before she made this trip.

A multitude of shops lined the street on both sides. Toward the end of Main Street, there was a big, reddish barn located next to the livery stables. Adjacent to the building stood a large corral for horses and behind it another corral, which held oxen. There were several covered wagons scattered behind the building.

They stepped through the large double doors of the building. The smell of sawdust filled the air and the sound of continuous hammering and sawing surrounded them. Workers bustled about in every corner of the building. At least ten to fifteen men worked on two new wagons in various stages of completion. No one seemed to notice them come in.

Brandy knew people went out west, but she was surprised at how many. This must be a big business, she thought.

"Excuse me," Brandy attempted to shout over the loud banging, but the noise was deafening. "Where can I find the man in charge?"

She didn't receive a response, so Scott whispered, "I don't think they heard you."

Billy stepped forward. "You want me to try?"

Brandy frowned. "Excuse me," she yelled a little louder this time. "Who's in charge?"

"I'm in charge, little lady." A medium-built man stepped out from behind the first wagon. He had an apron tied around his waist and a pencil resting over one ear. "What can I do for you?"

"I need to buy a wagon."

"Well, you've come to the right place. Follow me." He motioned for her to follow him.

Brandy breathed a relieved sigh. Finally, she was getting somewhere. This was going to be easier than she'd first thought.

"Gee! Look at the wagons," Scott said, his eyes wide with wonder. "Did you make all these wagons, mister?"

He looked at Scott and smiled. "Yes, I did, young man."

The man gestured for them to sit at a small, make-shift table consisting of nothing more than a rough slab of wood on sawhorses. He took out a sheet of paper and a quill pen. "Let me introduce myself. I'm Joseph Butler, at your service."

"It's good to meet you, Mr. Butler," Brandy said as she stuck out her hand. "My name is Brandy B-Brown, and this is my brother, Billy."

"You forgot me!" Scott said, tugging on her hand.

She looked down at him and smiled. "And this is Scott."

"You sure have a big barn, mister," Scott blurted out as he propped his chin on the table.

Joseph looked at Scott and laughed. "Yes, son, it's a mite large, but sometimes not nearly big enough. Now . . ." He picked up a quill and dipped it in a black bottle of ink. Then he glanced up at Brandy. "When will you be needing this wagon?"

"Today."

A deep rumble of laughter sounded in Joseph's chest, and it took a moment before he recovered enough to speak. "That's a good one, ma'am!" His laughter quieted down, and he looked at her to see if she was serious. "Aren't you a little late, ma'am?"

"I don't think so. We'll be leaving next week, and I thought if we could get it today, we could start packing the wagon . . ." Brandy's voice trailed off as she saw the look of incredulity on Butler's face.

"What I meant, ma'am," Joseph interrupted, "is that it takes darn near three months to build a wagon, and most folks 'round here place their orders ahead of time."

"That can't be! I saw three such rigs outside." Brandy stood up quickly. "You don't understand, Mr. Butler. We have to travel on this wagon train! Can't I have one of those wagons?" she pleaded, pointing to the canvas-covered wagons.

Mr. Butler stared opened-mouthed at her. Apparently, he wasn't used to women arguing with him.

"What's wrong, Brandy?" Scott tugged on her skirt. "Aren't we going to get a wagon? You said we would."

"Everything's wrong, Scott. Be quiet!"

Mr. Butler shuffled through several orders on his desk. He picked up a slip of paper. "Just a minute," he said as he rose and went over to another man working on a nearby wagon. After they conversed, Mr. Butler returned. "I'll tell you what I can do. There's a prairie schooner out back complete with a well-broken oxen team and a team of horses. It was ordered for another family, but they are now on to three weeks late picking her up. If you have the cash, it's yours."

Brandy sank back to her seat and gulped in air. "How much is it?"

"One hundred fifteen dollars for the wagon, and you'll have to have oxen or horses."

"What's the difference?"

"Oxen are right on fifty dollars a piece and horses are ninety."

It didn't take Brandy long to decide on the cheapest thing. "I'll take the oxen."

"Well, I hate to tell you, ma'am, but you'll need extra teams of oxen, and since I only have one, I'd advise you to take the horses, too."

"Why?"

"Oh, boy, horses!" Scott shouted.

"Shh," Billy hissed. Billy reached over and swatted Scott's arm. "Be quiet."

"Ouch!" Scott rubbed his arm and scowled at Billy.

Brandy gave Scott a look of warning that she'd seen Father Brown do many, many times. "I'm sorry, Mr. Butler. I believe you were going to explain why?"

"It will increase your chances of them lastin' the entire journey if you work them in shifts. And you'll have something to ride when you're tired of walking."

Brandy frowned. "It appears I have no choice. I'll take the extra team. How much?"

"Two hundred ninety bucks," he told her.

Brandy hadn't expected to pay so much, but Sam had been generous with the money he'd sent. However, a return bank visit would be necessary before she could purchase the rest of the supplies. That would leave them broke again. Money always seemed to be the root of all their troubles. Why couldn't she have been born rich? Then she wouldn't have to rely on anyone. She opened her black bag to pay Mr. Butler his fee.

"Much obliged," Joseph said. He counted the money, then leaned back in his chair. "Have either of you ever driven a wagon?" His bushy brows drew together in question.

"I've driven a buckboard," Billy said.

"Well, that's a help, but it's going to take some practice to handle this enormous wagon." Joseph stood up.

"I wanna drive. I wanna drive." Scott, who had been quiet for all of three minutes, decided to start again.

Mr. Butler must be a patient man, Brandy thought, because he calmly said, "I'm afraid you're a mite young."

But Scott wasn't to be put off and continued to protest as they went out to look at the covered wagon. Brandy looked up at the prairie schooner. It was bigger than some wagons, but still there wasn't much room, considering the size of their family.

"It's not very big," Brandy commented.

"Sure it is, Brandy. There's nothing in here . . . come see," Scott called from inside the wagon.

"It's average, ma'am," Joseph informed her. "I reckon it be 'bout ten by four feet. Heard tell some folks sew pockets and slings to the inside canvas for extra storage space."

"That's a good idea." Brandy looked over the inside, trying to picture where she would put everything. "Mr. Butler, could you provide me with a list of supplies we'll need?"

"You betcha. Then I'll teach this young man here—" Joseph squeezed Billy's shoulder "—how to drive."

"Did you change your mind, Mr. Butler?" Scott asked as he climbed from underneath the wagon.

"Correction, I'll teach *both boys* how to drive."

Brandy smiled warmly. She was thankful for this man's help. Instead of turning his back on them he was trying his hardest to actually show them what they needed.

"I'm going back to town, Billy. I'll see you at home. Come on, Scott," Brandy called to the child, who now had his head stuck out the back of the wagon. "Are you coming?"

"No. I want to drive the wagon. I'm staying with Billy."

Brandy glanced at Billy, a question in her eyes.

Billy smiled. "He'll be fine."

Joseph handed her a piece of paper. "Here's your list, ma'am."

Taking the list Joseph had written out, Brandy hurried on. As she walked, she unfolded the paper and began to read over the items. Her eyes grew wide at all the things they needed. Sweat beaded her worried brow. A fan should be the first thing on the list, she thought. She tugged on the neck of her dress. The first thing she was going to get was a cooler garment.

She began the long walk back, making a right turn at the gunsmith's shop. She stepped up on the boardwalk, passed the newspaper, funeral parlor, millinery shop, and two saloons. Up ahead she saw the dry goods and clothing store, with its sun-blistered sign.

The day had grown hotter than she'd expected, and each step became an effort. She was absolutely miserable as she yanked at the top of her dress again, which was now soaked with perspiration. Her flushed face spoke of her predicament. Even her hair protested its confines and had escaped the hairpins to straggle down her back.

Watching her feet, Brandy had to will each foot to move. How much farther, she wondered as she raised her head to look at the building. However, the building wasn't what she saw.

Walking down the boarded walkway, heading straight for her, was the scout . . . Thunder. She had really rather not see him now, knowing her appearance wasn't the finest. She needed to be at her best when she approached him again about being their guide. But there was no escape now.

She was trapped.

His footsteps slowed, then drew to a stop when he reached her. He said nothing while he took in her bedraggled appearance. She could feel his gaze slowly roaming over her, and she had to concentrate to keep from squirming. His eyes showed his mirth. "It *has* been warm today."

"Warm! It's been downright hot," Brandy retorted, forgetting that she needed a favor from him. "I'm sick of this sweltering heat!"

He stared at her as if he needed to study her face. "You'd be cooler if you wore a loose-fitting dress," he suggested. "Perhaps something in a lighter color, or are you still in mourning?"

"Yes, I'm still in mourning, and I'm sorry for my harsh tone. I guess the heat has made me irritable," Brandy apologized, realizing she'd snapped at him. "The heat has made me grumpy, but I intend to take care of this hot dress in about five minutes." She pointed at the dry goods store, then looked back up at him. Her gaze met his silver-blue eyes. They seemed to see through her, as if he could read her unspoken thoughts.

Living behind the mission's wall, she'd not seen many men, but she was sure this man was considered handsome, or at least she thought he was. She could see an inner strength, and she wondered if he belonged to another. Perhaps he had a wife out west, one who waited for his return. She almost reached up to touch his strong jaw, but stopped herself. Then she frowned.

Thunder stared long and hard, feeling his body tighten. His response to this woman didn't please him. He hadn't been attracted to a white woman in a long time, and now wasn't the time to start.

He saw her hand move as her many thoughts were reflected in the depths of her violet eyes. Those eyes of hers made his heart pound much harder than it should. Her beauty outshone her drab appearance, and he wondered why she tried to hide her loveliness. He had the strangest urge to ask who she mourned. Perhaps a husband, a mother, or maybe a father. It wasn't any of his business, he reminded himself. He was probably better off not knowing. "Have you found someone to escort you and your family?"

Her eyes held his in a way he'd not experienced before. "I've found you," Brandy said softly. "I had hoped you would reconsider."

He reached down and brushed back a damp strand of hair which clung to the side of her cheek. Her skin felt like velvet beneath his fingertips and, once again, desire raised its ugly head.

He watched Brandy tense. Her parched lips parted. She swallowed. Nervously, she ran the tip of her tongue over her lips as he watched her intently. Her eyes widened, and she blushed a bright pink. This kind of heat was much hotter than the outside temperature.

"Will you be our guide, Mr. Thunder?"

"Just Thunder."

Thunder liked the way she said his name and, for a fraction of a second, he considered her offer. His gaze drifted over her, and he found himself wanting to reach over and pull the pins from her hair and watch as it tumbled around her shoulders. What would it hurt to help her, seeing as he was already heading that way?

Thunder drew in his breath. That answer was much too easy. He wasn't comfortable with the way this girl made him feel. It was better for him, and for her, that he keep his distance.

"I hope you find someone, ma'am, but I'm not the man you need." Thunder stepped around her and strode down the sidewalk, his boots sounding heavy on the wood.

Once again, he hadn't given Brandy a chance to argue the point.

Once again, she vowed she wouldn't give up. Somehow, some way, he was the one to help them . . . the trouble was, he didn't know it.

SIX

Brandy watched Thunder walk away from her. "Oh, but I *have* found the man I need," she whispered. Convincing him was still her biggest problem. Her gaze bored into his back as he strode off. She admired the proud way he carried himself, and felt a stirring in the pit of her stomach. She felt strange and breathless—and always disappointment whenever he left. Funny, she couldn't remember feeling like this before. She shook her head. "It must be the heat," she murmured.

Brandy entered the dry goods store, which was the backbone of Independence because it carried the majority of supplies. A big sign hanging near the cash register said, IF WE DON'T HAVE IT, YOU DON'T NEED IT.

"What can I do for you, Miss Brandy?" Mr. Gardner greeted her.

She pulled the list out of her pocket and handed it to him. "I'll be needing these supplies."

"Are you sure you need all of this, Miss Brandy? By the look of this list, I'd say you were taking a trip."

"As a matter of fact, we are leaving Independence," she said as she moved over to look at the dresses and material.

"Sorry I am to hear that."

Brandy looked back at him. "The parsonage is closing, and I couldn't find a job here in Independence, so we had little choice," she explained. She noticed that the tops of Mr. Gardner's ears turned red. He evidently did feel guilty about the job refusal.

Turning her attention back to the clothing, she purchased two dresses, each simple in design and made of light calico and muslin materials. She also ordered the supplies for the trip from the endless list. They would need: 100 pounds of flour; 100 pounds of butter crackers; 100 pounds of bacon sides; 50 pounds of dried beef; 50 pounds of kiln-dried cornmeal; 20 pounds of rice; 25 pounds of beans; 1 light rifle, 1 Colt pistol and ammunition for both; 1 butcher knife; and 1 small axe.

"An axe? I wonder why Mr. Butler put that on the list?" she murmured as the storekeeper laid it down in front of her.

"Never know when you might need it. Can even use it as a weapon. Things can be mighty rough out there, ma'am."

Brandy shivered and prayed they would never have to use the axe as a weapon. "I also need a tent with two poles, some bed-clothing, and a few dresses for the girls. It appears that Mrs. Gardner has been busy sewing," Brandy said as she held up several dresses the woman had made.

While Mr. Gardner fetched the supplies, Brandy noticed a ready-made dress from back East. She'd never seen anything so pretty. She ran her fingers over the soft material. The dress was a lavender color with a white apron. She couldn't help wondering what she'd look like in such a gown.

Mr. Gardner swept by her with a sack of flour

which he placed on the counter. "You'd look mighty pretty in that dress, Miss Brandy."

"It is lovely, isn't it?" She touched the frilly ruffles. "But I don't need it. These other dresses will suit my needs much better."

"If you say so," Mr. Gardner said, then went back to adding up the merchandise. "Now is there anything else you'll be needing?"

She looked at the stacked supplies, and her eyes widened. "I hope not."

"Good. I'll send these packages to your place later. They're much too heavy for you to carry, and I know you don't have a buckboard."

Brandy smiled at his kindness. "Send all but the dresses, please. I'd like to take them with me," she said.

Because I'm going to burn this hot dress once I get home.

After paying out the last of her money, Brandy grabbed her bundle and turned for the door. "Good day, Mr. Gardner." The bell jingled as she opened and closed the door. She couldn't wait to return home and take a bath to cool off, and then try on her new dresses.

Mr. Gardner waited for Brandy to leave before going over and fetching the dress she'd been admiring. Once, when his wife had been sick, Brandy and Father Brown had helped him. He hadn't forgotten that kindness. This dress, which he packed in a separate box, was his way of repaying her.

Later that night, after Brandy had bathed, she slipped on a cool white shift and stepped just outside her bedroom door and looked at the wagon parked in the courtyard. She sighed and wondered about the adventure to come. The wagon appeared enormous sitting in the courtyard, but at the same time small when she thought about all of them fitting into the miniature home. They had a hard time getting along in the rambling courtyard—smaller quarters would be a real challenge.

The night was quiet; only the trickling sound of water in the fountain broke the silence.

They were really going. If she could find someone to accompany them. Thunder was their only hope on such short notice. Somehow, some way, she had to convince him they would be no trouble. Why, he wouldn't even know they were around. She crossed her fingers behind her and hoped that would be true.

Perhaps if she went to the Golden Lady tomorrow around noon, she could talk things out with him. Since Thunder saw Billy every day and knew him, he just might change his mind if he thought she was Billy's sister.

Billy had told her the Golden Lady was located beside the harness maker's. He'd also told her respectable ladies didn't go there. But desperate times called for desperate measures, she rationalized. Tomorrow she intended to pay one of the Golden Lady's patrons a visit.

She couldn't worry about her reputation when they needed help. Besides, she'd be leaving Independence soon, and she didn't care what the good people of the town said about her once she was gone.

The saloon was dark and musty, but at least it provided relief from the noonday sun. The Golden Lady was a haven where a man could cool his parched throat without being bothered by the troubles of the day.

At a side table just to the left of the swinging doors sat Cody Wright with his sidekick, Stanley. Cody was boasting about his most recent gunfight.

"That makes three, Stanley."

"You're gettin' mighty good with that sidepiece, Cody. You keep on and you just might have a reputation 'fore long."

"Shit, Stanley. Yuh suppose they'll be writin' stories about me in those dime novels?"

"It's possible." Stanley laughed. "As long as you're the fastest."

"I'm slicker than grease, all right," Cody boasted. He looked around the room, feeling far superior to any of the other cowhands. Then his eyes caught an outsider . . . a stranger . . . someone he didn't recognize. "Who's that newcomer over younder at the bar?"

"Which one?" Stanley counted more than fifteen men at the crowded bar.

"The one with the faded cavalry pants sittin' alone. I don't recollect ever seein' him before."

Stanley scanned the people at the counter, then spotted the fellow in question. A slight smile crossed his lips. "Goes by the name of Thunder."

"Whatcha know about him?" Cody could smell another victim. "By the way he wears his gun low, I bet he's a gunslinger."

"I don't think you'd call him a gunslinger, even though I hear he's real fast," Stanley said. "Heard tell he comes from up North, and was a real hero in the war."

"What's he doing here?"

"Scoutin' for the next wagon train headed west. They say he's part Cheyenne."

Cody placed tobacco in a wrapper, tapped it to distribute the weed, then licked it and rolled a cigarette. "I wonder if he's any good with that gun? Maybe he's just full of piss an' vinegar." His lips twitched in anticipation.

Stanley scrutinized the man called Thunder. Something about the nonchalant way he stood, and the dark hat he wore pulled down just enough to hide his face, spoke of the menace that lurked just beneath the surface like a snake ready to strike if provoked.

Stanley weren't no fool, but he couldn't say the same of Cody. "I don't think I'm aimin' to find out."

Thunder felt the eyes of the two men across the room on him. He sipped his third whiskey slowly. The clear brown liquid burned his throat, but eased his muscles which had been coiled like tight springs. He hated this waiting. Maybe a fight with those two cowboys might ease his tension. Hell, if he hadn't already committed himself to Ward, he'd pack his gear and head out. It had been too long since he'd been home.

"Want another whiskey, Thunder?" the bartender asked.

Thunder nodded at the sound of his name. He thought of his family and wondered if they would think he'd changed. He had his mother's white features, a small chiseled nose with high cheekbones. But his father's features were strong also, providing him with a square, firm jaw. His eyes were the combination of both parents. The black eyes of his father and his mother's vivid blue had left Thunder with eyes of silver-blue. He was bigger than most Indians, standing six foot, two inches, and every inch was lean and firm.

Broad, muscular shoulders provided the power it took to take his enemy down.

At one time, Thunder hated the white man and all he stood for. But now that he'd come to know them, he could truly say they were not all bad. Oh, there were some, but there were braves he didn't like, either. Now he felt torn between his two worlds, and he hoped going home would provide some of the answers to where he truly belonged.

A brown whiskey bottle thumped the bar as it was set in front of him, its appearance breaking into his thoughts. He looked up and found it wasn't the bartender who'd brought his drink but Billy.

"You look like you could use this." Billy smiled.

"Hi, kid. It's good to see you," Thunder said. "If you're smart, you'll never touch this stuff." He flicked his eyes to the bottle. "It's only good for rotting one's soul," he remarked as he straightened and looked at Billy across the bar. Thunder had come to like the scrawny kid. "Where were you yesterday? I kinda got used to seeing your ugly face around here."

Billy gave an impatient shrug. "Rather been here than what I was doin'."

"Which was?" Thunder asked.

"Learning how to drive some bullheaded oxen." Billy frowned. "They were supposed to be trained, but trained in what is yet to be determined. Personally, I think both shoulda been shot!"

Thunder chuckled. "I hope you showed them who was boss."

"Well . . . let's just say we now have an understanding." Billy laughed, too. Studying Thunder, Billy decided now was a good time to ask about the wagon.

He folded his arms and leaned on the bar. "Have you reconsidered my sister's offer?"

"Sister?" Thunder stared hard at the kid. His brows drew together into an affronted frown. "Offer?"

"Brandy said she asked you to help us on the wagon train."

His silver eyes widened with astonishment. *"She's* your sister?"

"Yeah, I guess you can say that." Billy shrugged his shoulders almost apologetically and added, "We're from the same orphanage."

"Orphanage? She's an orphan, too?"

"Yeah. She's got some crazy notion she's going to marry some guy out in Wyoming she ain't never met before."

"Why?"

"Long story," Billy said with a frown. "But it's why we need your help."

"I don't think it's a good idea, kid." Thunder didn't want to go into his reasons why. Especially when one of the main reasons was Billy's beautiful sister.

"I'll do most of the work," Billy offered, hoping to sway him.

"I've no doubt." Thunder smiled. "Your sister doesn't look like she's done a day's work in her life."

"Dang right," Billy agreed, then caught himself. "That may be true, but things have changed."

"I'm sure your sister can find someone else," Thunder said as he looked past Billy to the mirror hanging over the bar. He caught a glimpse of Ward approaching him.

"So, I find you here loafing." Ward thumped Thunder on the back. "Some help you've turned out to be."

"I'm a scout, remember? And right now there's

nothing to scout except a drink." Thunder glanced at the mirror behind the bar to make sure the two cowboys were still seated. The more he thought about a fight the better the idea appealed to him. He needed to release this tension somehow. And busting a guy in the mouth just might do the trick.

The saloon looked normal, Brandy thought as she stood outside the doors. She smoothed the front of her new cream-colored dress, thankful for the lighter material.

She heard laughter and music, so how bad could the place be? Taking a deep breath for courage, she lifted her hand and pushed. The swinging doors opened easily when Brandy touched them and stepped inside The Golden Lady.

The smell of stale beer and unwashed bodies replaced the fresh air she'd come from, and Brandy gagged.

She squinted, trying to see in the murky light. It took a few moments for her eyes to adjust to the dim, smoke-filled room.

For the moment, she hadn't been noticed, giving her time to survey the surroundings. The place was very noisy with the many conversations taking place at the tables. And on a raised platform, a piano player pounded out a tune. There were at least a dozen tables scattered around the spacious room, each occupied by men of every size and dress. The brightly-costumed dance hall girls mulled around the room, entertaining the gents.

Brandy's eyes widened when one of the girls sat down on a patron's lap and wrapped her arms around his neck. She laughed when he bent down and kissed the top of her breast. Brandy looked away quickly.

A long, wooden bar sat at the back of the room. Its patrons were propped against the counter, some facing out, some facing toward the bar. At the very end stood the one man she sought . . . Thunder. Then her gaze drifted to the man next to him. Ward was there, too.

That was all she needed. He'd probably already asked Thunder about being her escort only to find out she had lied.

Damn. Damn. Double damn! Would her luck never change? Brandy bit her bottom lip before summoning the courage to saunter over to Ward and Thunder.

She had barely taken a step when a hand reached out and grabbed her wrist, jerking her down onto a pair of masculine thighs. "If you're looking for someone, honey, I'm your man."

A small squeal escaped her lips. Her heart pounded. "I—I don't think so. I—I need to speak to that man over there." She pointed toward Thunder and tried to regain her footing.

Stanley's eyes quickly followed hers. A quick grin formed on his lips. He felt like he'd just found the bait to accomplish his goal. The little lady was pointing to the gunslinger he'd been wondering about earlier.

"So you're partial to breeds," he growled. His cruel tone sounded harsh and none too friendly.

"That is none of your business," Brandy informed him as she managed to get to her feet. However, the man still had a tight grip on her arm. She tried to jerk away. "Let go of me!" Glancing around, she saw they were drawing the attention of others. Great! Just what she needed.

Billy had just poured Ward a drink when he glanced at the door to see what had caused the ruckus. "Gosh almighty. It's Brandy!"

Thunder snapped around in time to see what was going on. He homed in on the man hanging onto Brandy's arm, and Thunder's jaw tightened. He shoved off the stool, only to find Ward's hand on his arm in an attempt to stop him.

"He's bringing her this way," Ward whispered. "Wait and see what he wants."

Thunder didn't like it, but he stayed put.

"Unhand me!" Brandy demanded as she was being pulled across the plank floor. She struggled and managed to kick over two chairs, but did little toward gaining her release. The man's fingers bit into her arm. Finally, she swung at him, her hand connecting with the side of his head, momentarily stunning him.

Cody glowered at her and tightened his grip. "You little hellcat!"

"Get your hands off her!" Billy shouted.

"Who the hell are you?" Cody sized up the boy behind the bar. He'd expected the Indian to say something—not the kid.

"She's my sister," Billy said with a stern-faced expression. "Let her go!"

"If I were you, young'un . . ." Cody paused, an ugly smile on his thin lips. "I'd shut my mouth and stay behind the bar. It seems she wants to see the Injun."

With her captor temporarily distracted, Brandy seized her opportunity, and kicked him hard in the shin.

"Why, you little bitch!" he yelled. Cody's grip slackened as he reached to rub his injured leg. She jerked free and dashed over to stand between Thunder and Ward.

Cody grabbed for her, but lost his balance and fell facedown on the floor. He scrambled to his feet and reached again for the prize.

"I wouldn't do that if I were you," Ward warned.

"Stay out of this, old man. I saw the bitch first."

Brandy flattened herself against the bar. She'd never heard such language! And certainly never directed at her.

"Whatcha doin' in here?" Billy whispered over her shoulder.

Brandy turned toward him. "I'm trying to get someone to escort our wagon." She shuddered as she looked around again. "This isn't a very nice place," she whispered back.

"No shit!" Billy told her heatedly. "I told you I'd talk to him. This ain't no place for a lady."

Silence hung thick in the room as everyone turned to watch the two men arguing over a woman. It wasn't an uncommon thing in any saloon and usually the death of one or the other would follow, providing the men had backbones. It was the best entertainment of the week.

"Yuh just goin' to sit there starin', or are yuh goin' to give her to me?" Cody asked.

"I'm not going anywhere with you," Brandy told him, hoping she was right. So far, she didn't seem to be getting much protection from Thunder or Ward, who hadn't taken their eyes off the man.

Undaunted, Cody reached for her again. Thunder caught the cowboy's wrist and squeezed tight until the other man winced. "I believe the lady said she had come to see me. Find another way to amuse yourself, my friend," he said evenly through clenched teeth.

"Get your hand off me, Injun," Cody spat, jerking away from Thunder and wiping his sleeve like he was trying to get the dirt off. "I don't like yer looks." Cody lowered his hand to his side and flexed his fingers just over his gun handle. "Why don't we settle this outside like real men?"

"Unlike you, I have no doubts about my manhood," Thunder said, wishing the scum would just go away. He had seen his loudmouthed kind before, and knew he looked for trouble. The girl had only provided an excuse.

The crowd chuckled at Thunder's insult.

"Either draw on me fair, or I'll put a bullet in yuh now!"

Thunder slammed down his glass and pushed away from the bar. He held his hands out, fingers flexing, ready to react in a heartbeat.

The gleam in Cody's eyes spoke of his excitement over his impending accomplishment . . . another notch in his gun handle. The whole thing made Thunder's skin crawl. He'd seen enough senseless killing. He didn't need more.

Brandy reached over the bar and grabbed Billy's arm. "Do something!" she pleaded.

Billy's eyes were wide. "I am. I'm going to duck behind the bar."

The next thing she knew, Ward had jerked her out of the way.

"Why are they making such a fuss, Ward? I didn't mean to cause any trouble. I only wanted to talk to Mr. Thunder."

"It's not so much *you* as the man's just looking for a fight. And it appears this time he's picked the wrong feller."

Thunder eyed Cody for a few long minutes, then moved past him, heading for the front door of the saloon.

"Where are you going?" Cody demanded.

Thunder didn't bother to answer. He just pushed through the batwing doors.

Chairs started to scrape on the floor as everybody stood up to follow Thunder.

Ward took Brandy by the elbow and escorted her outside. Billy followed close behind. "There's always excitement when a good fight is about to happen," Ward said.

"Can't someone do something?" Brandy pleaded.

"Not at this point," Billy said as he leaned up against a strong post. "It's gone too far."

The spectators from the saloon lined up along the boarded walkway while people who had been moving across the street now stopped to stare. The main players took their places on the dusty street.

A hot breeze blew tumbleweeds down the street. Wagons and drivers came to a stop, not wanting to get in the middle of gunfire.

Brandy listened to the mumbling all around her as each man placed his wager on who would win. Appalling—that's what it was. This whole thing was just one big game to them, and they couldn't care less if someone died. What was wrong with them? Death was not entertainment.

Finally, stillness prevailed. A hush came over the crowd and lingered in the air as the waiting began.

Ward leaned down to Brandy. "Are you sure you want to see this? It could get real ugly," he told her.

"No, I don't want to watch. I don't want them to fight at all." But in spite of her words, she couldn't pull her gaze off Thunder. He looked dangerous. Very dangerous. And yet she had the strongest urge to protect him.

Ward looked from man to man before he commented, "I'm afraid the cards have been dealt. There's no stopping it now."

"I heard Thunder's fast," Billy said, his voice filled with awe.

"Yes, he is," Ward agreed, nodding. "But there's always someone somewhere just a little faster."

Thunder stood, his feet braced apart, his hands hanging loosely by his sides. He flexed his fingers as he waited. Poised and ready, he appeared completely lacking in emotion.

Brandy shivered.

What was the secret to this man who stood so ready to fight for someone he hardly knew, she wondered. She was sure a compassionate man lurked in there somewhere, but so far he had hidden it well.

Brandy realized Thunder wouldn't have been in this fight if she hadn't entered the bar. If something happened to him, she'd never forgive herself. A strange kind of magnetism drew her to him. She didn't want to think she'd never see him again.

She jerked her eyes away from Thunder and focused on his opponent. The man didn't look half the man Thunder was. She'd heard someone call him Cody. He appeared cocky. But could he shoot? Would he win? God, she hoped not.

She silently whispered a prayer for Thunder.

Cody was beginning to have second thoughts. He shifted his feet as he recklessly attempted to stare down his opponent. His stomach quivered with uneasiness. He'd thought the breed would have backed down by now. Had he misjudged his opponent? He couldn't possibly be that fast. If he were, he would have heard about him. Cody wished the breed would move . . . draw first, but he just stood there, seemingly unconcerned.

He needed provoking.

"Yuh might look like a white man, but you're a stinkin' Injun! We don't need your kind 'round here!" Cody shouted. His finger twitched to feel the cold metal next to his hand. "Any last words?"

When Thunder spoke, his voice sounded cold and deadly. "You have a big mouth for such a small man."

Cody's temper blew and his trigger finger jerked. "I'll teach yuh! You'll be no better than buzzard's bait." His hand sliced through the air as he went for his gun.

This was it.

Brandy watched with horror.

Thunder had his gun palmed before Cody's cleared the holster. The bullet whistled through the air, carrying death to its target.

"Did you see that?" Billy shouted. He'd never seen anyone that quick.

The roar of the blast . . . the acrid smell of gunpowder . . . the ripping of flesh as blood splattered from Cody's chest sent a numbness running up Brandy's back, spreading like wildfire. Her head throbbed as a blackness engulfed her so quickly she couldn't do anything to stop the darkness as it sent her crashing to the ground.

SEVEN

Brandy couldn't see anything, nor could she move, but she vaguely heard voices and the shuffling of feet coming from the fog that had engulfed her. She wanted to move, but no sounds came when she tried to speak.

"She's been hit!" Billy shouted.

Thunder heard Billy's cry. A cold knot formed in his stomach as he hurried to Brandy's side. How could she possibly have been hit? There hadn't been any stray bullets. Could someone else have fired a bullet at precisely the same time? A bullet meant for him?

When he reached Brandy, he bent down on one knee and lifted her head, cradling her in his arms. He ran a hand over her body probing for a wound, but discovered none. Puzzled, he felt her forehead and found it cold and clammy.

"She's just fainted, Billy," he said. "Probably should get her inside."

Thunder rose, clutching Brandy in his arms against his chest. Before he could move, he heard the marshal call to him.

"Take her over to the jailhouse. I'll need to be talking to yuh, mister."

Thunder's expression hardened to a mask of stone. "You coming, kid?" he asked Billy.

"No, I'll go back to The Golden Lady. Need to pick up my pay. 'Sides," Billy grinned, "it appears she's in good hands. Take care of her, Thunder."

Thunder nodded. He didn't bother to answer the lawman, but headed toward the jailhouse with his unconscious burden. Brandy was as light as a feather, he thought when he looked down at her. He also noticed the new dress and smiled because she had taken his advice. He was especially glad to see it wasn't black.

"Need some company?" Ward called as he came up behind Thunder. "The marshal could spell trouble," he pointed out, then added, "Did you have to kill the man?"

Thunder passed Ward, then looked at him. "Should I have let him shoot me?"

"Guess not." The corner of Ward's mouth twisted upward. "But you could have wounded him instead of killing him."

"He needed killing before he killed somebody else."

"But that wasn't up to you."

In Brandy's fog-filled world she felt herself being carried. Someone's arms were firm and his shoulder hard as her head rested against him. What was wrong with her? Why couldn't she walk, see, or talk? She felt weak, drained of all energy. She wanted to say something, but her body refused to cooperate.

Voices drifted in and out of the murkiness; one of them sounded like Thunder. She felt so peaceful wrapped in strong arms, but whose? Were they Thunder's? Why would he hold her so protectively when he didn't like her and wanted nothing to do with her?

Giving up her feeble musings, she succumbed to the darkness once again.

Inside the jail, Thunder placed Brandy on a chair. She started slipping sideways, and he had to place his hands on her shoulders to pull her forward until her head was positioned between her knees. She began to struggle against his hands, and Thunder knew she would be all right.

He shoved her back up until he could see her face. Her hazy, violet eyes attempted to focus on him, but she still seemed woozy as her head bobbed from side to side. A fine sheen of perspiration coated her face. Thunder could see she hadn't fully recovered, so he kept his hands firmly on her arms to prevent her from falling over and cracking her skull. Now that he was so close, he could see that she was even prettier than he'd first thought. The gods had given her the rarest eyes he'd ever seen.

"She still looks peaked," Ward commented from beside him.

"The color is starting to come back to her face. She'll recover," Thunder said, then added, "When she does, I want to know why she came into The Golden Lady. She should have had better sense."

Brandy felt as though her head was two sizes larger than normal. She could tell someone was holding her up as her vision started to clear, and then she saw Thunder and Ward.

"What happened?" Brandy asked as she struggled to hold herself upright. "I feel terrible."

Thunder turned sideways to talk to her. "You've fainted, little one." She was surprised that his voice sounded soft and tender. "It seems you don't like the sight of blood."

A flash of the gunfight reminded her how scared she'd been for Thunder. "You were not hurt?" she asked.

"No. I don't have a scratch."

"And that's what I need to talk to you about." Marshal Pete's voice came from somewhere behind Thunder.

"Why are we in the jailhouse?" Brandy asked when she heard Pete's voice. They didn't bother to answer her.

"You're under arrest for murder," Pete said.

"What?" Thunder started to stand, but as soon as he let go of Brandy, she clutched his arm. Not able to do anything else, he held his arm around her, letting her head rest once again, on his shoulder.

Ward snapped around at the sheriff's words. "Wait a minute, Pete! I can vouch for Thunder. He works for me."

"He might work for you, Ward, but he's just killed a man in cold blood. The whole blame town saw him. They want blood."

"It wasn't cold blood. The dead man provoked him," Ward insisted. "He was doing everything he could to make Thunder draw on him."

"The fight was fair," Thunder added.

"That's not what everyone else says." Marshal Pete picked up a set of keys to the cell. "Remember, you're a stranger in this town."

"The fact that I'm part Cheyenne wouldn't cloud your good thinking, would it, Marshal?"

"You insult me, son." Pete glared at Thunder before heading to the cell. "Afraid I'm goin' to have to lock you up."

Brandy felt Thunder's shoulder muscles tense. She

still felt weak, but the cobwebs had finally begun to leave her brain. She was grasping bits and pieces of conversations, and she knew the conversation had turned sour. If they put Thunder in jail, he'd be hanged, and she would be stranded without help. Thunder was her only hope. Besides, he wasn't guilty. That other man had caused the fight and Thunder had done everything he could to avoid shooting him. And she couldn't bear the thought of Thunder in jail.

"Wait, Marshal Pete," Brandy's shaky voice stopped him from moving forward. Instead, he came back to stand in front of her and Thunder.

"You need to save your strength," Marshal Pete said in a soft voice, much different from the tone he'd used with Thunder. "I'll take you home after we lock this here fellow up."

"No!" She struggled to sit a little straighter.

Startled by her outburst, Pete straightened and gaped at her.

Brandy cleared her throat. "You know me?"

Pete smiled. "Yep, for a long time now."

"Then you realize that I'm an honest person?"

He nodded his head. "Yes, ma'am, I can definitely say that. But what are you getting at?"

Brandy's pulse began to beat erratically. She had to make Marshal Pete understand. "Thunder was defending me from that . . . that . . . awful man. If it hadn't been for me, Thunder wouldn't be in this pickle," she said. She drew in a big breath for strength and went on. "You cannot lock him up. I've hired him as my guide, and he's going to help my family go out west. If you arrest him on this trumped up charge, you'll sentence my family to starvation!" The marshal scowled, but Brandy rushed on anyway. "We have to be on that wagon train. And if I don't have Thunder, Ward will not let us travel with the train."

"Surely it can't be that bad, Miss Brandy. Can't you find someone else?"

She let out a long, audible sigh. "I've tried. There is no one else. I don't want anyone else." Brandy paused, surprising herself with her last remark. It was true. She didn't want anyone else for a guide. For some strange reason, she needed this man. She trusted him.

"Thunder was in that fight because the other man attacked me in the saloon. He merely protected my honor," she rushed on. "I assure you, it was a fair fight, Marshal. I want this man and no one else. In a few days, we will be leaving and you'll never see him again."

Ward cleared this throat. "You should listen to the little lady," he said. "Thunder is the scout for my wagon train and has graciously volunteered to escort Miss Brandy. Otherwise, she would have to stay behind. She and that bunch of kids are tenderfeet. They need him."

"We'll be pulling out in two days, and I'll assume full responsibility for Thunder until we depart," Brandy said.

The marshal rubbed his jaw. "This puts a new light on everything. I've never known you to tell a lie, Miss Brandy, and considerin' this fact, I'm trusting you now. I'll release him in your custody on one condition. He must stay at the parsonage and out of sight until the wagon train leaves. Probably not safe anywhere else. Someone might want to get even." He folded his arms across his chest and looked sternly at Brandy. "Is it a deal?"

Brandy looked at Thunder. Was that smoke she saw coming out of his ears?

He wasn't pleased.

Afraid he might say something and change the marshal's mind, she quickly replied, "That will not be a problem."

Thunder couldn't believe what had just happened. He was being railroaded, and he didn't particularly like the way his future was being decided right in front of him without him having any say. No matter which way he turned, he was no longer in control of his destiny. He didn't like it one bit, but going to jail for something he didn't do wasn't to his liking, either.

"Guess you both can go now," Marshal Pete said, but added, "Don't make me regret my decision."

Thunder felt like shoving a fist into the marshal's gut. Instead he pulled Brandy to her feet. "Are you able to walk now?" he asked roughly.

"I think so." As soon as Brandy took a step, she stumbled and reached for Thunder. "Sorry, I must still be a little weak."

"That is usually the case right after a fainting spell," Thunder snapped. He helped Brandy back to the bench. "I'll get my horse. He's still at the saloon." Thunder stopped and looked at the marshal. "That is, if you trust me to come back."

Ward followed Thunder out the door. After a few moments he said, "I must say you're taking this very calmly." He wondered what was going on in his friend's head. He didn't like it when Thunder got this quiet.

"Well, I sure as hell didn't want to hang," Thunder said. His lips thinned with anger. "That little lady may have gotten what she wants for now, but will she be able to handle what she has gotten?" He glared at Ward. "She could have just made the worst deal she has ever made in her life!"

Ward chuckled, then stopped as he realized what Thunder was saying. "Wait a minute." Ward took his hat off and rubbed the top of his head. "I thought you had already agreed to be her guide. That's what she told me."

Thunder took his horse by the reins. "I told the woman no."

"I see." Ward's mouth twitched as he mounted his horse. "I'll check on you later."

Once he was away from his hotheaded friend, Ward laughed until his sides ached, and it was all he could do to stay on his horse as he rode back to the wagon train. To say Thunder was mad, damned mad, was an understatement. He was furious! The little lady had hoodwinked him and she was going to have her hands full.

Thunder returned with his horse and went inside to get Brandy. She was standing and appeared to have improved but still seemed a little shaky as he escorted her to the horse. He mounted first, then reached down. "Give me your hand."

Brandy could almost feel the anger in Thunder. She reached for his outstretched fingers, and in one swift movement he pulled her up and in front of him. She squealed at the shock of his amazing strength. He ignored her, wrapped his arm around her, and nudged his horse in the sides. They took off at a slow walk.

He remained quiet as they rode to the parsonage. Brandy wasn't sure what to say. She tried not to touch him, but finally gave up and leaned against his chest. She felt his muscles tighten immediately, but she held on. She was sure he was angry at the way she'd manipulated the situation to her favor, but she felt she was justified. Surely he would forgive her later.

She hoped.

Brandy was going to have to try very hard not to provoke his wrath, but as least she had a guide, and they would be making the trip to a new life. A small twinge of guilt crept over her, but it didn't last long. She had saved his arrogant hide, and she wouldn't hesitate to remind him of that fact. He could be sitting in jail right now instead of carrying her home. At least, he could be grateful for that small favor.

Her gaze swept over his face. The firm set of his jaw demonstrated that he wasn't grateful. Yet.

Brandy liked being cradled in Thunder's arms. He had been very gentle with her, in spite of his anger. She wondered if this was what it would feel like when Sam held her, and she prayed she would feel something for the man. She found Thunder's easy breathing comforting, and something deep in her soul seemed to draw her to him.

Sneaking a peek up at his strong profile, Brandy wondered what it would be like to be kissed by such a man. Would it be pleasant or would he be rough, demanding, and ruthless?

"Have you ever been married?" Brandy wondered out loud.

"I thought you were asleep."

"No. As a matter of fact, I'm feeling much better."

"Good."

As they rode on, Brandy realized that Thunder hadn't bothered to answer her question.

* * *

The parsonage was built into a square with a large courtyard in the middle. He had passed the front doors before, but figured another door would be on the side for supplies. And, sure enough, when he rode around the corner he saw that a second pair of double doors were mounted at the back of one of the side walls. Formidable, Thunder thought.

He dismounted and knocked.

A young girl opened the doors. "Who are you?"

"Your new scout," Thunder said as he tightened his hold on his skittish horse's bridle.

"Open the doors, Mary," Brandy said from high atop the mount.

They entered through a side door and immediately Thunder's gaze swept the spacious compound. Good; at least he wouldn't feel so confined, he thought as he led the horse inside. He tied the horse to a hitching post. Reaching up, he caught Brandy under the arms and helped her down. Every muscle in his body screamed as the length of her body touched his. For some obscure reason, though his head told him to let go, his hands wouldn't obey. He looked down into her upturned face and stared at her expressive violet eyes. "You are very beautiful, little one."

Shocked that he'd actually said something nice, Brandy's lips parted to say something, but words were not forthcoming. She'd thought Thunder was going to kiss her. Worse, she'd wanted him to do just that. She'd never been kissed, and she wanted to experience it. Her curiosity was shameful, she reminded herself.

Instead of kissing her, Thunder set her away from him and asked, "Where's my room?"

Dizziness assaulted Brandy. Her heart beat a wild rhythm unfamiliar to her, and she realized it had nothing to do with her fainting spell. This new feeling made her feel hot and cold at the same time.

"Who did you bring home?" Mary said, coming up behind them. "Your new husband?"

Brandy turned too quickly and swayed.

Thunder reached for her. "You are going to bed until tomorrow," he said, his firm voice brooking no arguments.

"No, I can't," she protested and brushed his hands away. "I have to get you settled in first. You have to meet the children."

Thunder wouldn't be put off. As he looked around he wondered if part of her dizziness might come from hunger. "Where is your room?"

"Who are you?" Mary snapped.

They both ignored Mary.

"I really don't need to lie down," Brandy protested, but she pointed the way when Thunder would hear none of it as he swung her up into his arms.

"Come on, I'll show you the way," Mary finally said.

He followed Mary and laid Brandy gently onto the bed.

"Who are you?" Mary asked again. "And what's wrong with her?"

"She fainted this afternoon."

"She has always been a weakling," Mary snapped, her feelings clear from the tone of her voice.

"We can do without your snide remarks," Brandy said, pushing herself up. "This is our new guide, Thunder. He'll be staying here until the wagon train leaves. You can take him to Father Brown's room, Mary, and I'll fix dinner."

"You're not getting out of this bed," Thunder said in a tone that allowed no argument, and pushed Brandy gently back down. "I believe I told you I didn't want this job. Now that I'm roped into it, you might as well learn that I am responsible for your little group, and you will follow my orders."

"Wonderful! Just what we need . . . someone else to give orders," Mary said.

Thunder looked at Mary. "Since you seem so talkative, perhaps you can show me to my room. Then you can help your sister wash up."

"She's not my sister!" Mary informed him. "I just had the bad luck to end up here with her."

So, there was bad blood here, Thunder thought as he followed Mary to his room. That was just what he needed—two fighting females.

When he was alone, he looked around the sparsely decorated room. He kicked off his boots, then lay down on the hard bed. He linked his hands behind his head and stared at the ceiling. How had he gotten himself into this mess? What should have been a simple journey home was becoming more complicated every day. He should be irritated at Brandy, for making this mess.

Hell, he *was* irritated at her! He'd told her a dozen times he did not want this job. He didn't need the headaches. Now he had them all. But, worst of all, Thunder realized that he did want one thing from Brandy. How many times had his eyes focused on her lips, on her eyes, and the silky hair that should never be pinned up, but left long and flowing?

Yes, he wanted something from Brandy . . .

And that fact scared him most of all.

EIGHT

Brandy stretched lazily, like a cat, then sat up in bed. Last night had been the first night she'd slept peacefully in a long time. Perhaps because the last of her problems was finally over.

Yawning, she slid her feet to the smooth wooden floor and listened to see if anyone else was up. Birds chirped outside her window, but that was all she heard. This morning would be a good time to try to make breakfast before everyone else awoke.

She stepped lively as she made her way past the new wagon at the rear of the courtyard. Now that they had a guide and would be heading west, Brandy realized with a pang of sadness that she was really leaving the parsonage. This had been the only home she'd ever known, and the thought that she would never again see the beautiful courtyard and everything familiar to her made her sad. A sigh escaped her lips.

"Shame on you," she scolded herself. She should be happy to be finding a new life. Shouldn't she? She continued across the courtyard before all her doubts could surface again. There was no turning back now.

Entering the kitchen, Brandy decided to attempt one more time to prepare hotcakes. She placed wood in the stove and lit the fire under the black griddle, then grabbed the big, yellow mixing bowl from the shelf.

She sifted flour into the bowl. Next she poured the milk. When it didn't look like enough, she poured some more, then added eggs. She began mixing up the batter, wondering if she'd forgotten an ingredient.

Something wasn't right, but she didn't know what.

Brandy placed thin slices of slab meat in a big, black skillet. Then she continued to stir the flour mixture. Soon the sound of sizzling bacon and its rich aroma filled the room. She smiled and tucked a stray strand of hair behind her ear, leaving a smudge of flour across her cheek. Maybe she was finally getting the hang of this.

She dropped a little of the mixture on the hot griddle to see if it was ready, then began to pour what should have been a thick batter onto the black surface.

"Oh no, it's too thin!" She paused and blew a wisp of hair from her eyes. "Well maybe, just maybe it will thicken as it cooks," Brandy said, attempting to convince herself as she watched little bubbles pop up in the batter. She could remember Rosa saying that when the bubbles appeared it was time to turn the hotcakes over. Grabbing a spatula, she attempted to flip the first hotcake, but found it had stuck to the pan.

"What's wrong with this damned thing?" Brandy realized she'd picked up Billy's bad habits. Father Brown wouldn't have approved of her swearing. Scraping up the batter became next to impossible as it turned black and smoke started to fill the kitchen. She worked harder.

Grease! She'd forgotten to grease the griddle.

She began to cough and tried to wave away the smoke.

* * *

Thunder had little choice but to sleep in his clothes since his gear hadn't been sent over. Ward had promised to bring a few of his things over today.

Of course, Thunder would prefer a bedroll under a starlit sky, but white men seemed to like soft beds. He hated to admit it, but he had slept well last night, soft bed or not.

He rubbed his jaw, then stretched. He was surprised he hadn't awakened in a bad mood today. His disposition was far from being sour. He attributed everything to the fact that he had been so tired. There wasn't much of a possibility he liked it here, especially when he was being forced to do something against his will.

One thing he knew for sure: he was hungry. Deciding it was time for breakfast and hoping the meal was ready, Thunder pulled on his black cavalry boots. He could use some good food this morning.

He stepped out into the courtyard ready to inhale the fresh morning air, but something tainted it.

Smoke! He smelled smoke.

Gray clouds of smoke filtered out of the small cookhouse. Wasting little time, Thunder ran to the kitchen door just in time to hear Brandy swearing from somewhere in the midst of the grayish-white haze.

"I take it you don't have much experience with cooking," Thunder said from the doorway.

Brandy jumped with surprise. "You scared me!" She squealed and, in the process, inhaled more smoke, producing another bout of coughing. "I—I seem to be having a few problems. Don't just stand there," she blustered between spasms. "Help me!"

In two long strides, Thunder stood beside her. He took the pan from her hand and tossed it into the sink.

He jerked open the window and began to fan the fumes outside. As the haze cleared, he looked down at the griddle to find a small piece of something black. Evidently, *that* had been breakfast.

Brandy groaned.

Thunder looked up. The first thing he noticed was she'd forgotten to put her hair up, and wisps of it clung to her damp face. She had a smudge of flour across her cheek, and her eyes were red. She looked like she'd been in a battle this morning, and she definitely hadn't been the victor.

"I guess I burned it." She sighed and added quietly, "Again."

"You could say that," Thunder agreed. "Surely, you have a talent for something."

"I'm beginning to wonder," Brandy said doubtfully. "I can't seem to do anything correctly."

"What will you do when you have to cook for your husband?"

She shrugged. "I don't know. Perhaps he will know how to cook." She took the ends of her apron and wiped her face. "I'll worry about that problem when the time comes."

Thunder finally chuckled. "You live dangerous, lady. Hell, he'll probably pay me to bring you back here."

"That's not funny!" Brandy snapped and straightened her stance to show her irritation.

He moved toward the stove. "As a peace offering, I'll cook breakfast. You can do something safer—like set the plates on the table. You have done that before, haven't you?"

Brandy ignored his sarcasm and watched as he made breakfast look like something a child could do.

In no time, the bacon had fried crisp, and the hotcakes were a golden brown. "You can cook?"

"Among other things. I can even eat with a knife and fork," Thunder added dryly. "My grandparents taught me many things, some of which were civilized manners."

Brandy didn't understand his statement about his grandparents. And she wondered why his mood had changed so quickly. He seemed insulted. She wanted to inform him that she hadn't meant to offend him at all, but before she could, Scott, Ellen, and Amy entered the kitchen.

"Something sure smells good." Scott sniffed the air. "Brandy must *not* be cooking."

Thunder laughed. "I see you have eaten her cooking before."

"Sure have." Scott put his hands around his throat, pretending he was choking.

"I'm sure there are other women in this country who can't cook besides me. And I don't see your ribs showing," Brandy protested primly.

"That's because Ellen and Mary saved us." Scott giggled. "How come it's smoky in here?"

"It's a long story." Brandy wasn't about to tell the children what had happened. They already thought her useless as it was.

Thunder figured young Scott was apparently the lively one. It showed in his eyes. "Have a seat, young man, and we will see if I can fill you up."

"Who are you?" Scott must have finally noticed Thunder for the first time.

Evidently Mary hadn't told the rest of the children about their new guest last night, Brandy thought.

"This is our guide, Thunder." Brandy nodded toward him. "He'll help us on the trip to Wyoming."

Ellen set Amy on a high stool, then took her seat beside Scott. She watched Thunder suspiciously. However, she remained quiet.

Brandy placed the food on the table, then introduced the children. "This is Scott, Ellen, and Amy, and I believe you have met the other two, Mary and Billy. They'll be here shortly."

"It is good to meet you." Thunder set a small stack of hotcakes in front of Amy. "Are you hungry?"

Amy nodded her head as her chubby little hand reached for the fork. "Silver eyes," she said, looking up at Thunder.

"Yes, they are silver, little one."

The door banged open, announcing Mary's entrance. Her gaze darted to the table. "Good. I don't have to cook." She sauntered over and poured a cup of hot coffee, then took her place at the table.

"Would you like some hotcakes?" Brandy asked.

"Not if you cooked them," Mary answered sullenly.

"My, you have such a pleasant disposition," Brandy said as she sat down at the table with her own plate. "I don't know how I could make it through the morning without seeing your smiling face."

"These flapjacks are good." Scott stuffed a huge bite in his mouth, then looked at Thunder and smiled. "He's our guide." Scott pointed his fork at Thunder, but didn't wait for her comment as his mind moved back to the food. "You don't know what you're missing, Mary."

Mary frowned, then sipped her coffee. "I'll take my chances."

Thunder watched the sulking young lady but remained silent. The girl definitely needed her manners improved, he thought.

"Good morning," Billy said, yawning as he came through the doorway. "Thunder! What are you doing here?"

"I am your guide, kid. Hadn't you heard?"

"You mean Brandy talked you into helping us?" Billy's surprise showed on his face.

"Brandy and the marshal."

"Marshal?"

"It was either agree or hang . . . I had a choice."

"Great! A prisoner. Just what we need," Mary muttered.

Billy chuckled as he sat down, reaching for a jar of honey. "Some choice."

"Yeah. That's what I thought," Thunder answered sarcastically. Then he, too, joined them at the table.

"You don't like us, Mr. Thunder?" Scott asked. He seemed disappointed.

"You can call me Thunder. And to be honest, Scott, I don't know your family, so I will save my judgment until later."

Scott seemed satisfied with Thunder's reply. "You'll like us." Scott grinned. "Especially me."

"Somehow, I don't doubt that," Thunder said matter-of-factly.

Billy poured honey over his hotcakes. "But why are you here? I thought you were staying at the wagon train with Ward."

"The marshal released me on the condition that I remain at the parsonage until the wagons pull out." Thunder took a bite of food, but felt his irritation returning. "While we're on the subject of the wagon train, let's set down a few rules. Since I will be responsible for all of you, my orders will be obeyed. When I tell you to do something, there will be no questions asked."

"Why?" Mary challenged him right away.

Thunder wasn't surprised at her reaction, but he chose not to answer her immediately. He shot her a silver glare that promptly silenced her. "Your lives may one day depend on all of you following my instructions."

"What are the rules?" Brandy asked. She wouldn't dare argue. She was glad to get the responsibility off her shoulders.

Thunder leaned back in his chair. "This journey isn't going to be easy. You must do your share. We leave in two days. Today, I want each of you to decide what personal items you want to take. Then we can begin loading the wagon. Any questions?"

"Are you the one who will protect us from the Indians?" Ellen asked.

"Yes, I will protect you. But it might not always be Indians you need protection from; after all, I am an Indian, too."

Ellen's eyes grew wide with fright. She rose so quickly, her chair fell over. She fled from the room.

"Wait!" Brandy yelled and tried to grab Ellen's arm as she ran past.

Thunder looked to Brandy for an explanation. What had he said that was so bad?

Brandy faced Thunder. "A war party killed her parents," she told him. "You couldn't have known. I'll go and talk to her."

"No!" He held up his hand. "I will go." Thunder stood and looked at the boys. "Billy, Scott, don't forget to feed the animals. I shall see the rest of you at the wagon."

When Thunder reached Ellen's room, the knob turned and the door opened easily.

"Don't hurt me!" Ellen screamed as she scurried to the corner of her room. "Just go away!" She raised her arms to cover her face.

"What makes you think I would harm you, Ellen?" Thunder said smoothly as he eased into the room. He left the door wide open to calm her fears.

"Indians are bad! They hurt people, and they killed my parents!" she sobbed.

Thunder noticed a chair beside the door and sat. He realized he'd be less intimidating if he weren't looming over the frightened child. He was used to the prejudice from men, not children.

"I am sorry your parents were killed, little one," he said softly. "Life is not always easy. Unfortunately, you'll find bad people in every race, so do not judge all by just a few."

Ellen's eyes were haunted with fear, and she clutched her doll to her chest.

"If Billy took your doll, would you blame Scott and Mary, too? Do you think that would be fair?"

Ellen said nothing, but shook her head. She continued to stare with her huge eyes, still very wary of him.

Thunder hated to see terror in any child's eyes. "My mother was white, and her life was saved by Indians," Thunder continued. "They took her into their family and, eventually, she married my father. I was a product of that union.

"If mankind could be measured by loyalty, courage, and their love of family, they would all be Cheyenne,"

Thunder said with pride, wanting very much for the child to understand his people. "Does that sound like the same kind of people you saw? I know a different kind of people than those of which you speak. Yes, they kill, but white men kill Indians, also." He raised his hands and motioned. "Come here, Ellen. I will not hurt you."

Hesitantly, she stood. And for a long moment she stared at the man who held his arms out to her. Confusion flickered across her face as she seemed to think over what he'd just told her. Timidly, she took a step, then stopped. Finally after several minutes she walked over and stood in front of him.

"Close your eyes," Thunder said gently. "Touch me." He gently took Ellen's trembling hands and placed them on his cheeks. "And tell me what you feel."

Slowly, Ellen moved her small hands over his warm face. "I-I feel a nose, e-eyes, forehead, and a strong jaw."

"Very good," he praised. "Now keep your eyes shut and touch your face and describe what your fingers feel."

Ellen's fingertips followed the same direction she'd taken on his features. "I feel a nose, eyes, forehead—I feel the same thing!" Astonishment touched her pale face and her eyes flew open.

"Precisely. We are made just alike, you and I." He pointed to himself and then to Ellen. "The difference lies within our minds. True, there are bad red men, but there are also bad white men, and you do not hate all of them." He took her small hands in his. "I am truly sorry about your parents. Killing is such a terrible waste. Do not blame me or my people. I promise I'll not cause you harm."

Ellen bit her bottom lip as she tried to judge the man in front of her. Finally, a small smile hovered on her lips. She was evidently willing to take a chance. "I'm sorry I misjudged you, Mr. Thunder, but my memories are still painful."

"Of course they are, but grow from the pain. Never let it destroy you with hate," he said softly as he touched her cheek.

Ellen smiled. A hint of trust shone in her eyes. And a little of the ice Thunder had built around his heart seemed to melt. If only for a minute.

Brandy sat on her bed and folded the clothes she would take with her. Her mind kept drifting back to Thunder. He intruded on her thoughts more often than she cared to admit, and he most certainly was a complete enigma to her. His appearance was rough and dangerous, yet this morning he had taken over the cooking, and when Ellen had been frightened, he had been the one to calm her.

Brandy hoped that she hadn't made a mistake. Ellen was terrified of Indians. Yet, Thunder appeared to have cared what Ellen thought which made Brandy think there was more to the man than he let people see. But she shouldn't be sitting here daydreaming about *him*. He was their guide, nothing more. Nor could he ever be.

Brandy's belongings were few, and her packing was accomplished in no time as she folded and packed her dresses in the trunk. The only thing she owned was a small, brown trunk with a "B" carved in the top. It was her only link with her past. A few articles of children's clothing had been the only items in the trunk except for a beautiful quilted blanket of blue-and-white patched squares. In the very center of the quilt was a larger white square with the initial "B" sewn in. She assumed the "B" stood for Brandy.

Curious to see how the others were doing, she hurried outside. Thunder and Billy were busily stocking the wagon as they lifted barrels of cornmeal and flour and tied them to the sides of the wagon. Stacks of boxes along with hammers, saws, nails, string, and rifles were strewn everywhere.

"How is Ellen?" Brandy asked as she approached.

"Ellen is fine," Thunder said shortly. He did not pause at all while he worked.

"You mean, she talked to you?" Brandy found it hard to believe Ellen had opened up to a stranger. She had never talked to Brandy about her fears, but then Brandy remembered, shamefully, that she'd probably never given the child a chance.

"She talked," Thunder answered in his solemn tone.

"And she isn't afraid?"

"She's still scared, but not like before," he said as he stacked crates. He acted as if she were bothering him. "Are you packed?" he asked before climbing up on the wagon.

Brandy was still astonished at how easily he'd handled the situation with Ellen, so it took a few moments for Thunder's question to register with her. "Yes, I'm finished. It doesn't take long when you have so little."

"Then how about giving us a hand up here." Thunder offered his hand, and Brandy accepted his help into the wagon.

Once inside, she saw how everything was beginning

to shape up. A small bed had been built behind the driver's seat for Amy. There were two cots made into the side of the wagon that lifted to reveal storage space for sheets and blankets. A hook dangled in the very middle where a lantern could be hung to provide light at night.

Brandy busied herself folding sheets and quilts, and then she stored their clothes. When Mary and Ellen showed up they were quickly put to work packing bacon and eggs in the barrels of cornmeal for preservation. Scott busied himself filling the water barrels, and Amy played and ran around the courtyard.

Brandy paused. She watched everyone busy at their tasks. For once in their lives, they were all pulling together. And for a brief second, she felt like she had a family. Laughing at such a silly thought, she continued her packing. What a crazy notion! She didn't want to be responsible for these children. She shook her head. The smoke from this morning must have gotten to her senses.

The rest of the day, they worked hard, taking little time to talk. Of course, grumbling could be heard from all sections. But everyone did as Thunder instructed.

Brandy decided to take a break, so she sat on one of the beds in the back of the wagon to rest a minute. Mary, Ellen, and Amy had gone to their room to take a nap. Brandy could see Thunder through the back. It was amazing how much calmer she felt just having him around. He wasn't bad to look at, either, she thought and immediately felt her cheeks warm.

His black hair glistened in the sun. He was tall and muscular, and she could see how most men would hesitate to cross him. She'd seen firsthand what could

happen when some fool did. She could tell by he way
he handled the children that he was a natural leader,
and it made her wonder what his life had been like
before coming to Independence. Maybe one day he
would open up a little and tell her something of himself, but she couldn't see that happening anytime soon.
He was still very angry about being tricked into helping them.

Later in the afternoon, Thunder checked the rifles
and their supply of gunpowder. He hoped there would
be no need to use the guns, but that was an unlikely
hope. As one man, he could provide little protection
for his . . . Brandy's family. "Billy, have you ever shot
a rifle before?"

Billy looked up from what he was doing. "A few
times."

"I think you and Brandy should practice. There may
come a time we'll need every man."

Billy nodded. "Reckon I never thought about that
possibility, but you're probably right."

"Let's go out back," Thunder said. He propped the
rifle on his shoulder and went over to the wagon,
where he stuck his head inside. "Come on, Brandy."

"I heard what you said, but I don't want to shoot
that thing," she protested, and didn't bother to move.

"And who will protect you if Billy or myself are
not near?" Thunder reached up to pull her out of the
wagon. "Tomorrow you will learn to drive the prairie
schooner as well."

Brandy didn't resist. She sensed it wouldn't do
much good anyway. "Why? Billy will be driving the
wagon."

"And what will you do if he becomes sick or dies?"

"Don't say that—" Brandy snapped.

Thunder placed both hands on her shoulders. "You're the one who wanted to make this trip. You'd better face reality. You are going to be doing many things you've never done before."

Brandy clamped her mouth shut as her stubborn streak took hold. Was he going to point out that fact at every given moment? She lacked a choice in making this trip!

She jerked away from him. Right this very moment, if Thunder were a target, she'd have no trouble hitting her mark!

Behind the cookhouse, Thunder set up a few glass bottles, then took his place beside his two charges. He still couldn't believe he'd been roped into helping this family. "You first, Billy. We'll start with the handgun since it's the easiest to use."

Billy handled the Colt awkwardly. Slowly, he raised the gun and aimed. He fired twice before hitting a bottle on the third try.

"Not bad, kid." Thunder patted Billy on the shoulder. "It'll take a little practice, but we'll keep working on it. Give the gun to Brandy."

The metal felt cold and strange in Brandy's hand, but she was still angry and didn't hesitate as she lifted and fired, doing little more than pointing at the bottle. Bull's-eye. The glass shattered on the first try.

"Horsefeathers! I wouldn't believe it if I'd not seen it with my own eyes!" Billy shouted what Thunder had been thinking. "It had to be a lucky shot." Her arrogant smile told them she was feeling quite superior.

Brandy was a little surprised herself, but she

wouldn't let them know that. Again she lifted the gun and pulled the trigger. Another dead hit. "This is easy," she boasted and finally smiled at their dumb expressions. Maybe she had finally found what she could do well.

Thunder stared at her in complete surprise. "You seem to have a natural aim. Do you suppose your ability is the same with all guns?"

Brandy shrugged. "How should I know?"

"There is one way to find out. Try the rifle."

Brandy found the rifle heavy and awkward to hold when she tried to position the butt against her shoulder.

"Here, let me help you." Thunder stood behind her, and he placed her left hand with his under the barrel and the butt against her shoulder. "Take aim," he whispered very close to her ear. "Squeeze the trigger, slowly."

Brandy became acutely aware of Thunder's arms around her. His rugged, manly smell made her knees weak, and when he spoke, his breath was a warm caress on her neck. She turned to say something to him and her lips brushed his cheek, causing them both to jump. She felt heat rush to her cheeks.

Evidently Thunder didn't feel the same. He displayed no feelings as he repositioned himself and whispered, "Squeeze the trigger."

The explosion threw Brandy back, and she would have fallen if it hadn't been for Thunder holding her. "Ouch!" she exclaimed. Her ears rang from the noise and her shoulder throbbed. She wanted no part of the rifle. "I'll stick with the handgun."

Thunder's gaze riveted on her face, then moved slowly over her body. He wanted to think he was just checking to make sure she wasn't hurt, but he knew that wasn't the case.

His unexpected reaction to her when she'd been in his arms had startled him. His body was still reeling from the impact of touching her in such an intimate way.

He was sure her shoulder would be bruised by tomorrow. "I think you've had enough for today. I will work with Billy a while longer." He watched as she walked away. She was like no woman he'd ever met before.

And that could be real dangerous.

That night, dinner was a feast.

Ward had brought Thunder's gear, as promised, and he also furnished steaks for the whole crew. After checking around town and asking questions, Ward figured it had been a while since they had had a good meal. He'd found out that Brandy hadn't exaggerated the desperation of her family. Tonight, he heard no complaints about the spread.

After dinner, Ward and Thunder strolled out into the courtyard to talk away from Brandy's curious eyes.

"Let me see what the lady got herself for a wagon. I hope nobody took advantage of her," Ward said. "I find it hard to believe she was able to get a prairie schooner on such short notice," he commented, not expecting an answer. "Of course, who could refuse her?"

That remark produced a hard stare from Thunder.

Ward attempted to look innocent. At dinner, he'd tried hard not to smile as he'd watched Thunder at the head of the table as he'd interacted with the children.

Ward thought about pointing that small fact out to Thunder, but figured he would take off his head.

Thunder turned and led Ward past the fountain to the wagon. They went over the vehicle with a fine-tooth comb.

"Looks like Brandy did a good job finding herself a wagon." Ward chuckled. "And . . . a guide."

Thunder had just lit a cigarette. "Keep at it, Ward, and you will leave here with a fat lip," Thunder warned."However, I will give you that she is quite a capable young woman."

"You look like you're adjusting well here. I'd have figured you'd be ornery as a mule by now. But you look relaxed and, I might add, satisfied with your new family."

Ward watched as a stony mask slid across Thunder's face. "They are not my family. I'm forced . . . no, hired help."

Ward stared hard before speaking. "I think I know you well enough to say you wouldn't stay here if you didn't want to. These walls aren't high enough to keep you inside." Ward became silent as he, too, lit a cigarette and propped his arm on the wagon wheel. "So, why do you stay?"

Thunder blew a thin ring of blue smoke and watched it drift through the air as he pondered Ward's question. "That is something I've been asking myself all day. I know I don't have to remain here. As you said, I could climb the walls and be long gone with no one the wiser. Yet, I'm still here." Thunder blew another ring of smoke before adding, "Frankly, Ward, that scares the shit out of me."

"And well it should, son. And well it should."

NINE

The ink-black sky provided little light across the courtyard below as the wind whipped through the compound. A storm was rapidly approaching. Thunder could smell the dampness. The gods must be in as much turmoil as was he.

Ward's words echoed again in Thunder's mind long after his friend had left.

Why did he stay?

Driven by an unknown need to escape, Thunder didn't bother with a saddle as he led his horse, Lightning, to the side gate of the parsonage. The gate barely creaked as he shoved it open and led his mount through the opening. He secured the gate behind him and swung his long legs across his mount and nudged the animal into motion.

Thunder rode around the back side of town before he urged Lightning into a full gallop, the open prairie, horse, and rider becoming one with the wind. The wind was strong tonight and tore at his clothes, daring him to shed his shirt. He loved the freedom of the open spaces and the feeling that came right before a storm.

The darkness, the danger, the excitement.

Soon he'd lost track of time and direction. His senses reeled with the exhilaration of his wild ride.

It also brought back memories of another such ride, a long time ago, when his Indian name had been chosen. Thunder pulled back on the reins, bringing Lightning to a halt. He looked up at the sky as if his grandfather could hear him.

"I remember the night we stayed in the canyon, Grandfather," Thunder whispered into the stormy sky. "The lightning streaked across the sky, illuminating the heavens, and the strong winds forced the trees to bend down and kiss the ground. It was the darkest of nights, but I had no fear. I found the storm exhilarating as I rode my pony down the long caverns. Hearing the rumble behind me, I dug my heels into my mount, urging him to go faster as I raced the thunder down the canyon. Just when I reached you, a loud crash occurred as the Great Spirit shook heaven and earth.

"I remember seeing the amusement in your deep-set eyes as your clay-colored skin wrinkled with laughter. I wondered as I slipped from my pony what had amused you so. Your words still ring clear in my mind."

When his grandfather had spoken it had been with great wisdom . . . "Tonight, my grandson, I've decided on your warrior name. You are Cheyenne, and I have taught you many things. You must not forget them, for they will give you strength. This night, you have shown no fear of the thunderstorm. When the trees would bend . . . you stood tall. From this day forward, you will be known as Rolling Thunder. Be proud of your name for there will come a day when white people fear Rolling Thunder."

Thunder sighed, wishing it were that night many moons ago when his life was so simple. "Grandfather, one day I will make you proud!" he shouted to the hills.

Then, from a distance, came the slow roll of thunder, rumbling across the sky and crashing with earth-shattering noise. He wondered if the upcoming storm could possibly be as strong as the one brewing in him tonight. His emotions seemed twice as powerful as any force of nature.

The rain began slowly at first and then the dark clouds let loose their water until Thunder was completely soaked.

His intentions had been to leave this town and not look back, but here he sat on a knoll that overlooked the graveyard where he'd first laid eyes on the violet-eyed beauty probably sleeping like a baby in her soft bed while he prowled the night.

He'd realized he'd made his decision. But why did he want to stay? Was it the sense of family he had learned from the Cheyenne? Did he feel sorry for this group of vagabonds?

Was that the real reason?

He needed answers, and he had none.

Shaking his head, he swore, "Damn you, Brandy!" He bumped his horse in the sides and urged him back. "Everything is her fault." Life had become too damned complicated since he'd made the mistake of making Brandy's acquaintance.

By the time Thunder returned to the parsonage, the storm had blown over and the first rays of daybreak were streaking through the sky. After rubbing Lightning down, Thunder changed into dry clothes, then stretched out on his bed and hoped to gain a few hours sleep. His last thoughts before he drifted off were of rare violet eyes that glowed with unexplained emotion

every time she looked at him. And he couldn't afford
to find out what that emotion might be.

A cynical inner voice cut through his thoughts. He
couldn't get wrapped up in this family. He was going
to accompany the wagon train to Ft. Laramie, and then
go home to see his mother. Once the trip was over,
he would never see any of them again.

Come morning, a cup of hot coffee helped chase
the cobwebs from Thunder's brain; however, having
had little sleep, his mood was far from pleasant. And
she was the reason for his sleeplessness.

After breakfast, he and Billy silently hitched the
horses. Thunder didn't want to talk. He didn't want
to feel. He straightened, just in time to see Brandy
walking toward them. "It's about time. Are you ready,
Brandy?"

"Yes." Brandy detected a hint of irritation in Thunder's voice and wondered what caused him to be so
short this morning. After his comment yesterday, she
was determined not to complain. He had been right.
The trip had been her idea and somehow she'd survive
it. However, she had never intended to drive the
wagon. That was supposed to be Billy's job, but she'd
show Thunder she could do it. Or die trying!

"Where are your gloves and hat?" Thunder
snapped. Once again, he sounded impatient. This time,
he didn't even bother to look at her.

"It's hot. I won't need them today."

That comment earned her a raised brow and a
frown. "We will see." Thunder's voice was as cool
and clear as ice water. "Climb into the wagon. Billy
is already up there."

She almost asked if she had done something to make him so disagreeable this morning, but decided her best course of action was to ignore him.

The seat was high above Brandy's head, and she wondered how she would get up there. Evidently Billy hadn't had a problem since he was already seated. She looked back to Thunder, but he had turned away again. Apparently, he wasn't going to help her. And when she glanced up at Billy he was grinning at her.

She hitched up her skirt and stepped on a wagon spoke. Grabbing hold of the side of the wagon, she managed to swing her leg over the jockey box just as Billy reached for her hand.

By the time Brandy had made it to the top, her skirt had slid up to her waist. It might not be a pretty entrance, but she'd made it. Straightening out her clothing, she took the seat next to Billy, who was laughing so hard he had to hold his sides. He muffled his mirth when she snapped her head around and glared at him.

Thunder had just grabbed his horse's bridle when he heard Billy's laughter. Thunder turned in time to be greeted by Brandy's backside. The woman must learn a more graceful approach to driving, he thought. Or she'd have every man on the wagon train watching her. Then he would have his hands full.

"If the seat is too high, you might try entering the wagon from the back."

Brandy looked up and glared at him. "I didn't think of that. Why didn't you say so in the first place?"

"I didn't realize you'd show your drawers to everyone," Thunder snapped as his piercing eyes swept over her. What was the matter with him? She wasn't his woman. Why should he care what others thought?

He was sure being nasty today, Brandy thought. She

had a good mind to tell him she didn't need his help. She'd do it herself. Then she realized that was probably what he wanted . . . to be released from his obligation. There was no way she was going to let him off the hook no matter what mood he was in.

He was taking his horse, so at least she wouldn't have to ride with him. However, he didn't mount. Instead, he took Lightning to the back of the wagon and tied the animal.

Thunder strolled back to the front of the wagon. He didn't bother to say a word; he simply climbed into the driver's seat.

"What are you doing up here?" Brandy asked. At the same time, she scooted toward Billy, making room for Thunder.

"Since you are both greenhorns, I think it's better if I drive until we get out of the town. I'd hate to have a spooked team tearing through the streets."

Scott ran toward them, jumping and shouting excitedly, "I want to go! I want to go!"

"Not today," Thunder said, then realized his tone had been short when he saw the child's smile fade. "We'll be leaving tomorrow, and then you can ride in the wagon all you want," he said. "Be a good brave and open the gate for us."

"What's a brave?"

Thunder smiled for the first time today. "Someone who is big and full of courage."

Scott grinned. "I like being a brave." He didn't bother to argue any further, much to Brandy's surprise. She watched him struggle to open the big doors, and then he waved as they passed through.

As the wagon swayed, bumped, and thumped, Brandy became uncomfortable squeezed between

Billy and Thunder. If she scooted much further in Billy's direction he'd be on the ground, but she didn't want to touch Thunder. Being close to him did strange things to her that she didn't understand.

Every time they hit a bump, her thigh brushed his, and she became very aware of the man next to her. He was staying on her mind far too much for her liking, and lately she'd even begun to dream about being kissed by this handsome stranger. She wondered if she'd lost all of her sanity.

"We will be there soon," Thunder snapped.

Evidently, he thought her squirming meant she was impatient.

She smiled to herself. *If he only knew!*

Ten wagons hitched and ready to begin their drills stood in a clearing just outside of town.

"I didn't realize there would be other wagons," Brandy remarked with a perplexed frown.

"These are the newest drivers. All of you will learn together. There will be another ten to twelve wagons which have already gone through their training period."

"Mind if I drive first?" Billy volunteered.

"Good idea. Here." Thunder turned over the reins to Billy, then jumped to the ground. "Stay thirty feet from the wagon in front of you," he said, and then he was gone.

The little band of wagons drove a couple of miles outside of town. Every driver maintained a straight line, keeping thirty feet between each wagon. If they didn't, they were reminded quickly by Thunder and Ward.

Billy handled the team like an expert, and Thunder praised him each time he rode past the wagon. Over and over again, they would circle the wagons, then straighten them out to form a single line.

The drills went on for at least two hours before the dreaded call was issued. "Switch drivers," Ward shouted over the din of wagons and animals.

"I'd rather not do this," Brandy tried to object. However, Billy ignored her as he handed her the reins and climbed past her. "What do I do?" she asked, feeling the same panic she imagined the animals must feel.

"Just click your tongue like this." Billy demonstrated the sounds for her. "And pop the reins."

Surprisingly, the animals moved forward, and it pleased Brandy. This might be easier than she'd first thought. She felt in command of the beasts in front of her, something she hadn't managed to feel with the children.

They moved along at an easy, plodding gait, and for the next half an hour, they formed orderly lines, then sweeping turns; then they did it all over again. Every few minutes, Thunder pointed out something she had done wrong or was about to do wrong.

Ward rode past her once and gave her a sympathetic smile. Then he issued the command to start again.

The hot sun showed no mercy as the day grew hotter, and Brandy's hands grew damp. She kept wiping them on her skirt, but the leather straps constantly sliding back and forth between her fingers soon caused blisters. Now she understood why Thunder had suggested gloves. However, she'd never admit the fact to him. No matter how much it hurt.

"Keep that line straight, Brandy!" Thunder shouted.

Was it her imagination, or was Thunder only yelling at *her?* Maybe she needed a new guide—one with a better disposition. The thought appealed to her at the moment. But it was soon forgotten as they kept up the grueling pace for another hour.

"Turn right and form a circle," Ward barked again.

Brandy groaned. The blisters between her fingers and on the palm of her hand had started to ooze.

"Are you all right?" Billy leaned forward to look at her.

"Yeah. Just a little tired," she mumbled. Boy, was that an exaggeration! By now, every muscle ached, and her shoulders burned from the constant pull of the animals. Then there were her hands! Maybe, if she switched to her left hand, which was in much better shape, she wouldn't be so uncomfortable.

Acting on the idea, she made the switch, but the straps slipped from her grasp and fell down on the jockey box. She immediately put her foot on top of the reins to catch them. She watched Billy out of the corner of her eye. He was looking out to the side, not paying her any attention. When she looked back to the team, she could see Thunder riding back from the first wagon.

Without wasting another minute, she reached down and tried to gather the loose straps. If she stretched just a little further, she could get them. She leaned over, but lost her balance and tumbled forward. Clutching at the jockey box with both hands, she screamed from her upside-down position.

Billy jerked around and grabbed Brandy's skirts. He tried to hold onto the fabric and reach the reins, but they, too, fell to the ground. Given their heads, the horses picked up pace and broke away from the line.

"Do something, Billy!" Brandy shouted.

"Be still!" Billy yelled. "If I lose my grip, you'll be crushed. Hang on, Brandy!"

"I can't. I'm slipping!" she yelled at the same time she heard the material of her skirt rip. "Catch me!"

Before she could scream again, she was no longer on the wagon, but sitting on a horse in front of Thunder.

"You're supposed to control the animals from the seat . . . not below it!" he bit out dryly.

"I know that! I lost—oh, never mind." Brandy refused to explain. Couldn't he see that she'd almost been trampled?

"If you're through with your little show, I suggest you get back on that seat and get your wagon in the circle with the others. We still have work to do," Thunder reminded her.

Brandy fumed as she jerked around to face him. "Why didn't you just let me fall? At least, I'd have been out of your hair, and you could devote your time to the rest of the wagons!"

Thunder rubbed his chin. "That's a thought. But you have five children in your charge, so get up there and do your job," he growled before shoving her over to the wooden seat and nodding for Billy to give her the reins once again. "See if you can hang onto them this time."

She glared at him, but wisely took control of the wagon again in her left hand.

Thunder looked past Brandy to Billy. "How about paying more attention to your sister? We could have lost the whole wagon because of her carelessness."

Billy looked sheepish. "Sorry."

Brandy was sick of their guide. She must have been

crazy to ever want him to start with. How was she going to put up with the insufferable mule for the entire trip? Maybe she should fire him. No, on second thought, they would never get to Ft. Laramie without him.

Drat! She sucked in her breath and blew it out. This was going to be a very long trip. Slapping the reins, she moved her wagon forward and then into the circle just like an old cowpoke.

Thunder sat off at a distance and smiled. Maybe it helped to get Brandy angry once in a while so she would forget her helplessness.

Ward rode to where Thunder sat on his horse. "Don't you think you've been a mite hard on the little lady? You could have hitched the oxen instead of the horses."

"Horses are more difficult. It is better that they learn from the hard team first," Thunder said curtly. "And, no, I'm not being hard. Just trying to knock some sense in that thick head of hers. I got a feeling I have yet to see the real Brandy. I have a gut hunch she has a stubborn streak in her a mile long, and I know she isn't as helpless as she thinks.

When they returned to the parsonage, Brandy was dog-tired. Billy had said he'd unhitch the team, and she didn't bother to argue. She really didn't care if she saw this vehicle anytime soon. She climbed out the back of the wagon and made her way to her room. She didn't know where Thunder was at the moment, and she wasn't sure she cared. He'd find something else for her to do.

The minute she closed the door, she started stripping her clothes to bathe. This morning she'd been smart enough to move the tub over by the window and fill it with water.

The warm sunshine had done a perfect job of heating the water. She sighed as she eased her aching bones down into the warm liquid. But the minute her hands hit the water, she cried out, and tears sprang to her eyes.

Looking down at her bloody, beaten hands, she could see the blisters that had formed and burst, leaving raw skin. She wouldn't be so foolish as to disregard Thunder's warning to wear gloves again. Perhaps she shouldn't have been so stubborn and listened to him.

Leaning her head back, she thought of the dark, handsome man. She began to lose her anger as an unfamiliar emotion began to unfold within her body. He hadn't asked for any of this, so she really shouldn't blame him for his bad mood. And he was nice to look at. She smiled at that wicked thought.

Thunder really didn't seem to show much interest in her, though, and she supposed she should be thankful for that.

But she wasn't.

Was she vain because she wanted him to think she was pretty?

Confused was the only way to describe her jumbled thoughts. They had been that way since the man had entered her life. She could barely remember her dull life before him. Perhaps, once they were under way, she wouldn't see Thunder that much, and she could concentrate on her future husband instead of the raw masculinity of her guide.

Carefully, she dried her body, making her hands

perform even though they hurt. Picking out a soft blue muslin dress, she slipped it on, then placed a cloth around her brush handle so she could pull the bristles though her hair.

Tomorrow she knew she'd hurt more, and getting dressed would prove difficult. Maybe one of the girls could help her.

Strange . . . she never could remember asking the girls to help her before. Was she really changing? Or was it just this difficult situation?

TEN

Brandy was the last one to arrive at the table. Everyone else was seated and already eating. They seemed to be enjoying themselves, and Brandy admitted that supper smelled exceptionally good tonight.

Billy glanced up as she entered the room. "Figured you'd decided not to join us after your rough ride today."

"What happened?" Scott asked, his mouth full of food.

"She was dern near trampled by the horses when she fell off the wagon," Billy explained between bites of cornbread. "Good thing Thunder managed to pull her back."

"Wow! You should be careful," Scott said, his look very serious.

"I realize that. And I will be careful from now on," Brandy said as she seated herself at the place they had prepared for her. "Sorry I'm late, but I took a much-deserved bath and then fell asleep for a little while."

"Boy, is your face red!" Scott said. "You should've wore a hat."

Billy grinned.

Thunder chuckled, but didn't comment, much to Brandy's surprise.

"It seems I should have done many things today that I didn't do. You all should take a lesson from me, and do wear a hat until you're used to being out in the sun so much."

Ellen placed her fork beside her plate. "Mary and I have hats already. What about Amy?"

"Amy will be in the wagon most of the time," Thunder said. "However, you should make her a small hat to wear when she's outside playing."

"Maybe we can use material from an old dress," Ellen said.

While everyone continued their chatter, Brandy served her plate, wincing every time the spoon hit a tender spot on her hands. She remained quiet during the rest of dinner, as she had to concentrate on getting the food to her mouth without hitting any raw spots. She'd just admitted that she should have worn a hat, but she wasn't ready to hear an *I told you so* about wearing gloves. At least, not tonight.

Thunder glanced at Brandy more than once. Something wasn't right with her, but he couldn't figure out what was wrong. She was much too silent. He knew she must be tired, but it was something else. Today, she'd probably done more work than she'd done in her entire life. Unfortunately, the days ahead wouldn't be any easier, something he'd been trying to tell her all along. He watched her face as she took each mouthful of food. Was that pain he glimpsed?

"Everyone should turn in early tonight," Thunder said when Brandy was finished eating.

Scott set down his glass of milk. An eager look on his face, he asked, "When do we leave?"

"When the sun first touches the morning sky,"

Thunder said, smiling down at the child's milk mustache.

"What does that mean?" Mary asked in her usual querulous tone.

"Try five o'clock," Billy answered.

"Why such an ungodly hour?" Mary said, not bothering to mask her displeasure. "Can't we leave later?"

"In a week, Mary, you'll not have to ask that question," Thunder answered with more patience than he felt.

"But I am asking now!"

"Oh, do be quiet," Brandy snapped. She knew she was tired, and her patience wasn't as good as it should be, but tonight she couldn't handle Mary's whining.

Billy glanced at Brandy with surprise and then jumped back into the conversation. "It will be much cooler to travel in the morning."

Mary's lips twisted into a cynical smile. "Brandy will never get up on time."

"If you go to bed now, perhaps you won't miss your precious sleep. And don't worry about me. I'll be up." Brandy's lackluster voice sounded much like she felt, and she really didn't have the energy to argue. "We all need to get used to this routine."

Mary got up abruptly, and threw her napkin on the table. "Thanks a lot getting us into this situation!"

"Wait a minute, Mary. I'll walk with you," Billy offered, and pushed back his chair.

Once Mary and Billy had gone, Ellen said, "You look real tired, Brandy."

Brandy glanced at Ellen and managed a weak smile. Before she could respond, Thunder answered for her.

"She's had a very busy day. I think Brandy has also

learned a few valuable lessons . . . such as the reason for wearing a hat."

Brandy frowned at him. She knew he was bound to say something sooner or later and, worse, she knew she deserved it. Her stubbornness had caused her pain.

"I'll put Amy and Scott to bed," Ellen volunteered. "You go on to your room."

"I can put myself to bed," Scott said as he jumped up and dashed from the room.

"In that case, I'll just put Amy to bed." Ellen laughed as she picked up the baby. "Brandy, you look like you can barely hold your head up. You'd better get some sleep, too."

"Thank you." Brandy smiled. The children could be sweet and cooperative when they wanted to. At least, some of them could be. "I intend to do just that as soon as I clear the table."

Ellen swung around. "Do you need me to help?"

"I will help her," Thunder said as he rose to his feet. "Run along and get some rest."

Scott ran back into the room. "Almost forgot. Good night," he told Brandy and kissed her on the cheek. Then he went over and motioned for Thunder to lean over so he could kiss him on the cheek, too. "See you in the morning."

"Good night, Scott." Thunder rubbed the top of the child's head and then patted Scott's backside as the boy ran off. Thunder was surprised and touched by the young one's open affection.

As Thunder cleared the table, he noticed that Brandy was still much too quiet. She sat at the table, staring off into the distance. Was she still angry with him? He'd really been hard on her today, but he had done it for her own good. "Come, Brandy. It will only take a moment to clean up, and then you can go to bed."

Slowly, she got up and reached for the plates. "Ouch!" she cried out, and the plates crashed to the floor before she could catch them.

After hearing the crash, Thunder quickly set his dishes down and turned. "What's wrong?"

"Nothing." Brandy's gaze flew up to his. Guilt dulled her eyes. "Apparently, I can't do anything right," she grumbled before bending down to pick up the scattered dishes. Carrying the ones that survived to the sink, she went back to get the pieces, but Thunder blocked her way.

He placed his hands on her shoulders, then tilted her chin up. "You can do many things well when you put your mind to it. Are you going to continue being silent all night, or are you going to tell me what is bothering you?"

"I don't know what you mean," she said, but avoided his eyes.

"Do you not?"

"I don't have anything to say," she sputtered, bristling with indignation. "Now, let's finish the table. I'm tired." She raised her hands to push him out of her way, but the minute she shoved him, she winced. Tears sprang to her eyes as she jerked back her hands.

Thunder grabbed her wrists and turned her palms so he could see them. He frowned at what he saw. He didn't like the looks of her hands. They were bloody and raw. He searched her face and saw the tears welling in her eyes.

Evidently, her skin had been so soft the straps had blistered her hands immediately. He gazed into her accusing eyes, feeling completely guilty. He wiped the tears from her cheeks and realized he felt a spark of admiration for her. She had handled her team although she had to have been in terrible pain.

Thunder admitted he had wanted to teach her a lesson, but not like this. Perhaps he had been too hard on her. However, if she'd worn her gloves, she wouldn't be in pain now, he quickly reminded himself. Maybe she had to learn everything the hard way.

"I will mend your hands," Thunder said as he let them slip from his grasp. "Where are your bandages?"

Brandy was shocked at the impact of his gentle grip. She watched the many emotions crossing Thunder's face, but she couldn't be sure what he was thinking. For a moment, she thought his eyes glowed with tenderness. And something more. She hoped he felt guilty because he'd fussed at her all day. Seeing the soft light reflected in his dark eyes made her wonder. Did he actually have a heart?

"The bandages are in a box behind the driver's seat of the wagon," she said softly, her heart beating in her throat.

"Do you have any other supplies?"

"Yes, I have quinine, opium, whiskey, and hartshorn for snake bites, God forbid, and laudanum."

"Go. Light the lantern. I will be with you in a moment," Thunder said, then turned for the door. "I must get something from my saddlebags."

Back in his room, he found the small pouch he needed. He returned to the kitchen to get a bowl. Measuring a spoonful of flour, he sprinkled herbs from his leather bag into the container. Next he added water, then stirred the mixture to the consistency of paste. All the while he cursed himself. He should be whipped for pushing Brandy so hard today. He knew she wasn't used to what he'd put her through. Yet, he'd been angry and had taken his anger out on her. It had been a long time since he'd actually felt any emotions at all, and he didn't like this guilty feeling. It was much better to be numb.

At this very moment, Thunder wished he'd never stopped in Independence, Missouri.

His life was starting to get complicated. He should have kept going until he'd reached his homeland.

All was silent as he made his way to the wagon. A full moon spilled a bountiful light over the beautiful courtyard.

Thunder found Brandy sitting on one of the bunks that folded down in the wagon. The lantern hung just above her head, casting a soft, warm glow to the interior.

"Let me see your hands," he said as he sat on the bunk across from her. He took her hands and turned them, palm side up, then placed them on his knees. He stirred the mixture in the bowl until it was a creamy white paste. "Why didn't you tell me your hands were in this condition?" he asked gently while he applied the white mixture, making sure he coated her fingers completely.

"Would you have listened?" Brandy challenged him.

Looking up, he stared into her violet eyes for a long moment. There, beneath those black fringed lashes, defiance sparked within, telling Thunder she still had fight in her. He liked that. "Probably not, but the next time, try."

"And have you yell at me like you did all day?" She laughed half-heartedly. "No, thank you."

He carefully rubbed the cream into her skin. Her closeness was like a drug, lulling him into euphoria. "Was I really that bad?" he asked with a soft growl. She nodded. Her burnished hair lay softly around her shoulders, coming to rest on the tops of her breasts. The hollow at the base of her throat caught his eye. Thunder couldn't suppress the smile that curved his mouth.

Brandy liked Thunder's smiles even though they were few and far between. The smile softened his features and made him look less intimidating.

"How does that feel?"

She noticed a change in his voice. It was huskier than before. "It still hurts, but is much better. What is that stuff?"

"It's made from special herbs," he answered as he tenderly held her hands, his tan fingers closing carefully around hers.

Brandy never dreamed Thunder's hands would feel so warm, so gentle.

"I put in mint leaves to help with the burning. Did it work?"

"Yes," she whispered. Hypnotized by his touch, she stared at his hands. "My fingers don't burn half as bad now, thank you," she whispered. Glancing up at Thunder's bronzed features, she could sense the barely controlled emotions he seemed to be fighting to rein in. Somewhere deep inside her, she wondered at her fascination with this man. Did he feel the same things she did?

"Leave the cream on overnight and it should help with the soreness," he told her as he wrapped her hands in strips of linen. "Your fingers will have to heal completely before you can drive the wagon again.

Brandy—" he paused as if he didn't know what to say "—I am sorry."

Thunder was so close Brandy could feel the warmth from his body. A delightful shiver of wanting something more ran through her. Something undeniable was building between them. Reaching over, Thunder pulled the ribbon from her hair and ran his fingers through it, letting the silky, reddish-brown strands fall freely. A brief shiver rippled through her.

"You should always wear your hair unbound," Thunder murmured in a husky, sensual voice.

A strange inner excitement filled her and she felt her eyes grow misty. Her heart beat faster as Thunder slipped his hand under her hair. Slowly, he rubbed the back of her neck, and warmth flowed through her body that had nothing to do with the outside temperature. His touch relaxed and soothed her, and she was surprised to realize that she wasn't as afraid of him as she'd been before. She sensed he wanted to communicate with her, but he didn't know how.

Brandy took a deep breath. He was strong and rugged, yet his touch was soft and gentle. And just now, he'd been patient and tender as he'd bandaged her hands. She couldn't say the same thing about earlier today. This man was very confusing. She couldn't figure him out. Her eyes misted with confusion over all these newfound feelings that this man seemed to produce in her.

All reasoning left Thunder while he stared into Brandy's dark violet eyes. Her emotions registered like a mirror, and he found she wasn't good at hiding what she felt. Of course, living in a parish, she would never have had to hide anything. In many ways, she seemed little more than a child, but her body was definitely that of a woman, and he couldn't seem to help himself as he gathered her into his arms.

Brandy's eyes grew large with passion. Thunder knew he should stay clear of her, but somehow he couldn't find the strength to resist her soft pink lips as they parted slightly and waited for his next move. *A move he shouldn't make.*

He brushed her lips lightly with his. She trembled as he breathed in the lavender scent of her soft skin. Struggling to hold himself back, he savored the tantalizing taste of her mouth, then placed soft kisses across her face.

Finally, losing the struggle, he crushed her to him, his mouth pressing against hers. He deepened the kiss, sliding his tongue inside for a tantalizing exploration.

Brandy returned his kiss with reckless abandon. She became lost in a swirl of emotions she'd never experienced before. Her arms moved around his neck and, at the same time, she felt herself being lowered to the cot she was sitting on. Hot sensations spread through her body like wildfire. She was shocked at her own eager response to the touch of his lips.

She twisted her fingers into his long hair and deepened the kiss as his hands explored her back.

Thunder's breathing grew heavy. Feelings he thought long dead raced through his body like a raging prairie fire. His senses reeled. The pleasure building in him had long since gotten out of hand. When his hand brushed her breast, he heard her passionate moan, and he wanted to give her more but . . . with a great deal of strength, he pulled back.

Puzzlement showed in Brandy's soft, moist eyes. She looked at him with an unspoken question.

"You are so innocent, and I am taking advantage

of that innocence," Thunder said as he stared down at her. He traced her lips with the tip of his tongue, and she parted her mouth, letting him give her one final kiss. God, she felt good in his arms. He hated letting her go. But that was what he must do. "I will resist touching you in the future."

"Why?" Brandy whispered, wondering what she'd done wrong. She definitely liked how Thunder made her feel, and it frightened her, too. There had to be more. She felt so empty. There just had to be more.

Thunder laughed harshly. "Because kissing is only the beginning. There are other things I could teach you, but that job will be for your future husband. You do remember him?" He hated the thought of another man teaching Brandy, touching her, and making her his wife. But what could he do? She'd chosen before she'd met him, and when they reached the fort he would not stay. He would be out of Brandy's life forever.

Brandy's face grew warm. A rush of guilt washed over her. The fact was, she hadn't given her future husband the first thought. "I—I forgot about him," she said in a small voice. She tried to feel ashamed, but she longed for Thunder's touch.

"Come, I will help you to your room so you'll not disturb your bandages," Thunder said in a little gruffer tone than he should have. Reality once again had returned, and he remembered that he was different. Brandy needed to marry her own kind.

In her room, Brandy sat on the bed while Thunder pulled off her shoes. "Will you be all right now?"

"Can you unbutton my gown?" Brandy held up her bandaged hands. "My fingers are too clumsy and the buttons too small."

Thunder groaned. He wasn't made of stone. But he knew there was no way she could do it with her hands bandaged. He sat down beside her and unfastened the garment, then quickly dropped his hands to his sides.

"Thank you for taking care of my hands, and thank you for the kiss. I've never been kissed before," she whispered in a tiny voice.

Thunder looked at her. He wasn't quite sure he'd ever felt like this when kissing anyone else. Hunger burned deep within him. And for the first time, he found he longed for the white world and this white woman.

He pushed himself up and left the room.

It was going to be a *long* journey.

ELEVEN

The sun was just coming up over the horizon as Thunder walked across the courtyard, casting just enough light so he could see where he was going. He'd already gotten Billy up.

Brandy was next.

Impatient to be on his way, he knocked on Brandy's bedroom door.

No answer.

Frowning, Thunder opened the door. Just as he'd expected, she lay curled up on her side, sleeping like a baby. Then he smiled. It didn't appear that she had moved all night. As he drew closer he noticed her thick, dark lashes resting on her creamy cheeks. Her lips were parted slightly, and she appeared not to have a care in the world.

If only life were that simple.

"Get up, Brandy."

She didn't move.

Thunder shook her shoulder after he still hadn't gotten a response.

"Go away," Brandy mumbled.

"Not on your life. Get up!" Thunder ordered. He threw off the cover and swung her feet around to the edge of the mattress, then pulled her to a sitting position.

Brandy groaned. "Please. I'm so sore," she complained, but didn't open her eyes. "Why are you torturing me?"

"Either get up now, or I will leave you behind. I do not have time to be your keeper," he said curtly, but added in a gentler tone, "How are your hands?"

"Hmmm?" she said sleepily.

"Your hands?" When she didn't move, Thunder swore, "Oh hell, I feel like I'm talking to a child." He took off the bandages and looked. Her fingers didn't appear as angry-red as they had yesterday. "Are they sore?"

Brandy blew a stray piece of hair out of her face. She seemed more awake now. "A little, but they are so much better than last night. Thank you." She gave him a half-smile. "Are the children ready?"

He noticed she was becoming alert. "Billy's getting them, and I hope they are moving faster than you are." Thunder slipped her last shoe on, knowing her fingers would be very stiff, and her face was still very red. "Come, stand." He pulled her to her feet.

"I don't have any clothes on," she protested.

Thunder looked down at her white chemise and saw how her firm, round breasts pushed against the thin material. "I can see that," he finally said, his gaze returning to her sweet-tasting mouth. He'd been attracted to her since the first moment he'd laid eyes on her . . . an attraction that needed to stop.

She crossed her arms across her breasts. "Well, you shouldn't be looking. Hand me that cream-colored dress, and I'll put it on, but you must look away."

Thunder sighed as he retrieved the garment off a peg and handed it to her. Then he turned his back to her.

After a few moments, she said, "You can turn around but you'll have to button my blouse."

God, he must be made of iron, Thunder thought as he moved to her. Carefully, he buttoned the front of her dress, his fingers brushing her creamy skin more than once. Every time he fastened another button his temperature rose a notch. After all, he was only flesh and blood.

"What about my hair?"

"You are a lot of trouble," he grumbled, his voice holding a note of impatience. "Turn around." Swiftly, he parted her hair in three sections and began braiding.

"Where did you learn to do that?"

"When I was small, I braided my mother's hair."

Brandy saw the heart-rending tenderness in his eyes when he spoke of his mother. It reminded her of the way he'd looked at her last night. Had the kiss meant anything to him? Suddenly, she felt awkward. "Well, you are very good at it." She started to leave, but he stopped her.

"One more thing," Thunder said as he strolled to the peg and retrieved a bonnet. He placed it on her head and tied the ribbons under her chin. "Now, you are ready."

She frowned at him for making her feel like a child. Is that the way he really saw her? Obviously, he wasn't thinking about their kiss. It had probably meant nothing to him. Hadn't he promised it would never happen again?

Thunder held open the door, and Brandy stepped outside. In another moment, they were at the wagon.

Everyone was there. Scott and Billy sat in the driver's seat and the girls looked out the back.

"See? I told you she'd never get up on time," Mary jeered.

Brandy ignored her and climbed into the back of the wagon with the girls.

Thunder fell in behind the wagon as Billy clucked the animals into motion. He herded the extra horses and a milk cow. Brandy admired the way Thunder looked this morning. He wore buckskin britches, cavalry boots, and a light blue shirt which made his blue eyes sparkle. Again, she thought of their kiss last night. She wasn't sure that it meant anything, but the kiss had been wonderful. Much more than she could ever imagine a kiss could be.

As they went through the gate for the last time, Brandy watched as her home grew smaller. She sighed, not knowing what the future would bring. She'd been surrounded by those walls for as long as she could remember. She just prayed Sam was a good man and that he would want a ready-made family. And if he didn't? Well, she refused to think of that problem just now.

Later . . . she'd think of it later.

The other wagons were lined up and ready to leave when Brandy's rig finally reached them. They took their position in the back of the line and waited for the signal from Ward to move out.

"See you later, kid," Thunder said to Billy before riding around to the back of the wagon. "To save the animals, the wagon must be kept as light as possible, so everyone but Amy and Scott will have to walk."

"What!" Mary screeched.

Brandy was surprised, too, but said nothing except, "Let's go, girls."

"I don't mind walking, Thunder." Scott scrambled from the back. "Isn't that what a brave would do?"

"Yes, it is." Thunder nodded and noted that Mary had yet to move. "If you refuse to move on your own," he told her in a deadly voice, "I'll be glad to assist you out of the wagon."

"I don't like this," Mary complained as she climbed out of the back. "Just what have you gotten us into, Brandy?"

Brandy heard Ward's voice ring out loud and clear. "Wagons, Ho!"

Brandy smiled as Mary trudged ahead. "Apparently a long, hard walk."

Slowly, they started moving all twenty wagons, one by one, until they were stretched out in single file. There would be no turning back now. Ahead lay an uncivilized land and the unknown. And that's what scared Brandy most of all: the unknown.

She tried to picture her future husband's face as she wondered what he would be like. Would she be able to love a man she didn't know? She almost laughed at the absurd thought. Had she not fallen willingly into Thunder's arms last night? Lord knows, she didn't know the first thing about him. But she would like to. She did know that she was attracted to the mysterious man. Why couldn't she have met Thunder first? She shook her head as she trudged along, trying to keep her face down so the bonnet would shade her already-tender face.

She looked up and saw Thunder in the distance. It probably wouldn't have mattered. Except for the tender moment last night, the rest of the time he seemed to wish she didn't exist.

Brandy and the children marched along beside the wagon. The dust wasn't as bad as if they walked directly behind. She tried singing songs and talking to Scott to alleviate the boredom, but so far there hadn't been much to see but flat prairie. She wondered how long they'd go before they stopped to rest.

It was nearing late afternoon when Thunder rode back to check on them.

"How's it going, Billy?"

"Not bad. Scenery doesn't seem to change much."

"Perhaps Brandy will be able to relieve you in a couple of days, so the job will be easier. And we do have another saddle so sometimes you can ride, but today won't be as long as others. We will stop when we reach the river," Thunder said before turning his horse. "I'll check on the girls."

He darted behind the wagon and found Mary and Ellen walking with their sunbonnet-covered heads down. Scott stumbled, and Brandy grabbed him before he hit the ground. She stopped and swung him up piggyback and then continued walking. Thunder leaned over and lifted Scott onto his saddle in front of him.

"Hi," Scott said, his voice sounding weary. "I'm still a brave."

"Are you tired?"

"Can braves be tired?" Scott asked.

Thunder nodded.

"Then I'm a little tired," Scott admitted.

"How about keeping me company for a little while?" Thunder's gaze moved to Brandy. "How are you doing?"

She glanced up at him as he rode beside her. "Do you suppose your cure for my hands will work on my feet, too?"

He smiled. "I will take care of that tonight. And see if I can find you some moccasins."

Mary swung her head around. "You could at least ask about us, too. Did you come back here just to gloat?"

"Only to see if the sun had sweetened your disposition, Mary. And I see it hasn't," Thunder told her, then nudged Lightning back toward the front.

"I hate him," Mary grumbled.

"It's not nice to hate," Ellen reminded her.

Brandy smiled and looked up at the blue sky. *How am I doing so far, Father?*

She could almost picture Father Brown beside her, walking along with her, step for step, his head bent, hands clasped behind his back. His voice came out of nowhere, *You're doing fine, my child. I knew you could keep your promise.*

Later that night, the call finally came to circle the wagons. The sun was just starting to set, and Brandy had never been so glad to stop in all her life.

Just as they practiced, the wagons started turning slowly until they had formed a huge circle. The extra horses, oxen, and cows were put in the circle so they could feed upon the grass without running away.

Campfires flickered to life as everyone prepared for dinner. Mary and Ellen volunteered to start the fire and cook.

Scott came running over to Brandy. "I want to help. I want to help."

"Scott, why don't you go and gather a few more sticks for the fire while Billy and I pitch the tent," Brandy said.

"Be right back," Scott said.

"Don't go close to the river."

Billy and Brandy spread the tent out flat on the ground. Brandy wrapped extra rags around her hands to protect them as she held the stakes for Billy to hammer into the ground. Finally, they raised the poles that held the tent up and it stood and actually looked normal.

"Not bad for a couple of greenhorns," she said as she punched Billy in the side.

"Darn near perfect." Billy grinned and shook her hand, careful not to squeeze. Then he threw back a tent flap. "Let's spread some blankets out on the bottom because after supper I intend to test this tent out."

"Just think, they said today was easy going." Brandy laughed. "I wonder what we will look like after a hard day?"

"Probably dead," Billy said as Scott came running up with his arms full of sticks.

"Look, I found a bunch."

Billy touched Scott's shoulder and pointed. "Take them over to the campfire."

Scott nodded, then stuck his head into the tent. "I like this."

"Good, because it is where you and Billy are going to sleep tonight."

"Oh, boy." Scott grinned and ran off with his bundle.

Brandy looked around. "Where is Amy?"

"Don't know. I thought she was with Mary and El-len," Billy said matter-of-factly.

"Have you seen Amy?" Brandy shouted to the girls. They both answered no. "We'd better look for her. You go that way and I'll go the other way," she pointed.

"Amy!" Brandy called as she hurried to the wagon behind them. So far, she hadn't really met the other travelers, and she hoped these people were nice. Surely, Amy hadn't wandered away from the wagon toward the river.

When Brandy reached the next wagon, she saw a big man with a ruddy face surrounded by a bristly red beard and mustache. A round cap made of some kind of plaid with a small ball on top perched on the side of his head. His trousers were homespun, and he had a little black pipe stuck out from the corner of his mouth.

"Hello, lassie. My name is Cameron MacTavish." He smiled as he held out his hand. "Just call me Mac-Tavish."

He had such a warm smile that Brandy knew she would like this man right away. "Hello. My name is Brandy Brown, and I'm from the next wagon." She pointed behind her. "I'm looking for a little girl about waist high." She held her hand just below her waist to demonstrate.

"And would she be havin' short brown hair and brown eyes to match?"

"Yes." Brandy nodded. "Her name is Amy."

"Then yer prayers have been answered, lassie." MacTavish took Brandy's arm and pulled her over to the back of his wagon. "Nettie, my girl. Believe we've found Amy's mother."

Nettie was a plump little woman with the same red hair as her husband. "What a lovely wee one ye be havin'," she said as she climbed out of the wagon with Amy, who had fallen asleep on Nettie's shoulder. "I have already fed her, and she went right off to sleep."

"Amy isn't my child," Brandy said as they walked back to her wagon. "We are from an orphanage that closed."

"Ye poor dears." Nettie shook her head and looked around at the other children. "There are so many of ye, why don't ye let Amy stay in our wagon? 'Twill give ye more room, and she's such a dear little thing, we wouldn't mind one bit."

Brandy thought for a moment. "Are you sure you don't mind? We do not want to impose."

" 'Tis no problem atall," Nettie assured her, then turned to her husband. "MacTavish, get our pot of stew and we'll eat with our new friends. I'll just go and lay Amy down and be right back."

Brandy strolled over to the girls. "Looks like we've made some friends. Do we have enough plates?"

Ellen spread out a second big blanket. "Look in that box in the back. There should be a couple more. Where is that woman taking Amy?"

Brandy explained as they got out the plates and silverware. Both girls agreed it would be best for Amy as well as give them a little more room.

When MacTavish and Nettie returned, Brandy introduced everyone and they all sat down to eat on the blankets, except for Mr. MacTavish who sat on an upside-down bucket.

"You talk funny," Scott said immediately.

"Do I now?" MacTavish laughed, a hearty chuckle

that made them all smile. "And I might be saying the same of you, laddie."

Billy was serving up his plate of stew when he asked, "Where are you from?"

"Scotland."

"It that near the Oregon territory?" Scott asked, then bit off a chunk of bread.

"No, lad, Scotland is across the sea. Nettie and myself came to America almost three years now."

Brandy leaned against the wagon wheel as she ate. "Where are you goin'?"

"We're heading to Oregon where we intend to farm. Are you folks going that far?"

"No, we're stopping in Ft. Laramie," Mary said.

Brandy couldn't believe that Mary was actually being civil tonight. Maybe she was just too tired, or maybe she liked the MacTavishes.

Brandy halfway listened as the conversation went on around her while her thoughts drifted off toward a certain guide. She wondered why Thunder hadn't come to have dinner with them. Of course, she couldn't blame him. He had already tasted her cooking. But, she realized, she'd gotten used to seeing him at dinner, and she sort of missed him. She sighed. He was probably eating with Ward, and not thinking of them at all.

She put her fork on her plate. "That was wonderful, Nettie. You are a very good cook."

"It's a pleasure to have someone to share our supper with. If ye not be a mindin', we could eat together every night," Nettie suggested.

All the children agreed at once that the idea was splendid. Brandy couldn't remember when they had all agreed on anything, especially so quickly. "We would like that, as I'm sure you can tell. As long as you use our supplies also," she added.

"It's a deal, then," MacTavish said. "Nettie here has always wanted a big family. Didn't know we'd find it in the next wagon." There was a trace of laughter in his voice.

Out of the darkness, Thunder appeared. "How is everyone doing tonight?" he said casually as he moved into the light of the campfire.

Brandy couldn't believe he'd been so quiet. She hadn't heard him approach. But she was glad to see him, even if he did tend to be a tyrant at times.

"MacTavish, Nettie." Thunder nodded.

"Cup of coffee?" Nettie held up the pot.

"Thank you." Thunder accepted the tin cup and sat down next to Nettie.

"What do we have in store for us tomorrow?" MacTavish asked.

"Tomorrow at daybreak, we cross the Missouri River. That will take the better part of a day by the time we get all the wagons across. If we're lucky, we'll make a couple more miles before we camp."

"Aye, sounds like a busy day." MacTavish nodded. "How would you children like a story before going to bed?"

They nodded their heads, and Brandy smiled. MacTavish seemed to have a natural charm. She was grateful to Amy for wandering off and finding these wonderful people.

"Come, Brandy, walk with me," Thunder said as he handed the cup back to Nettie.

They strolled down to the river. "How are your hands?"

"Just a little tender, but much better," she answered.

"I put rags on my hands when I helped put up the tent."

"I think you should use the cream again tonight. When your hands are better, you can ride one of the horses when they are not being used as a team. It will break up the weariness of walking. The other girls can ride, too, but we have only one saddle so you'll have to take turns."

"I'm sure everyone will enjoy riding." Brandy looked toward the dark water. "That's a big river. How will we cross?"

"You will see tomorrow. I am responsible for you, but I'm going to be busy helping the other families as well, so you'll have to help keep an eye out for everyone. How did the children do today?"

"I think they are holding their own. The grumbling ended about noon." Brandy laughed.

Thunder looked at her in the moonlight, thinking how nice it was to gaze at her face at the end of a long, hard day. He wondered if his life would have turned out differently if he had met her in Boston. She didn't seem the least bit prejudiced. He reached out to trace the curve of her jaw with his fingertips. She was too naive to know how to hide her feelings, and her lips parted. She looked very inviting. He longed to accept the invitation, but he was older. He knew better.

Brandy's skin tingled. She found herself wanting to kiss him as they'd done before. Thunder's eyes had darkened, and the sight of them made her breath catch in her throat. Her heart twisted just a little. She couldn't deny that something about him appealed to her. She just wasn't sure what that something was or what to do about it. This strange uncertainty was a very new feeling to her.

"Brandy." Thunder's hand fell away from her face. "Promise me you'll take care of yourself tomorrow," he said, his voice thick with something Brandy didn't understand.

Disappointment washed over her, and it was all she could do not to beg him to hold her for just a little while.

She wanted him.

She desperately needed him.

She drew in a deep breath and held her hands behind her to keep from reaching for him. "I will," she whispered. "You be careful, too."

She watched him walk away from her, knowing that it would be a long time before sleep chased away the thoughts of the man she could never live with, and could never live without.

TWELVE

The morning was bright and beautiful with a slight breeze blowing. Just enough to ease the heat so it wasn't quite as hot as the last few days had been. The milder weather was greatly appreciated since everyone was rushing around trying to prepare for the crossing.

Brandy and the children sat around the fire and ate their breakfast of biscuits and molasses. They had been allowed to sleep later than normal. She figured it was because they had to cross the river and the darkness would only add to the danger.

The lead wagons had already started moving toward the water. She and the children finished their breakfast quickly, then packed everything back into the wagon. Ellen and Mary washed the dishes and placed them in the special box at the back of the wagon. Brandy went to get the oxen.

"Brandy, you must get in line. You have to go across the river, too," Thunder snapped as he rode past them.

"And good morning to you, too," she called to his back. Damn man! He was so frustrating!

Billy chuckled as he hitched the oxen instead of the horses. "Mary, get the cow and lead him behind the wagon. Brandy, you ready?"

Brandy raised a brow. Billy was beginning to issue

orders like Thunder. Or maybe she was just being oversensitive. "Yes. Let's go."

They had to wait since they were the next to last wagon. She would have pointed out that small fact to Thunder, if she'd had the chance. Why hurry when they just had to wait for their turn? Maybe he just didn't know how to say good morning. She smiled at that.

It was interesting watching the other wagons float across the river on the large boats she'd heard Ward call scows. The extra horses, cows, and oxen swam their way to the other side. So far, everything seemed to be going smoothly.

It was midday when their turn finally came. With a wave of the hand from the boatman, they were motioned to move forward. Billy guided the wagon to the edge of the riverbank, where he unhitched the team. Several men rolled the wagon upon the scow, which was basically a flat barge with no sides. They placed blocks of wood in the front and the back of the wheels so the wagon wouldn't roll into the water. Brandy paid the fee of a dollar for the wagon, twenty-five cents for the yoke of oxen, and twenty-five cents for each horse.

Once the wagon was secured, Thunder told them what to do. "Everybody get in the wagon. Brandy, Mary, you can stand by the sides, and Billy and I will follow with the rest of the horses."

The boatman shoved them away from the riverbank, and the scow glided through the water, pulled by a tow rope on the other side. The muddy-colored river spanned out in front of them. Brandy was surprised at how routinely everything seemed to be moving. She glanced at the opposite shore and saw that the other wagons were hitching up their teams and starting to move out. They would have to catch up with them by nightfall.

"What's that in the water?" Mary asked as she peered over the side of the scow. Suddenly, her scream pierced the air.

"Woman overboard," the boatman shouted.

Brandy swung around just in time to see Mary topple off the side of the boat. Her head went under immediately.

Panic seized Brandy. There wasn't anyone to help Mary. Without thinking, Brandy jumped into the water. Father Brown had taken them to a lake many times when it was hot, but Mary had never been able to swim.

As Mary's head surfaced, she screamed, "I can't swim!" Water covered her mouth and silenced her screams and she went under again.

Brandy jerked her skirt up to her waist and tied it in a knot so it wouldn't catch around her legs again. Then she started swimming toward the girl. It seemed like forever before Brandy finally reached Mary and was able to grasp her arm and yank her up.

Mary coughed and thrashed her arms wildly as she panicked, hitting Brandy in the head.

"I've got you, Mary. Calm down," Brandy told her as she struggled to keep her own head above water. "Tread water with your arms like this." She demonstrated with her free hand. "Or we're both going to go under."

Mary calmed a little. Brandy looked to shore but they were in the middle of the river, which was much too wide to swim. The scow was being towed by a rope, so it kept on going across.

Out of the corner of her eye, she saw Thunder and Billy, but they were too far away.

She heard the boatman call to shore. "They're going to drown."

Scared, Mary started thrashing again. "We're going to die, Brandy. We're going to die!"

This time they both went under.

Brandy was determined that they would get out of this alive.

They hadn't come this far to drown.

God would give her strength. She shoved Mary to the top and then followed, gasping for air. She was losing strength, and she wasn't sure how much longer she could hold on. She just knew that she had to, no matter what.

Thunder watched helplessly as the two heads bobbed in the water. His heart was beating so fast he could imagine it bursting from his chest as he urged his horse to swim faster, but it still wasn't fast enough. With the clothes that the women had on it would be like a weight dragging them down. What if Brandy died? He felt a sensation so unfamiliar to him it almost robbed him of his breath.

They were going under. He reached out.

Suddenly, a hand swept down and grabbed her. The next thing she knew, she was being hauled beside a horse. "Wait! Get Mary first," Brandy insisted.

"Billy has her," Thunder said.

Brandy didn't realize how the sound of Thunder's wonderful, deep voice could calm her. Even if he didn't sound pleased. She floated beside his horse as they swam to the other bank. When the horse had gained his footing, Thunder let Brandy slip to the ground. She stumbled, but managed to get back up by herself. She wrung the water from her hair and shoved it behind her back and out of her face. Next she wrung the water from her skirt.

Thunder was beside her in a split second. "Next time, I will make you both get into the wagon! That was a damned foolish thing to do. And where did you learn to swim?"

"Father Brown took us to a lake when it was hot," Brandy informed him and gave him a puzzled look. Then anger sparked in her eyes. "But I knew how to swim before then. I was taught when I was a child. The only thing I know is that Mary went overboard, and I just couldn't let her drown," Brandy stormed back. "What is it about the daylight hours that make you so ornery?" she demanded as she brushed her wet skirts down. She glared at him. He merely smiled, making her that much angrier.

Brandy marched over to Mary. "Are you all right?"

Mary had been on her knees, throwing up water. Once she had settled her stomach, Brandy reached down and helped the girl to her feet. Mary wiped her mouth with her skirt. Finally, she turned and faced Brandy. There were tears in her eyes as she answered, "Yes." Then, after an awkward moment of silence, Mary said, "Thank you."

Ellen and Scott came running. "Brandy, you saved Mary," Scott shouted and looked at Brandy as if she were a hero.

"You sure did. Mary would have drowned if you hadn't been there," Ellen seconded.

"She would have done the same for me." Brandy shrugged. Thinking that they needed a little bit of humor, she added, "Or at least thrown me a rope."

The children laughed.

"I hope we don't have any more rivers to cross," Ellen said, worry in her eyes. Poor Ellen was afraid of everything.

"I'm sure we will." Brandy squeezed Ellen's shoulder. "But probably none as deep or as wide as the Missouri." Brandy smiled and said, "Let's go change clothes. There is only one wagon left and then we'll have to be back on the trail."

"The excitement is over," Thunder told them. "It's time to catch up to the rest of the wagons."

Mary and Brandy left the others and went to the wagon, where they changed clothes. When Brandy had trouble with the buttons, Mary brushed her hands away and buttoned Brandy's blouse.

Brandy smiled, and together they moved on with the wagon train. She sensed that something had changed between them, but it was still too fragile to talk about.

The train only gained two miles before it was time to circle up. Today had been long, but not as long as the days that lay ahead, Brandy thought.

Mary and Billy dug a pit for the fire and placed two forked sticks in the ground on each side of the rocks. Then they laid a pole across the two sticks to hold the heavy black kettle to cook in.

Brandy, Ellen, and Scott gathered buffalo chips to burn in the fire.

"What are buffalo chips?" Scott asked as he placed one in the basket.

Brandy laughed. "You don't want to know. Nettie said they burn just as well as wood, and there aren't any trees so we have to have something," Brandy explained, not bothering to tell him that the chips were dried dung.

"What we having to eat?" Scott asked.

"Nettie said that MacTavish killed a wild hen of some kind, so we will actually have meat tonight." Brandy looked down at the basket of chips. "I think we have enough for now."

"Good. I'm starved," Scott shouted and ran ahead of them.

Brandy turned to Ellen. "I can finish this up if you want to milk the cow."

"All right." Ellen headed in the same direction as Scott.

Brandy caught sight of a horse and rider and knew by instinct that it was Thunder.

"How are you doing since your near-drowning in the river?" he asked when he got close enough.

"I'm fine. Are you going to eat dinner with us tonight?"

His gaze traveled over her face and searched her eyes. Warmth crept through Brandy's veins.

Finally, he said, "I have to do some scouting ahead, so I'll be gone for a couple of days."

She swallowed hard, feeling very uncomfortable inside. "Please be careful."

He gave her that half-smile that she liked so much. "I will, but I think I should be saying the same to you after what happened today."

She laughed. "You may be right."

"Do stay out of trouble, and if you find that impossible, Ward said he would look out for you."

Brandy gave him a sassy frown, and then she shifted the basket to her other hip and moved over to his horse. She placed her hand on Thunder's leg and gazed up at him as she tried to read his unreadable features. "Come back soon," she said, almost in a whisper.

He placed his hand on hers, and she couldn't help but notice the tingle of excitement rushing through her. "I will be back. Take care of yourself," Thunder said in what sounded like a strained voice.

She backed away from his horse and nodded, and then he rode off. She willed him to look back. If he did, it would mean he cared.

But he didn't look back.

That night after dinner the story of Brandy rescuing Mary was told over and over again. The children told it so much that Brandy was embarrassed and uncomfortable. She needed to do something to shift the attention off herself. "Let's hear one of your stories, MacTavish."

"Please," all the children chorused. Amy clapped her little hands as she sat in Nettie's lap.

"Let me see now . . ." MacTavish rubbed his red beard as he thought. "How about a ghost story?"

"Yeah," Scott answered, his eyes as wide as saucers.

Everyone gathered around the fire with MacTavish at the head of the circle.

"I know many tales, but I believe I'll tell ye the story of the Gray Lady." He paused, then began. "There is a Scottish baronial mansion that stands overlooking Brodrick Bay. 'Tis an enormous castle. That's where the ghost lives to this very day. Sometimes, when yer in the library you can hear clump, clump, clump . . ." MacTavish thumped the cooking pot with a spoon very slowly for effect. "Eerie foot-steps in the room above yer head."

"Have you heard it?" Billy asked.

"Aye. And Nettie, my girl, actually saw the ghost." Ellen gaped at Nettie. "Really?"

"Aye," Nettie said with a nod. "The Gray Lady came in through the side door of the sitting room I was in. She seemed to float across the room, but paused midway to look at me. And then she did the strangest thing . . ." Nettie paused.

"What?" Scott prompted, leaning a little closer.

"She walked right through the wall."

Several of the children gasped.

Brandy had gotten caught up in the story herself. "Are you certain?"

"Aye. Right though the brick wall. Found out later that there used to be an archway in the wall, but it had been bricked up for twenty-some years."

"I would have liked to have seen that," Scott said as he sat back on his heels.

Nettie rose with a sleepy Amy on her hip. " 'Twould make the hairs stand up on the back of yer neck." She chuckled. "Ye can finish the story, MacTavish. I'm going to put this wee lassie to bed."

"What did the Gray Lady look like?" Mary asked, mesmerized by the story.

" 'Tis said she looks like a dairymaid. She's been seen many times going down a back stairway, dressed in gray with a white collar." MacTavish paused. "One morning the butler—"

"What's a butler?" Scott asked.

"He's a mon who opens the doors of great houses."

"Why? Are they heavy?"

MacTavish chuckled. Brandy stepped in. "People

with lots of money have servants who do different jobs around the house so that they will not have to."

Scott thought about it for a moment and then asked, "Why don't we have servants? Then we wouldn't have to milk the cow."

"Because we don't have any money," Brandy said simply. "Now be quiet so MacTavish can finish his story before bedtime."

MacTavish stroked his red beard. "Where did I leave off?"

"With the butler," Billy prompted.

"Ah, yes. One day the butler noticed someone walking down the stairway." MacTavish leaned forward as if he were going to tell a secret. "It was the Gray Lady. She paused beside a mon who was doing odd jobs around the castle. This time he was scrubbing the floor. The lady seemed to stop and talk to the mon before moving on. But when asked who had spoken to him, he gave a funny look and said no one."

Everyone was quiet for a few minutes. Then Mary broke the silence. "Do we know why she haunted the castle?"

" 'Tis said that the girl was a serving wench at the castle at the time that Cromwellian troops were billeted there. The general in command had an affair with her, and she became with child. In those days, such girls were simply thrown out of the castle. She was so heartbroken that she killed herself, and that is the reason that her spirit still haunts the castle. She is looking for the man she loved."

"That was a good story," Brandy said as she rose, and stretched her back. "Let's thank Mr. MacTavish and get ready for bed."

Later that night, Brandy dreamed of ghosts and castles, then the ghosts faded and were replaced with dreams of Thunder and his wonderful kiss. She was going to miss him over these next couple of days.

Maybe even his bossiness, too.

For the next several days, the routine was the same. They rose early in the morning and traveled until dark. Brandy's hands were healing, so she helped Billy out with the team and wagon.

Finally, after a grueling four days, they stopped early because they had come across some trees that flanked a small stream, the first they'd seen in the last four days.

Ward came riding back once the wagons were circled. He was covered in dust, the brim of his hat soaked with sweat. "We are stopping a little early tonight. You can get your washing done at the creek and hang your clothes out to dry."

"That's a good idea," Brandy said.

"We are also having a hoedown after dinner so everyone come and gather around my wagon. We'll have music, dancing, and games for the children."

"Sounds like fun," Brandy said and then finally asked the question she'd been dying to ask. "Have you seen Thunder?"

"No." Ward smiled. "But don't worry. He'll show up."

After Ward left, Brandy frowned. Evidently, he wasn't too worried that something could have happened to Thunder. Maybe she shouldn't worry, either.

She walked around to the other side of the wagon. "Girls, let's go get the washing done. Ward said there would be a dance tonight, and we can all go."

"Hot diggetty!" Billy said as he and Scott came over to where the girls stood. "Something different for a change. I'm all for it."

"Mary, why don't you get Nettie's laundry since she has been doing all the cooking."

"That's a good idea," Mary said. "It will be nice to hear some music," she added wistfully. She looked at Billy. "You going to dance with me?" She gave him a small smile.

Brandy watched the two of them. If Brandy had realized what a change could have come over that girl, she would have thrown her into the river a long time ago.

"You betcha." Billy grinned at Mary. "Scott will, too."

"I don't know how to dance," Scott said.

"Don't worry. Dancing's easy," Billy said. "You just have to move to the music." He held up his hands as if we were dancing with someone.

"Billy, can you heat us some water?" Brandy asked. "And Scott—"

"I know. I have to milk the cow," he said with a frown.

Brandy laughed. "You took the words right out of my mouth."

"We need a butler." Scott giggled.

They carried their baskets of clothes to the river and found an empty spot. Brandy took out the scrub board and Mary and Ellen used big rocks to scrub the clothes with lye soap. With everyone helping, it didn't take long, and soon they were hanging the clothing on ropes stretched between the wagons. As warm as it was tonight, the clothes would be dry by morning, Brandy thought as she clasped the last pin on a skirt.

After dinner, Mary and Ellen picked out two pretty calico dresses. Mary wore a plum-colored dress and Ellen wore apple-green.

"What are you going to wear?" Mary asked.

"I'm not sure," Brandy said. "I'm going to go through the trunk and come up with something. You two run along so you don't miss anything, and I'll be there just as soon as I get dressed."

When Brandy was by herself, she opened the trunk and looked at a couple of dress, but they were too similar to what she'd been wearing every day. Then she saw something wrapped in brown paper that she didn't remember putting in the trunk. The girls had packed some of the things that had been delivered from the general store, so she had no idea what it could be.

She pulled out the package and tore open the paper. Brandy smiled with pleasure. It was the dress. The one she'd liked so much back in Independence. Mr. Gardner must have slipped it into the supplies she purchased. She couldn't remember the last time she'd had a present.

She shook out the lavender-printed cotton fabric and the matching white apron. The top was a simple fitted bodice that opened at the front and was fastened with tiny white buttons. The dress had a round neck, with just a hint of white lace. The short sleeves were trimmed in the same lace.

Slipping the garment on, she noticed how much fuller the skirt was than her normal dresses. She smiled. It felt good to wear something new, and this dress would be perfect for dancing. Quickly, she brushed her hair, wishing she had a mirror to see herself, but knowing that it was vain to do so. She decided to leave her hair loose tonight instead of braided. As she started for the gathering, she had to admit feeling a little excitement. Too bad Thunder would miss all the fun. Then she wondered if he ever did anything for fun because he always seemed so serious.

Brandy heard the music before she got there. It was a good sound—so much different from the everyday sounds they had grown used to.

Mary and Ellen spotted Brandy immediately and came over to her.

"You look so pretty," Ellen said.

Brandy smiled and blushed. "Thank you." She wasn't accustomed to getting compliments.

"That is a lovely dress," Mary said. Brandy realized it was the first time that Mary had ever said anything nice to her other than thanking her by the river.

"Maybe you can wear the dress sometime," Brandy suggested.

Mary broke into a wide smile. "I'd like that."

"Go back to your friends and have fun. Look, there are people over there dancing. Everyone seems to be having a grand time. See all their smiles? Now shoo, go have fun. I'm just going to stand here and watch."

There were several men playing instruments. She saw a fiddle, a harmonica, a washboard, and a guitar. And she had to admit they sounded good together. They very seldom had music at the parsonage, so it had been a long time since she had heard anything other than hymns. Before long, Brandy was tapping her toes with the rhythm and smiling at the couples dancing. She noted how happy the couples appeared and the special way they looked at each other. Would someone ever look at her like that?

Nettie came up beside her with Amy asleep on her shoulder. " 'Tis a lovely sight ye be presenting to-night. Are ye having a good time?"

"I just got here, but it is wonderful," Brandy said. Reaching over, she touched Amy's head. "It appears she has had all the fun she can stand for one night."

"Aye, I'm going back. MacTavish will talk a couple more hours before he winds down." Nettie chuckled. "Here comes Ward. Get him to dance with ye."

Ward was dressed in a faded red shirt, and he wore a big grin as he stopped and offered his arm. "Would you care to dance?"

"I don't know how," Brandy admitted.

"Doesn't matter. Neither do I." Ward laughed.

He swung her up in his arms, and they whirled around and around, and soon Brandy was laughing and having a good time.

"Are you enjoying yourself?" Ward asked.

Brandy nodded. "Yes, I am. It's so nice to do something other than cooking and cleaning. And I haven't had Thunder to yell at me in days."

Now it was Ward's turn to laugh. "So you've been doin' all right without Thunder. He's trained you well, but I do expect him back soon."

"How did you meet Thunder?"

"He's been a friend for a long time. He made the mistake of falling in love with my niece so I used to see him often."

"Mistake?" Brandy asked, wanting to learn more.

"My niece professed to love Thunder. Then she found out he was part Cheyenne and she never spoke to him again. She never even bothered to tell him the reason why. Thunder kind of changed after that. He became harder on the inside."

"That is terrible. It must have hurt a lot."

"It did scare him. But we remained friends. He is a good man."

"I think so, too," Brandy admitted, but she wondered if Thunder would ever trust any woman again.

Thunder thought the sound of Brandy's laughter was the most beautiful sound he'd ever heard. He stood back in the shadows and watched as Ward and Brandy danced. He'd made himself stay away a couple of days longer than he needed to, trying to put some distance between him and Brandy. He'd told himself over and over again that he couldn't be bothered with thoughts of any woman. But somehow this little lady kept creeping into his thoughts. So he finally decided it was time to return. He didn't want to think about how he'd punished his horse, urging him on at full speed to get back sooner.

Brandy looked like a spring flower in the midst of brown, dry dirt. In the glow of the campfire, her skin appeared soft and creamy-looking. The memory of a soft yet passionate kiss came back to him. His unexpected reaction to Brandy startled him and so did his next move as he started toward her and Ward.

When he reached them, he tapped Ward on the shoulder. "Do you mind if I have a dance?"

"About damned time you came back," Ward grumbled. But his expression didn't match his words. "Did you find any buffalo?"

"Yes. We will talk later," Thunder said, his eyes

fixed on Brandy's face as he swung her into the circle of his arms.

"I can see your mind is elsewhere," Ward said with a grin before he moved off to dance with someone else.

Thunder couldn't believe how beautiful Brandy looked. The lavender color of her dress made her eyes a vivid purple, her cheeks were flushed, and her lips a soft pink. Perfect for kissing.

Stop it, he warned himself. "Have you been well, Brandy?"

She moistened her lips. "Yes, have you?"

"I have done much riding and scouting the trail." He tightened his grip on her, pulling her a little closer to him. "But it is good to be back."

"I've missed you," she said softly.

He smiled and gazed into her eyes. Suddenly, it was as if they were the only two people in camp, and without thinking about what he was saying, he said, "I have missed you, too."

The expression in her eyes told him just how much she cared for him. And knowing didn't ease him one little bit.

It was like throwing gunpowder into a fire.

Brandy rolled and tumbled back and forth in her narrow bunk. How long had she been trying to go to sleep? It seemed so long, but it had probably only been a couple of hours since they had turned in.

Every time she shut her eyes, she could picture herself and Thunder dancing. He'd looked so handsome tonight, dressed all in black. His silver eyes had held her mesmerized.

She rolled to the other side.

All right, quit thinking about Thunder. And go to sleep.

She remained motionless as she willed herself to sleep, but after a few minutes her eyes flew open. It was too hot!

That was the problem.

Rising on her elbows, Brandy looked at the other two girls, who seemed to have no trouble sleeping at all. So maybe it was just she who was restless. She felt like everything was sticking to her, and she needed some relief. Maybe if she cooled off, she could then get some rest because morning would be here much too soon.

She eased out of bed, carefully making her way to the back of the wagon. She pulled up her gown so she wouldn't step on the hem as she climbed outside.

Glancing around, she made sure no one else was moving around. Everything was so still and peaceful. But then it should be at this time of night. She was the only one who couldn't sleep, she thought as she headed for the river.

She didn't know the name of this river, but it was so different from the enormous Missouri. It was shallow in places and deep in other spots with rocky rapids here and there. She swished her foot in the edge of the water and thought about how wonderful it felt. A swim would cool her and make her feel better.

The river curved like a snake and was hard to see in some places because it was so dark, but the full moon provided enough light that she could see a small cove where she removed her gown and tossed it in the high grass.

Crickets chirped nearby as she waded into the

water. After the first gasp, she adjusted to the chilly water and decided it was just the right temperature. She dove under the water and swam for a ways before she surfaced again. As she treaded water, snippets of childhood memories came to her, and she could picture herself and her mother swimming in a river. Brandy smiled. She didn't have many memories of her mother, but this was a nice one. At least, she and her mother had been happy at one time.

She should be a little more modest, she thought, but who was to know? Everyone else was asleep. So being a little wicked wouldn't hurt. The water worked its magic, swirling, caressing her body. She relaxed and floated in the water.

Then she heard a splash. Raising her head, she looked all around her, but saw nothing but a small ripple.

If it were a snake or animal, she would have seen it.

Wouldn't she?

She was just letting her imagination run wild. But the interruption had ended the mood. Maybe she should swim back to shore.

That's when it struck.

Something slid around her waist and for a moment she couldn't breathe. As cold fear swept over her body, she desperately tried to scream.

But no sound came out.

THIRTEEN

At first Thunder thought he was dreaming. He shook his head. No. He wasn't dreaming . . . the little fool was still there.

He'd been lounging in the cool water when he'd first glimpsed Brandy. She'd stopped in the small alcove, then reached up and slipped the straps from her shoulders; her gown slid slowly to the ground and puddled around her feet. He probably should have made his presence known, but something stopped him.

He watched as she waded into the water, her body bathed in moonlight, her glorious hair resting on her breasts. He hadn't realized he'd been holding his breath until she dove into the water.

That's when his anger mixed with his desire. Damn fool. It was dangerous to wander away from the wagons alone. And more so when you were completely naked. There could have been other Indians out here besides himself. When she surfaced and floated on her back all his eyes saw were creamy white breasts and hard nipples extending above the water line.

That's when all his sanity left him.

Brandy had just pushed him too far. This time she was going to have to deal with him.

* * *

Suddenly the water rippled behind Brandy. She tried to straighten, but firm arms snaked around her waist, hauling her back, cutting off her air.

She gasped because she was too frightened to scream. "Who are you? What do you want?"

"I want to know why you are out here away from the wagons? Thunder's angry voice was next to her ear.

Brandy relaxed when she recognized his voice, but as soon as she did so and pressed against his body, she realized that he didn't have any clothes on either. "I—I was hot and couldn't sleep."

He took her by the arms and turned her to face him. She was glad of the darkness that hid the flush in her cheeks. She sank down in the water to hide her unclothed body.

Thunder's eyes glittered with anger. "Do you not realize how dangerous it is to be by yourself?"

She nodded. "But you're here."

"That is different. I can take care of myself."

"Well, I can take care of myself, too," she snapped back.

"Can you?" His voice held an ominous tone.

She couldn't quit staring at Thunder, remembering how it felt when she'd kissed him. His dark hair was slicked back away from his hard features, and his eyes appeared silver in the moonlight. The smoldering flame she saw in his gaze startled her. Her feet didn't touch the bottom, so he was holding her steady in the water away from him.

She shamefully longed to reach over and taste his lips. He was disturbing in every way, and she was well aware of his muscles beneath her fingertips. Trying to ignore her wanton longing for him, she stared at his chest instead of his eyes.

Thunder watched the way her hair floated around her breasts as she clung to his forearms. The flesh and blood beneath his hands told him he hadn't imagined her at all. An invisible web of attraction building between them was very powerful.

"You are so beautiful. Moonlight becomes you," he said in a whisper.

He lifted her chin so he could see her face more clearly. Was that desire he saw flash in her eyes? The knowledge that she experienced the same feelings that he did, felt like a prairie fire sweeping over him. His thumb slowly moved to her lower lip. He couldn't stop himself from rubbing his thumb back and forth across her lips. She was drawing him to her just like a thirsty animal to water.

And he was bone dry.

What would one little taste hurt?

He bent his head, his mouth mere inches from hers. "You should go back," he warned her.

"Y—yes, I probably should," she murmured as her arms went around his neck.

That was all he could take.

The small gesture pushed him completely over the edge. He jerked her next to him, their naked bodies fitting perfectly as he kissed the side of her neck. Hot skin next to hot skin.

"You really don't know what you're doing to me," he warned softly as he trailed kisses up her chin. She wrapped her legs around his waist and heat surged through him so fiercely that he felt he was standing in fire instead of water.

Drawing in a shuttered breath, she whispered, "Tell me what I do to you."

He felt her tremble as he softly kissed her earlobe. Her back was smooth. Her skin silky. He'd never felt anything so soft . . . so inviting. Her breast crushed next to his chest—much too tempting, he thought as his lips sought hers. The sweetness of her mouth caused him to groan. His tongue stroked and caressed hers until she responded with a passion of her own, feeding his hunger. "You make me forget that I am unworthy, you make me forget everything."

She looked at him. "You are the bravest, smartest man I've ever met." She was nibbling on the side of his mouth as she added. "I do not care that you are part Indian. I care for the man that you are inside, the one I've come to know."

Her words would remain in his mind forever. As would her scent. It seemed to fill his soul. But he had to give her one more chance. "You should walk away from me now before it is too late. You know I will not stay. I will leave you."

Brandy gave a harsh laugh as she hugged Thunder to her. "Everybody in my life has left me so what should one more make?" She kissed his chin. "Make me forget, Thunder," she pleaded, "if only for a little while. Make me forget."

He started moving toward shore. She still had her legs wrapped around him when they left the water. He spotted her gown and the sheet she'd brought with her in the enclosed trees.

Carefully he went down on his knees, laying her upon the sheet. Her body was beautiful beneath the moonlight; small beads of moisture dotted her skin as he once again leaned down to take her tempting lips, kissing her deeply, making her want him as badly as he wanted her.

Brandy was moving on instinct. She was uncertain what to do or how to please him, but she wanted desperately to learn. When she touched her tongue to his, instinct told her she was doing something right. As her tongue tangled with his, Thunder's hand slid up the side of her breast, covering it possessively. He massaged her breast as his tongue did wonderful things to her mouth. She was beginning to think she was in another world, as her hand moved over his thick, muscular arms.

Was this love?

His mouth left hers. She felt cold and begged, "Please." Ever so slowly, he lowered his head where he fastened his mouth to her breast. He began to suckle. A sudden heat like she'd never experienced before swept over her. She heard herself moan again and felt embarrassed that she had, but he was driving her crazy as he nuzzled the other breast, his lips tightened around her nipple. She was barely aware that his hand had moved lower until he touched her thighs. She stiffened.

"Don't," Thunder coaxed against her mouth.

She relaxed and opened her legs for him. His fingers slid between the curls and began to massage her. She arched against his hand. What was the crazy feeling? She tried to look into Thunder's eyes but he was trailing kisses down her stomach until his lips replaced his fingers and a jolt of pleasure shot through her, much stronger than before. She began to whimper for something . . . she wasn't sure what. But she felt that there had to be more to this torture.

When she thought she could take no more, Thunder

recaptured her lips in a kiss like none before. His lips were demanding, and she tried to give back all that she could.

Thunder had never known that lovemaking could be this good. And it was taking every ounce of strength to hold back. He cursed himself for wanting her. He cursed himself for not leaving when he had the chance, but none of that stopped him from claiming what he wanted.

He parted her legs and positioned himself to enter her. And just when he realized that he was making her his, it was too late because he had entered her and felt her tightness just as she gasped.

"I'm sorry, little one," he murmured and then he kissed her again and said, "Forgive me." He waited until her body had adjusted, but the heat was so unbearable now he couldn't stop once he began to move again.

He thrust deeper and deeper and he felt Brandy began to move. She wrapped her legs around him and arched her hips so he could move freely.

She had lost complete control. Never feeling like this before, she marveled at the completeness she felt as Thunder plunged one final time and shuddered at the same time that she saw white lights exploding all around her.

He collapsed against her, then rolled to the side, still keeping her within his arms, "I'm sorry I hurt you," he said huskily.

She heard his hard breathing as she rubbed her hands up and down his back. "It only hurt for a little while," she admitted, and then added, "I like it when you hold me like this."

"I like it, too," Thunder admitted.

When their breathing had calmed, they lay on the sheet, gazing up at the stars.

"We shouldn't have made love," Thunder finally said, breaking the silence.

"I know. But I'm not sorry."

"But your husband should be the first."

"I don't want to talk about that now." She turned on her side to face him. "Look, we may never have another time like this one together. Let's enjoy a couple of hours."

He wrapped his arm around her and gazed down at her upturned face. "And what do you suggest that we do?"

"Tell me about your childhood. I don't know anything about you."

"It was pretty normal. My father is Crazy Arrow and my mother is Little Woman."

"What a funny name."

"Indian names mean something. My name is Rolling Thunder. I was named after a storm. My mother received her name when she was captured and they brought her to camp. My mother is a white woman. She told me when she arrived at camp, my father walked over and looked at her then declared, 'I want this Little Woman.' "

"That is so sweet. Did they love each other?"

"Not at first. She was afraid of my father and of course she didn't speak Cheyenne so it was a while before there was peace between them."

"Your mother taught you her language, didn't she?"

"Yes. She wanted me to be educated in both worlds, so I could help both people."

Brandy snuggled closer to Thunder. "She sounds

like a very smart lady. How did you come to be in our part of the territory?"

"You are full of questions tonight," he said as he rubbed his fingers back and forth across her arm. "I went to my white grandparents so that I might learn the white man's ways. I enrolled in school and spent several years with them. Then the war broke out." He sighed. "That is a different story, and I do not want to speak of war." He brushed the hair from her shoulder. "Tell me how you came to be at the orphanage."

"There isn't much to tell. My life hasn't been as exciting as yours," she said as she traced circles on his chest with her finger. "I don't remember much about when I was little, but I was left on the doorstep of the parsonage with my chest. I was only five years old."

"The one that is so heavy?"

Brandy nodded. "Father Brown said I had blood stains on the front of my dress when he first saw me."

"Do you know where they came from?"

"Someone killed my father," she said in a small voice. Thunder tightened his hold on her as she continued.

"I don't know much. I remember my father arguing with three other men. I came running into the room, and he shoved me behind him so quickly I didn't see them. There was a loud noise and the next thing I knew my father was on the floor, and I was trying to wake him up."

Tears trickled down her cheeks, and she knew she was getting Thunder's chest wet. "I'm sorry I'm crying."

"There is no shame in crying, Brandy." He held her and wiped her cheeks with his fingers. "Sometimes it's a good way to cleanse the soul."

She smiled at him, and he pulled her up so he could kiss her tenderly.

When she was settled again she said, "You know, I've never spoken of that day before. Father Brown asked me what happened when I first came to him and I told him I didn't know. But over the years bits and pieces began to form. However, Father Brown never asked me again."

"Perhaps he thought you'd been through enough pain."

"Father Brown was a good man. I wish you could have met him."

"I do, too. He sounds much like my grandfather. My grandfather spoke with great wisdom. Would you like to hear the words I said to him upon his death? It is a good way to remember your loved one."

She nodded.

Softly, Thunder repeated the words with his cheek resting against the top of her head.

DO NOT STAND AT MY GRAVE AND WEEP.
I AM NOT THERE. I DO NOT SLEEP.
I AM A THOUSAND WINDS THAT BLOW.

I AM THE DIAMOND GLINT ON SNOW.
I AM THE SUNLIGHT ON RIPENED GRAIN.
I AM THE GENTLE AUTUMN RAIN.

WHEN YOU WAKE IN THE MORNING HUSH
I AM THE SWIFT, UPLIFTING RUSH

OF QUIET BIRDS IN CIRCLING FLIGHT.
I AM THE SOFT STARLIGHT AT NIGHT.

DO NOT STAND AT MY GRAVE AND WEEP.
I AM NOT THERE. I DO NOT SLEEP.

"That was beautiful," she said with a sigh. "And the way Father Brown would want to have been remembered."

"Brandy, tonight has been special. I will remember it always. But," he hesitated as if he wanted to say something else, "we both have duties—"

"And promises," Brandy whispered.

He sat up and pulled her up with him. "You should go back now. The sun will be up soon, and we'll be leaving."

Brandy slipped the gown over her head while Thunder pulled on his breeches. When he straightened, she wrapped her arms around his neck, and he hugged her so tight that she never wanted to break away.

Finally, when she pulled back she said, "I don't know what to say."

"Sometimes things are better left unsaid." He kissed her lightly then and drew away. Once again his mask had slipped into place, and she had no idea how he felt. He gave her a nudge in the right direction. When she turned around to say something he had disappeared as if he'd never been there.

Brandy felt empty inside.

The next morning, the wagon train was on the move again.

Last night when Brandy and Ward had been dancing, he told her that they had about two weeks left until they reached Ft. Laramie. As she walked this morning she kept thinking, *I only have two more weeks before I lose Thunder.*

Last night . . . Brandy sighed. Just how did she feel about last night?

Guilty, yes. Because she'd given in so easily to temptation when she should have waited for the man she was going to marry.

Sorry, no. She had experienced something very special, she realized. And as wrong as it may sound, she was glad that Thunder had been the first. She realized that she cared for him more than she should. But what could she do about it?

Absolutely nothing.

She was promised to someone else.

"Look." Ellen pointed to a group of wooden crosses and stone cairns.

Brandy hadn't realized that Ellen had been walking beside her, she'd been so lost in her thoughts, but she turned now in the direction that Ellen pointed.

"It looks like there are at least ten graves. That is the most we've seen in one group," Brandy said. Every day they passed graves beside the road, three here and four there. It was a strange feeling for everyone because they realized that they could end up being in one of those graves before the journey ended. "Let's walk over there and see if the markers say anything."

When they reached the first stone, Brandy found her answer. MARY LOU, DIED JUNE 6, CHOLERA. "They didn't put a year," Brandy said in a quiet voice.

"What is cholera?" Ellen asked as they caught up with their wagon.

"I don't know much about the disease except what I've read in books. It's an infection that attacks you down here." Brandy patted just below her stomach. "It makes you go to the bathroom so much that it eventually weakens your whole body, and you die within days. It is very contagious so that's why we see so many graves."

"How do you get cholera?"

"From unsanitary conditions, and bad drinking water. This is the reason we've been boiling all our water to cook with."

"I hope it doesn't happen to anybody on our wagon train."

"I do, too," Brandy admitted. "Look, here comes Mary."

Mary rode over on her horse and asked Ellen, "You want to ride for a while?"

"Sure," Ellen said and held the horse for Mary to dismount.

Mary started walking with Brandy.

"Did you enjoy your ride?" Brandy asked, making small conversation.

"Anything is different. I have met another girl about four wagons up who is my age. Her name is Lettie, and we've been riding together."

"It's nice to make new friends."

"You know we never had the chance at the orphanage."

"Yes, I know," Brandy said in a choked voice. "I will miss MacTavish and Nettie when we arrive at the fort." She could feel Mary's sharp eyes boring into her as she walked.

Mary finally asked. "What about Thunder?"

Brandy grew hot at the mention of his name. "What about him?"

"I've seen the way you look at him," Mary teased. "I would say that you like him very much and that you'll miss him."

"Like a toothache," Brandy snapped and then apologized. "That wasn't very nice. Yes, I will miss Thunder."

More than she cared to admit.

FOURTEEN

A week had gone by, and Thunder knew he was avoiding Brandy. He made sure he was gone before she woke up and he returned from his scouting duties late after everyone had retired. But today he was going to get back to his normal routine if it killed him. He was devoting too many thoughts to the woman, and that irritated the hell out of him. He had a job to do and he'd do it, come hell or high water.

He didn't need Brandy. He didn't need anyone.

"You look as ornery as a mule this morning," Ward commented when he drew his mount to a halt beside Thunder. "At breakfast this morning you hardly said two words."

Thunder turned and glared at Ward from under the brim of his black Stetson. "Didn't get much sleep last night," he muttered.

"You wouldn't have a certain lady on your mind that would be causing your lack of sleep?"

"How about I just couldn't sleep?"

"Yep. You're ornery. You're really going to like this bit of news."

When Ward didn't say anything further, Thunder said, "Go ahead, spit it out."

"Just rode to the back and one of the wagon wheels on Brandy's rig broke. MacTavish has stopped to help but the rest of the wagons will have to move on as I'm sure you know." Ward shrugged matter-of-factly. "Figure you'd want to know."

Thunder cursed as he pulled his horse around and headed to the rear of the train. He could already see the long distance that separated Brandy's party from the rest of the train.

When he arrived, he tied his horse to the wheel of the wagon and went around to the other side. Mac-Tavish had already started hammering on the wheel.

"How the hell did this happen?" Thunder asked abruptly, turning to Billy. Without waiting for Billy to answer, Thunder asked. "Did you hit a rock?"

Billy spread out his hands and shrugged. "I wasn't driving."

Thunder swung around, aiming to locate Brandy. He immediately spotted her. He might have known that Billy would have been careful. Thunder didn't have to look far; Brandy was standing right behind him with her arms folded and a defiant spark in her eye.

"So what happened?" Thunder barked.

"We hit a gopher hole and the wheel came off."

Thunder's expression was taut as he asked, "Do you not know that you are to avoid rocks and holes?"

"Really?" Brandy said with a sarcastic tone, her brows raised. "I thought I was supposed to hit as many as possible." She shifted positions and propped her hand on her hip. "It was hidden by a clump of grass."

MacTavish and Billy chuckled softly. Thunder glared at Billy, then back to the sassy Miss Brandy. She evidently was as ornery as he was this morning, and he could foretell a battle brewing between them. Maybe it was better to ignore her this morning and save the fight for later. Thunder moved over to Mac-Tavish. "How bad is it?"

MacTavish shook his head. "Not so bad. We were lucky this time. No broken spokes. I'm just straightening out the hub, and then Billy can put it back on the wagon."

Thunder turned to the girls. "Take as much as possible out of the wagon so that it will be easier to lift. Scott, you need to grease the rest of the wheels."

An hour later, while MacTavish and Thunder got ready to mount the wheel, Nettie motioned for Brandy to come over to her.

"I've been wanting to talk to you," Nettie confided. At the same time Amy came running by them, squealing because Scott was chasing her.

"What about?" Brandy asked.

"Ye know it isn't much longer before we'll be at the fort and parting ways," Nettie said with a catch in her voice.

"I know. I hate to see you and MacTavish leave. The both of you have been such lifesavers to my family."

Nettie reached out and squeezed Brandy's arm. " 'Tis a blessing ye've been to us. I've always wanted children, but it wasn't to be. That is why I'd like to ask if we can adopt Amy." Nettie paused, then rushed on, "She's been such a joy and we love her very much."

Brandy smiled. "I believe that Amy is happy with you, but I think I should ask the other children. We are all in this together, and what affects one usually affects the others."

Nettie nodded her head. "I understand."

"I'll do it tonight," Brandy promised.

"The wagon is ready," Thunder announced. "Get everything back inside. We have time to make up."

He and Billy lifted Brandy's trunk. "I don't know what this trunk is made of, but it is much too heavy. If we lose animals, this thing will have to go."

"No," Brandy said quickly. "That is the only possession I own. It's all I have from my family. If that trunk goes, so do I."

Thunder stepped very close to Brandy and said softly, his warm breath in her ear, so that only she could hear, "Do not tempt me."

She glared at him, then wheeled away before she said or did something she'd regret. Thunder must have remorse over the night they'd made love, and he was trying to show her just how much. How had she possibly thought she could have feelings for this pig-headed fool? The way he stared at her made her feel like she was some kind of inconvenience. As far as she was concerned, he could trot himself back to the front of the wagon train and stay there.

Billy hitched the horses, and Brandy climbed up on the seat and took the reins. Thunder galloped ahead and Billy followed as they headed back to the trail.

Not a breath of air stirred over the open prairie. The sun beat down upon them with sultry, penetrating heat. Brandy's dress was wet and stuck to her, making her even more uncomfortable.

Later in the afternoon, they finally glimpsed the dust of the rest of the wagon train. Black thunderclouds rose fast on the horizon, darkening the sky. At least the storm brought a strong breeze, a welcome relief from the heat.

* * *

By the time he could actually see the rest of the wagons, Thunder noticed that they were making a run for a group of distant trees. He didn't have to guess why. The whole sky was densely shrouded with a purple hue.

Thunder held up his right hand, halting the wagons. "Billy, Mary, take the team. Brandy, you and Ellen ride on one horse. Scott, come with me," Thunder shouted over the wind, then wheeled his mount around to MacTavish's wagon.

"Go ahead and pass us while we change drivers," he ordered, in a tone that brooked no argument. "Make a run for those cottonwood trees. There's a storm ahead, and it appears to be a bad one. We don't want to get caught out in the open." He gestured for them to go. "We will be right behind you."

"Aye. Be careful," MacTavish said with a nod as he flicked the reins. "We'll see you there."

"What's wrong?" Brandy asked Thunder as she mounted and reached down for Ellen.

"When that storm breaks, we don't want to be out here on the open prairie. The wind could topple the wagon, and by the looks of those angry black clouds this just might be a long storm. Help me herd the animals, and get them going in the right direction."

Thunder moved up beside the wagon. "Head for those trees."

Billy nodded, snapped the reins, and he and Mary rode off.

The oxen could sense the upcoming storm because they took off, running after the wagon.

It was a mad dash across the open plain. The gusting wind plastered the tall grass to the ground. Brandy eyed the moving clouds as she rode; there was a certain excitement in the storm that appealed to her. Thunder rode beside them, his long black hair blowing in the wind, and she was surprised to see he was smiling. Evidently, he enjoyed the oncoming storm as well. She admired how he sat on his horse with Scott in front of him. Scott laughed with happy abandon as he hung onto the pommel and faced the ferocious wind.

They made it to the safety of the trees just as the first drops of rain began to splatter the hot ground.

Brandy, Mary, and Scott pitched the tent in record time while Billy and Thunder unhitched the team.

Loud thunder rumbled overhead. Brandy glanced toward the sky to see that it had darkened to a purplish-black as the rain pelted them and the wind blew harder, its force mixed with the rain and plastering everyone's clothing to them.

They all ran for cover.

Ellen and Mary darted to MacTavish's wagon since it was closer. Scott and Billy dove into the tent, and Brandy and Thunder finished tying the canvas down on the wagon where they had rolled it up earlier in the day.

When they'd tied off the last ropes, Brandy entered the back of the wagon, followed by Thunder. They were completely soaked.

Brandy turned and gaped at him. "We can't be in here together . . . alone."

Thunder looked at her as if she'd completely lost her mind. "There is a storm outside, Brandy. Or hadn't you noticed?"

"Of course I've noticed. But it isn't proper," Brandy told him. Of course, she hadn't been worried about *proper* when they'd made love, but this time the chil-

dren were much closer. And Thunder's attitude had
left much to be desired lately.

Thunder moved over to stand right in front of her
as the wind buffeted the wagon. Rain pounded against
the canvas, looking for a way to gain entrance.
"Sweetheart, there hasn't been anything proper about
our relationship since we first met."

The storm rumbled overhead, followed by a bolt of
sharp lightning. It sounded like it hit a nearby tree.
Brandy jumped and threw her arms around Thunder's
neck.

"I take it we are not worried about being proper
anymore?" Thunder chuckled as he unwrapped
Brandy's arms from around him.

Brandy stiffened and backed away. "You're impossible."

"I know," he said with a smile as he began to re-
move his shirt. "This storm is a bad one, and I've no
doubt it will continue until morning."

Brandy's eyes grew wide as she stared at Thunder's
muscular chest, remembering how he had felt beneath
her exploring fingers. "Now what are you doing?"

"Taking off this wet shirt, and I suggest that you
get into some dry clothes, too. Hand me something
to dry off with."

She now understood what Thunder meant and she
complied, tossing him a sheet. Then she got one for
herself and dried her face and hair.

"Let me get to the back for a dress," Brandy said
and then squeezed by Thunder, their bodies brushing
as they traded places.

She removed a light green dress from the trunk and
didn't bother to shut the lid. "You'll have to turn your
back," she told Thunder.

"Don't you think it's a bit late for modesty?"

Her face burned, and she glowered darkly at him. At least he remembered, she thought. Still, she felt awkward. "Please."

"First trade places with me so I can get my clothes from the back," he said with a grin and squeezed by her again.

Earlier, he'd thrown his saddle in the very back of the wagon. "All right, my back is turned," he said as he opened his saddlebag and got out a dry shirt and breeches. However, he couldn't resist turning and looking at the magnificent ripe body only a couple of feet away. Of course, all he could see was her back. He shook his head to get rid of his dangerous thoughts, then changed his own clothes. He sat on the bunk.

He lit the lantern overhead, since it had grown so dark outside. He wrung the water out of his clothes and draped them in the back so they would have some chance of drying out. "Hand me your dress, and I'll hang it up."

In the process, he bumped his shin on the trunk lid Brandy had left open. "Damn!" he swore and bent over to close the lid. That was when he noticed that the chest's lining had been torn, and he wondered if Brandy would blame him for this, too. Bending over, he examined the lining and pulled at it. "You can probably fix this when we arrive. Wait a minute— there is something behind here."

He pulled out the knife he kept in his boot and worked on the edge until he could reach what was behind the material.

"I don't remember it being torn before," Brandy said. "It must have ripped when we had to move the box," she said, leaning over him so she could see better. "What is it?"

Finally, Thunder was able to grasp the object. "It appears to be a piece of paper." He handed the folded note to Brandy.

"This is strange. I wonder why it was behind the liner." she said as she unfolded the letter. Brandy quickly scanned the note to the bottom. "Oh, my God! It was written by my mother."

Her face had lost its color, and her hands shook so badly that she dropped the note. Thunder bent down and picked it up.

"Would you like me to read it to you?" he asked as he sat on the bunk across from her.

Brandy nodded. "Please."

He unfolded the paper, then began to read:

Dear Brandy,

When you find this letter, I hope you'll have grown into the lovely young woman that I fancy you becoming.

I know you do not understand why I left you, but it was never because I didn't love you. Never that!

We come from a wealthy family in Boston. Unfortunately, that was never enough for your father. He had to go west for adventure, and we went with him.

Well, he found his adventure when he dealt with the wrong business partners. I pray that you will forget his violent death and only remember that he did love you. Now, my life is also in danger. The men think I have what they are looking for and that is the reason, my darling, that I have

Brenda K. Jernigan

left you with the priest. These men would kill you, too, to get what they want.

Those parish walls will protect you from the evil that lies outside.

Have a good life, my daughter, and be careful to love the right man. Choosing the wrong man can lead to a life of misery. That I have found out the hard way. Always remember that I love you.

Love,
Mother
P.S. Keep the chest with you. One day it will bring you wealth.

Thunder folded the letter and glanced at Brandy. Tears were trickling down her face, and she reached up and brushed them away. His heart ached for her. "Come here, Brandy," he said gently.

She didn't hesitate, going straight into his arms.

"All this time, I thought she didn't love me," Brandy whispered, choking back a sob.

Thunder rubbed his hand across her back. "It sounds like she loved you a great deal. Now I understand what the chest means to you—I'll try not to throw it off the wagon. Provided I could lift it," he joked, trying to cheer her.

She pulled back and gave him a soft smile. "It is all I have of my mother." Brandy glanced back at the square box. "I don't see how it will bring me wealth, though."

"If you sell it by the pound, you could be very wealthy." Thunder laughed and was glad when Brandy responded with a smile. He pulled her back to him.

"My grandparents live in Boston. That is where I went to study."

"Wouldn't it be strange if your grandparents knew my relatives?" Brandy asked. "Basically, you and I came from the same place."

"In a manner of speaking."

Suddenly, lightning burst with a terrific crash directly above their heads. The rain poured from the sky, hitting the canvas and sliding to the ground. Brandy jumped at the noise.

Thunder tightened his arm around her. "The storm will not harm you," he said very calmly.

"I know."

"I believe that this storm will rage all night, so we had better get some sleep," he said quietly to calm her.

Brandy looked up at him, and in that fraction of a second, Thunder forgot all his vows not to kiss her again. His lips moved toward the nape of her neck as his fingers brushed her hair from the spot he sought. Placing soft kisses on her neck, he felt her shiver in his arms.

Again the rumble of thunder seemed to be all around them, but this time Brandy didn't jump. She clung to him and whispered, "Kiss me until I can't hear the noise."

Tenderness surged through Thunder for the temptress with the violet eyes. Hungrily, he took her mouth with a raging passion he hadn't known he possessed. He opened her mouth with his own while he gently lowered her to the cot that they sat upon.

Brandy parted her lips, sliding her arms up and around his shoulders. Somewhere in the back of her mind, she remembered she'd vowed she wasn't going to fall for Thunder's charms anymore. She reminded herself that she would be losing him in a few days, and there would be such an emptiness that no one could ever fill.

In spite of her determination to resist him, Brandy couldn't. Thunder's mouth had such a fierce tenderness that she melted against him. His hand roamed over her body, pausing when he reached the mound of her breast. "Get out of these clothes," he murmured.

At that moment, Brandy felt a special bond between them as she stripped her clothes and tossed them on the other bunks. Thunder did the same. She wondered why she trusted this man so much. Why did she feel so special when she was with him?

He drew her back into his arms and she gasped from the contact of her bare breast against his chest. She felt his heat.

She placed soft kisses at the base of his throat before her conscience nagged at her, and she shook her head in protest. "We can't." However, her actions didn't match her words.

Thunder's mouth came down on hers, silencing her protest and leaving her trembling with desire. He parted those tempting lips, teasing her tongue with his as he tasted all of her sweetness.

Wrapping her arms around his waist, Brandy seemed to want to get closer to him. Carefully, Thunder pushed her back so they could lie on the small bed, then he covered her body with his.

The wind howled and whistled through the trees and around the wagon. The storm seemed to have isolated them from everything else.

He ignored the outside elements. The storm raging

in him was many times stronger than what went on
around them. Brandy's lips were so soft that he
couldn't get enough of them. But he wanted to explore
all of her body, so he left her lips and trailed kisses
down the column of her throat. He heard her moans
of pleasure and her gasps when his mouth found her
breast. He liked pleasing this woman very much.

An aching desire racked his body as he tried to
make himself go slowly. While his lips tightened on
her nipple, his hand moved lower to settle between
her thighs. He rubbed her sensitive skin and felt her
wetness as she twisted and turned from the torment
he was causing.

"Please," she begged him, and he knew he couldn't
hold on much longer. He was losing control. He settled himself gently on her, his full manhood coming
to rest between her thighs, replacing his hand.

He caught her mouth in another searing kiss as he
entered her. "You feel wonderful," he murmured.

"As do you," she gasped, arching her hips up to
pull him deep inside her.

A surge of red-hot desire consumed him. He began
to move faster and push harder, urging her to feel and
want him as much as he did her.

She responded in kind, not holding anything back.

Lightning cracked above them. The storm surrounded them, invading their souls, pushing them to
the edge of no return. Together they found their release as wild abandonment overtook them and swept
them away to the magical place that lovers share.

Brandy hoped this moment would never end. Her
heart was bursting with many emotions that she
wished to share with Thunder, but she was afraid to
tell him how she felt.

Would be break her heart and walk away?

She would never know. As sleep claimed her, she knew she'd settle for what they had now and not worry about what was to come.

The next morning when Brandy awoke in Thunder's arms, she smiled. He was awake and watching her. She gave him a chaste kiss and wondered what thoughts raced through his head. Instinct told her that he would never divulge such information.

Thunder started to say something, but Brandy quickly put her fingers over his mouth and whispered, "Don't spoil what we have. Let's savor the memories."

He nodded.

Brandy heard Billy's voice just outside the wagon. She scrambled from Thunder's arms, thankful that they had put their clothes back on sometime during the wild night.

Billy stuck his head in through the back of the canvas. "Are you two behaving?" he asked with a chuckle.

Brandy felt the heat in her face, but she'd never let on that she was embarrassed. "Don't be silly. How did you do last night?" she asked as she made her way to the back of the cramped wagon.

"That tent leaks! Started to make a dash for the wagon, but figured what the hell, we'd just get wetter."

When everyone was on the ground, Thunder said in a low voice as he passed Brandy, "Billy would have been in for a big surprise last night."

Brandy's eyes widened. She didn't even want to think about what could have happened. She would have died from embarrassment.

Thunder smiled, then said to Billy, "Better take the tent down. After breakfast we'll be heading out. After that downpour, it will be slow going at first."

An hour later, everyone sat around the campfire eating the biscuits that Nettie had prepared. All except Thunder, who had gone back to Ward's wagon.

" 'Twas some terrible storm we had last night," MacTavish said. "Glad I was that we made it to the trees when we did." He paused and looked at Brandy. "And did you get any sleep last night."

"A little," Brandy said. "There were a few times I thought lightning was going to strike the wagon."

"At least you weren't wet," Billy mumbled.

Brandy waited for everyone to finish eating before she said, "We need to talk about something as a family."

Nettie nudged her husband, then she rose with Amy in her arms. "We'll be back at our wagon."

Brandy waited until she had everyone's attention. "MacTavish and Nettie want to adopt Amy and take her with them." The children just stared at her. Brandy realized that she usually didn't ask their opinion on anything. "I think it would be best for Amy. What do the rest of you think?"

"I think, at least, she'd have a family," Mary said.

Ellen agreed with a shake of her head and added, "And someone to love her."

Billy put down his plate. "Amy seems happy enough."

"But we wouldn't get to see her anymore," Scott said, looking extremely unhappy.

"No, Scott, we wouldn't. But we want what is best

for Amy. And we don't know what is ahead of us. It would be harder for a baby to survive. I think Mac-Tavish and Nettie are wonderful people and are much better equipped to take care of her."

"I'm sure going to miss them," Mary and Ellen said at the same time.

"I wish they were going to stay at the fort, but they have other plans. Let's take a vote," Brandy said as she stood. "All in favor of letting Amy go, raise your hand."

Everyone raised a hand and Brandy smiled. "Good. I think it's for the best. Mary and Ellen, why don't you go and tell Nettie the good news while I clean up."

Brandy gathered the dishes and took them to a washpan. She thought of Amy and smiled. She knew they had done the right thing. A tug on her skirt drew her attention, and she looked around to see Scott standing beside her.

"Why such a long face?" Brandy asked, already knowing the reason.

Scott looked up at her with big brown eyes, and for a moment he just watched her. She saw the tears gathering. "You're not going to give me away, too, are you?" he finally asked fearfully.

"Of course not." Brandy dried her hands on her apron, then stooped down and put her arms around Scott. "I wouldn't have let Amy go if I didn't think it was better for her." She held him away from her. "Wouldn't you like to have your own family?"

Scott shook his head as he started to cry. "I like it with you and Billy and Thunder."

Brandy gathered Scott into her arms and hugged

him tight. Scott sobbed on her shoulder, "Promise that you won't ever leave me. I love you, Brandy."

Brandy choked. For a moment she couldn't say anything. Because she realized that she had never had anyone to love her except for Father Brown, and now this little boy, the one she held in her arms, was offering her all the love he could give. As tears streamed down her cheeks, she finally managed to say, "I'll never leave you, Scott. On that you have my promise."

He pulled away and looked at her, then said, "Why are you crying?"

"Because you have made me realize that you and the others are my family and have always been. As long as we have each other, we'll survive," Brandy said around the lump in her throat as she pulled Scott back into her arms.

"One way or the other we will survive," she said in a broken whisper.

FIFTEEN

The sun was just starting to set when Brandy caught her first glimpse of Ft. Laramie and the Black Hills that lay just beyond it. The white building stood out from the brown grass and the green cottonwood trees that grew near the river. Ft. Laramie marked the gateway to the Rocky Mountains. The wagon train was now one-third of the way to Oregon and Brandy was at the end of her trail.

She breathed deep—the air was so dry and clear it seemed to crackle.

They had made it.

Faintly she heard the rippling notes of a bugle and glimpsed the blue-clad soldiers going through their drills on the parade ground in the middle of the buildings that they called a fort.

Ft. Laramie wasn't anything like Brandy had expected. She'd thought everything would be behind high walls. Instead, she saw open adobe buildings and wooden structures scattered in a square, with the middle open for a parade ground. The fort was beside the Laramie River, which provided them a good source of water. There were no watchtowers to warn of danger, so she felt Ft. Laramie was fairly peaceful.

A rider from the front of the wagons galloped back, yelling, "Circle the wagons!"

As was their custom, everyone began making their circle. They were experts by now, not making the same greenhorn's mistakes that they had at the beginning of the journey.

"Is this where we're going to live?" Scott asked from the seat beside her.

Mixed feelings surged through her. She was scared and very uncertain. She tried to force her confusion aside. Now was not the time for doubts. "I don't know exactly where, Scott, but this is where we will leave the wagon train."

Scott pointed. "What are those things with the sticks sticking out of them?"

"They're teepees. Evidently the Indians camp here, too," Brandy explained just as Ward rode up beside their wagon.

"Lookin' over your new home?" Ward asked as he dismounted his horse.

"I think so," Brandy replied, climbing down from the wagon seat. Then she turned and held her arms up for Scott to jump down to her. "You better go help Billy with the tent," she told Scott with a pat to the rump.

Once he'd left, Brandy asked, "Ward, can you tell me anything about the fort?"

"It's situated between the Laramie Creek and the North Platte, even though you only see one river now. I believe the fort was originally established in 1834 as an American fur trading post, but the government took over in '49."

Brandy stared at the sun-dried bricks. "The fort is much older than I thought. I imagined it to be protected by high walls from the Indians, yet I see teepees all along the river."

"So far they haven't had much trouble right around here, though that's not the case in other places. The tribes come here to trade furs," Ward said.

"Thank you for explaining." Brandy put her hands on the small of her back and stretched. "Where is Thunder?"

"He's ridden over to the teepees to see if anyone has news of his family," Ward said. He adjusted his Stetson back on his head. "Is your future husband a soldier?"

"I don't know," Brandy admitted in a small voice with a shrug. "I don't know anything about him. His letter said to come to Ft. Laramie, and he would meet us here. It is still hard to believe that we're here. I feel so far away from home."

"Young lady, you are far from the home that you knew. You should feel a little apprehensive—it's natural." Ward's teasing laughter made her ease a little.

"Your fiancé had no way of knowing when the train would arrive," Ward said. He thought for a moment. "I'll tell you what. The wagons will stay here for another day before moving on," Ward said, folding his arms over his chest. "Tomorrow I will take you to the fort to meet the colonel. I hear they have a new officer called Colonel Jeb Moonlight. Never met the man, but we'll do so tomorrow and see what he can tell us of your man. What's his name?"

Brandy frowned at the phrase "your man," but she supplied the name. "Sam Owens. Thank you, Ward, for helping. I'll see you in the morning."

Ward mounted his horse. "Cheer up—everything

will turn out all right," he said, then he rode off to another wagon.

Dinner didn't consist of much: dried beans and biscuits. Their little party was in a somber mood as they ate, eyes cast down toward their plates. Brandy wasn't sure she wanted to know what the children were thinking. Were they blaming her?

"Look at all those long faces," MacTavish suddenly said. "We should be rejoicing that we've made it this far and be very grateful we're not buried back on that trail with all those poor folks who didn't make it. Except for Mary trying to drown herself, we haven't had much trouble to complain about."

Laughter erupted from all as they looked at Mary, who immediately began blushing. "It wasn't funny at the time," she finally said.

"That's much better. No more long faces." MacTavish nodded with a chuckle.

"We're going to miss you after you leave," Ellen said, and the rest of the children nodded.

"Nettie and myself will definitely miss you children, too. But we'll send word once we've found our piece of land, and if things don't go right here, you're more than welcome to come and stay with us."

At the moment, MacTavish's idea sounded much better to Brandy than staying here, and it was on the tip of her tongue to ask if they could go with them now. Instead she said, "Thank you."

MacTavish pulled a pipe out of his pocket. "I have an idea. Tomorrow night I'll think of a very special story to tell."

"All right," the group chorused.

The next thing Brandy knew, Thunder was standing beside her. She hadn't even heard him approach, but that was usually the case.

"Good evening," Thunder said with a nod to everyone.

"Would you care for some supper?" Nettie asked him.

"I have already eaten, thank you." Thunder looked at Brandy. "Come ride with me, Brandy."

Slowly, she got to her feet and followed him over to Lightning, where Thunder mounted first. "Do I need to saddle a horse?" she asked.

"Not for this short ride." He held his hand down to her. She grasped his arm and he swung her up effortlessly behind him. "Hang on," he said, at the same time nudging his mount.

Her arms snapped around his waist in a death grip, lest she fall off the horse. Since Thunder's shirt was open she could feel his warm skin beneath her fingertips. She marveled at his muscles, and how good he felt in her arms. Smiling, she thought how much she liked touching this man. She would like it even better if she were sitting in front and he was holding her.

"Where are we going?" Brandy asked.

"To meet a friend."

They rode to the teepees where Thunder dismounted and helped Brandy down.

There were many campfires throughout the small village, which was spread along the river bank. The smoke from the many fires filled the evening air with a fragrant haze. The brown teepees were covered with well-worn buffalo hides, the willow poles framing them against the sky. Men, women, and children went about their tasks, barely glancing at the newcomers. Brandy thought the circle of teepees reminded her of the wagon train in a way. Everyone had a job to do. Maybe there really wasn't that much difference between the Indian and the white man.

A short brave strode up to them. His long, black hair hung over his sun-bronzed bare chest. He had feathers in his hair and wore buckskin breeches. His black eyes twinkled in his dark skin, and she thought he had a trusting face.

"Is this your woman, Thunder?" his deep voice rumbled in broken English.

"Not my woman, but the one I spoke to you about," Thunder said smoothly. He took her arm. "Brandy, I would like you to meet Little Big Bear. He is from my tribe. We grew up together."

"It is nice to meet you." She nodded at Little Big Bear. "How did you get your name?"

Little Big Bear grinned, a smile that went from ear to ear. "You like my name?"

She smiled easily. "It is different."

He chuckled. "My father's name is Big Bear. I look like him, only not so big. The Medicine Man one day call me by my name. He say I growl like a bear." Little Big Bear growled and held his hands up over his head. "Just like my father, but I was too small. Soon name stay with me," Little Big Bear explained, then motioned with his hand. "Come. Sit. We will talk."

Brandy sat down at the fire. She liked the way the Indians' names all had meanings to them. She wondered what her name would have been—probably Dumb Bear because of all the mistakes she'd made.

"Brandy, how did you come by your name?" Little Big Bear asked. "It isn't a white man's name."

"My mother said my hair was the color of brandy and thus gave me the name."

"It is rare." He nodded in agreement. "Maybe we would have called you Raging Fire." He smiled at her.

"That name would definitely fit her," Thunder acknowledged with a knowing nod. She frowned at his jest.

Thunder smiled at her displeasure. "Little Big Bear will be here for another month. If you find yourself in trouble, come to him."

"All right," Brandy said with a smile and a nod to Little Big Bear. Then she asked Thunder the question she had dreaded all evening. "When are you leaving?"

"Tonight."

Tonight. For a moment, she couldn't breathe. *Tonight* kept echoing through her brain. He couldn't leave so soon.

She was losing him. She'd never see him again.

It wasn't fair.

Life wasn't fair.

Would everyone that she truly cared about continue to walk out of her life and leave her behind? What was wrong with her?

She took several deep breaths as Thunder and Little Big Bear continued talking about their tribe and what had happened since Thunder had left. Finally, Thunder stood and said, "It is time to go."

Brandy was so numb she could hardly move, but somehow she managed to stand and go through the motions of acting normal as she followed him to his horse. She could plead with him to stay, but she knew deep in her heart that it would do no good.

They rode back to the wagon train in silence. They had just about reached the wagons when Thunder stopped and dismounted.

He helped Brandy down, then let her lean against his horse. And before she knew what he intended, he leaned down and kissed her. The intimacy was slow and languid. A shudder rushed through her.

His mouth moved hungrily over hers and her world careened crazily beneath the savage urgency of his demanding kiss. It was as if he were trying to tell her something through his actions that he couldn't say with words.

But she needed words.

How did he feel about her?

When he pulled back, he said, "I shall miss you."

Those were not the right words. Her world came crashing down. "Is that all you have to say?" she managed to get out.

"You will be meeting your future husband in the next few days, and then you and the children will have a home. As I recall, this is the reason you came on the trip."

For a moment, Thunder wished things were different. Perhaps if she loved him they could somehow work things out, but she belonged to another. When he brought the subject up, Brandy never denied that she had any other intention but going though with her agreement with this mysterious man.

"He doesn't know about the children," she said softly.

"What!" Thunder couldn't believe what he heard.

She flinched at the tone of his voice. And her heart thumped heavily as she raised her eyes to his. "I was afraid he wouldn't send the money. And we had to get out of town."

He stared at her in total disbelief. "You are one crazy woman. What are you going to do if he refuses the children?"

"I don't know."

"Well, it's a fine time to be thinking about it now," he gritted out slowly as he reached up and grabbed her arms.

"It isn't your problem," she hissed in frustration. She knew what a risk she'd taken. "So don't worry about it. I paid you to do your job and you've done it." She jerked away from him. She wanted to hurt him the way he was hurting her. How could he just walk away after all they had shared?

Thunder was torn. He knew he needed to stay. Brandy didn't seem to realize what she was doing or just what could happen to her. Would he ever understand the woman?

Hell, the man she was promised to would probably be glad to have the children just to get Brandy. His stomach twisted. He wondered why. Damn it.

He couldn't stay, he reminded himself. Little Big Bear had said Thunder's mother was very sick, and he needed to go to find her. Little Big Bear had not mentioned Thunder's father.

Brandy would survive. She knew what she was getting into. She had more spirit than any woman he'd ever met, and deep down he admired that spirit no matter how frustrated she made him. She just didn't know what she was capable of, because she'd never been put to the test.

He reached for the reins. "I guess my job here is done."

Brandy moved away from the horse without touching him. She swallowed her pride. "Please don't go."

He reached down and cupped her face. "There are reasons that I must leave."

And one of the reasons was that he didn't want to be with any of them, Brandy concluded. She slapped his hand away from her face. Her anger built inside her. Let him walk away. That was what he always wanted to do. "If you ride out of here, I swear I'll hate you until the day I die," Brandy told him with a cold and slashing voice.

"Hate is a strong emotion," he said. He stared at her for a long moment. She wished she could see his eyes, but the darkness prevented it so she had no way of knowing how he felt at this moment.

Without another word, he turned his horse and left her staring at his back. Panic like she'd never known welled in her throat as she watched him ride off. She crumpled to the ground and sobbed. Her heart was truly broken.

Why hadn't she told him that she loved him? Would he have stayed? She wept some more. Instead, she'd told him just the opposite . . . she'd said she hated him.

Now she'd lost him forever.

Suddenly, a hand touched her arm and she jerked. Had Thunder come back? She turned around, only to find Billy. She really didn't want him to see her crying, but it was too late for that, and seeing him made her cry just that much harder.

Billy pulled her next to him and gave her a hug. "You want to tell me what's wrong?"

"He—he left," she sobbed.

Billy rubbed her back. "Your future husband? I didn't know you'd seen him."

Why did everyone constantly remind her of that man? "No. Th-Thunder." She shook her head miserably.

"You knew he was going to leave sooner or later."

"I know, but I didn't expect it to be so soon. I liked him."

Billy held her away from him. "Liked?"

Brandy straightened and wiped the tears from her face. "Yes, liked."

"Humph." Billy grunted and arched a brow. "I seen you two. When you weren't fightin' I'd say you were sweet on him. Come on, let's go back to the wagon."

"Well, he's gone now," Brandy said.

"He had good reason."

"Yes, I know." Brandy nodded. "He wanted to see his people."

Abruptly, Billy stopped and turned to look at her. "He didn't tell you?"

"Tell me what?"

"His mother is very sick," Billy said as they started walking again. "Somebody down at the river told him."

"I didn't know," Brandy said, feeling a little better—not that his mother was sick—but now she knew the reason he'd left so quickly.

When they reached the wagon, Billy looked at her. "You ready to meet your husband?"

"I—I have to keep my bargain. But I must admit, I've a funny feeling like—"

"Like what?"

Brandy took a deep breath. "Like I'm getting ready to open Pandora's box."

"Who's she? And what about her box?"

"You really don't want to know the answer to those questions." Brandy gave him a sorrowful smile. "Let's just hope I'm wrong."

SIXTEEN

About mid-morning, Ward came to the wagon to get Brandy. She mounted her horse and they rode to the fort.

"Where are we going?" Brandy asked him.

"We're headed for that building over yonder." He pointed. "It's called the Old Bedlam."

It was a two-story, wooden building with porches stretching across the top and bottom. Painted a pristine white, it appeared very clean. "What is in that building," she asked.

"It's where the officers and post headquarters are housed." He pointed in another direction. "Over there is the Sutler's Store."

"What's that?"

"A civilian licensed by the army to deal with ordinary citizens and Indians. This fort used to be a trading post, and there is still plenty of trading going on, so I reckon you could still call the store a trading post."

"I see. Sounds like it would be a popular place," she said as they pulled their horses to a stop at the front steps of the white building.

"Very popular."

Several white buildings surrounded a rectangular parade field. A group of men marched by as Brandy and Ward dismounted and left their horses tied at a hitching post.

When they opened the screen door a man in a blue uniform glanced up from his desk, but didn't bother to stand. Finally, he asked. "May I help you, sir?"

"We would like to speak with the colonel."

"And who may I say wants to see him?"

"Ward Singer, the wagon master of the train just outside the post."

"Just a moment." The young private got up and disappeared into a room to his left. A few minutes later he was back. "You may go in now," he said as he gestured toward the door.

Ward stood back and allowed Brandy to enter the room first.

The man behind the desk rose. He was a big man and very overweight. His uniform stretched tight across his belly and his yellow sash had been loosened. He also smelled of liquor when he extended his hand to Ward. "Colonel Jeb Moonlight at your service. What can I do for you?"

Ward grasped the man's hand. "Ward Singer, wagon master, and," Ward paused and placed his hand on Brandy's arm in a protective gesture "This is Brandy Brown. She is here to meet—"

"Sam Owens," Brandy supplied the name. "Do you know him?"

"Yes, ma'am," Moonlight said and gave her a peculiar look. "He has a place a few miles from the fort."

"Then will you provide an escort to take me and my family there?"

"Yes, ma'am. But Sam isn't there. He's taken a little trip."

Brandy became alarmed. "And when will he be back?"

"Tomorrow. He told me he was expecting something on the train. Of course, he didn't say that something was you," he said with a leer that turned Brandy's stomach.

"We'll be pulling out early tomorrow, Colonel, so I'll have Brandy leave her wagon where it is. She has been under my protection, and I turn her over to you until her intended comes for her."

"As it should be." Moonlight pushed himself heavily to his feet, signaling that the meeting was over. "Anything else I can do for you?"

"No." Ward stood also. "Some of my travelers will be visiting the sutler for supplies."

"We've got a fine one."

"Is there any Indian activity up ahead?"

"Damned savages," Moonlight spat. "I think we should get rid of all of them, but it's not my call. Make friends with them, comes the word from headquarters. But that's an army issue. In answer to your question, the last two months have been quiet so your journey should be uneventful. Have heard of a couple of skirmishes near Denver."

When they reached the door the colonel nodded drunkenly, and Brandy realized he had been indulging heavily and it was still early. She would hate to be around him by the end of the day.

"Good day, ma'am. I'm sure I will be seeing *a lot* of you."

"Thank you, Colonel," she said, shrinking back from his sour whiskey breath, and wondered what he meant. She assumed that he and her future husband must be acquainted. However, Moonlight had looked at her as if she were a piece of merchandise, and she didn't like the uneasy feeling she was beginning to get.

Pandora's box . . . the thought ran through her head and she shivered.

Brandy spent the rest of the day helping Nettie and MacTavish straighten up their supplies and storing the new provisions that they had bought at the store.

As much as Brandy's heart ached at the prospect of losing these good friends, they made a promise that they wouldn't say their goodbyes until tomorrow morning. Tonight they would have dinner and a story as usual.

The weather had suddenly changed for the better. The oppressive heat they'd first experienced was gone. It was now mid-September and the days were pleasant and chilly, promising the first hint of winter. Brandy hadn't thought about it until now, but soon it would be turning cold and they would need heavier clothing to keep them warm. When she said as much to Nettie, Nettie told her to wait a minute.

Nettie came back carrying four quilts. "Here, I want you to have these so that you'll remember us when you stay warm."

"I can't take these. What will you use?"

"I have plenty of them. Where we came from was plenty cold, so I was always making quilts. This way, I'll still be taking care of you." She smiled.

Brandy hugged her. "Thank you. We will cherish them."

At dinner everyone seemed subdued until Mac-Tavish started telling them a story of Scotland. As usual, he swept them away to another land they could only dream about.

Morning came much too soon for Brandy. It was a beautiful day. There wasn't a cloud in the azure-blue sky, and the air was pleasant and dry with a slight, cool breeze.

"Wagons Ho," came the call from the front.

" 'Tis time for us to go," MacTavish said. He gave Brandy a hug. "You take care of yourself, do you hear?" He looked at her then gave her another hug. "We'll be writing to you to let you know where we are."

Brandy could do nothing but nod, because she couldn't say anything. MacTavish left her to hug the other children, and Brandy held her arms out to Amy for a hug. "You be a good girl."

Amy wrapped her little arms around Brandy's neck and kissed her on the cheek. Then she went looking for Scott.

Nettie blinked back the tears as she embraced Brandy. "All of you will be in our hearts," she whispered thickly. She reached into her pocket and pulled out a small wrapped bundle. "I want you to have something," she said and pressed the cloth in Brandy's hand.

Brandy unwrapped the bundle and removed the cloth. A pearl-handled derringer lay in the palm of her hand. She gave Nettie a puzzled look.

"A lady needs to protect herself. I have another just like it. Now promise me you'll keep this in your pocket in case you'll be needin' it," she said gruffly as she continued to fight her tears.

Brandy gave her a shaky smile. "I promise," she said, making no effort to disguise her own tears.

"Good. And if my guess is right, you'll be seeing Thunder again. Then you won't need it," she said with a wink.

"I don't want to say goodbye, but know I must," Brandy whispered, sobbing.

"Come on, Nettie girl," MacTavish said as he climbed into the driver's seat. Even his eyes glistened a bit.

They all waved farewell.

When Brandy glanced at the children, everyone had tears in their eyes, and she wanted to say something to make them feel better, but she couldn't find the words. She just gathered them to her, and held them tight.

Ward rode back and dismounted. "You take care of yourself, Brandy. And when I'm passing through this way again, I'll make sure I look you up."

"Thank you for all you've done for us, Ward. I will never forget you," Brandy managed around a lump in her throat.

Ward looked at the beautiful young woman in front of him. He really didn't like leaving her alone out here, but he had little choice. He had a train full of wagons, and passengers depending on him. A good rule was never to get too close to the people he led across the country, but somehow in Brandy's case, he'd broken his own rules. He wondered if Thunder's mother had not been sick, would the man have left them alone so quickly. If so, he would have to be a damned fool.

"I've got to go," Ward said as he gathered his horse's reins and mounted. "Billy, look after everyone.

Goodbye." Ward nudged his horse and cantered away. When he was a good distance from them, he halted and turned one last time. "Goodbye," he called.

Brandy wondered if he'd left so abruptly because he didn't want them to see him cry. Then again, men didn't cry—only women did.

They all stood beside their wagon, watching him ride after the wagons. Brandy couldn't help but think—now what?

Everyone she cared about was gone.

She was alone in an unfamiliar land, waiting for a strange man she knew she didn't love.

She wiped her face dry and swallowed her last tear. No, she wasn't alone. She had the children.

The land Thunder rode across was golden in color. The tall, rich grass, kissed by the sun, brushed his knees as he rode toward home. He'd been riding for days.

He'd thought he'd be very excited to be nearing his home, and he was in a way. He was eager to see his mother. He hoped she wasn't as sick as Little Big Bear had hinted, and fear that he might not reach her in time spurred him on.

But he couldn't quit thinking of Brandy. He'd see a sunset and he'd remember her hair, her eyes. Her stubborn chin.

And the children had come to mean something to him as well. He hadn't wanted them, either, but somehow they had crept into his affection. How many times had he taken Scott for a ride and marveled at his giggles and never-ending questions? Billy had become a man during the trip, pitching in to help wherever he was needed. Thunder smiled with satisfaction, knowing that Billy could drive a wagon better than anyone could. Mary had definitely changed and become bearable. Ellen had learned to trust.

Then there was Brandy. Always Brandy.

He hoped her memory would fade from his mind before long, because she would soon be another man's wife. And that ate at his insides like an all-consuming disease.

Sam Owens rode toward the wagon. He'd expected the wagon train a couple of weeks earlier, so he was glad Brandy was finally here. His business could use some fresh blood, and it was good to know his ad could still draw women. He smiled slyly. Maybe today was going to be a good day.

Once Sam reached the wagon, he dismounted and tied his horse off. A little boy came running up to him.

"Who are you?" the kid asked.

"My name is Sam Owens. I'm looking for Brandy Brown," he told the little boy, wondering who he belonged to.

"I'm Brandy," a voice came from behind the wagon, and a lady came walking toward him with the prettiest hair he'd ever seen. As a matter of fact, she was beautiful. Much more so than what he'd expected.

"It is nice to finally meet you, Brandy," Sam said. "I'm sorry I wasn't here when you first arrived." He couldn't get over how beautiful she was. Yessiree, today was his lucky day. "Have you been here long?" he asked, forcing politeness to cover his eagerness.

"We've been waiting here a day," she replied.

"We?" Sam questioned

"The children and I," she said with a sweeping hand.

"Children?" He glanced sideways in surprise as three kids came from around the wagon. "These are your children?" he asked again but didn't wait for her to answer. "Nothing was mentioned in the letter you sent me about children, or that you'd been married before."

Brandy swallowed hard. A sensation of sickness and desolation swept over her. She looked at Sam for a moment before she answered. He was tall and broad-shouldered; his hair was sandy brown and his eyes a light-colored brown, but they held little warmth. He was a nice-looking man, but she really didn't feel anything toward him. Of course, she'd just met him, and she couldn't expect much. But the day of reckoning had arrived.

His mouth was tight and grim. "You've not answered my question."

By now, all the children had gathered behind her. "These are my brothers and sisters. I have promised to take care of them."

Sam came closer, looking down at her intensely. "That wasn't the deal."

"I know. But I've promised I would take care of them. They have no one else."

Sam backed away from her and ran his hand through his hair. "That is four more mouths to feed. The deal is for you only. You can leave them at the fort. There's always somebody who'll need extra hands."

Brandy stiffened. "Then we don't have a deal. I will not leave the children. They are my family."

Sam took a menacing step toward Brandy and grabbed her arm. "I spent a lot of money for you, honey. You owe me. I want my money back."

"Get your hands off my sister," Billy said, propping a rifle across his arm.

Immediately, Sam let go of Brandy.

"I don't have your money. I spent it to get out here."

"Well you're not getting off without paying your debt. I brought you out here to work. I can have you thrown in jail. Or better yet, I could still put you to work at my hog ranch."

"I—I thought you brought me out here to marry." She hesitated, blinking with bafflement. "I don't understand. A hog ranch?"

"I see you don't know what that is." Sam laughed. "It's a place where men pay for the company of the women I house."

Mary gasped.

"As a matter of fact, I could use all three of you girls for work. They'd pay a pretty price for the young one."

Brandy slapped his face. "Don't you dare think of involving my sisters in such . . . such . . ." It was too terrible to put into words.

"You owe me, honey. Even if I really wanted a wife, I wouldn't consider one with baggage." He pointed to the children. "And one way or the other I intend to collect."

"That may be true, but your ad also asked for a wife, so I don't believe that you were entirely honest, either." Brandy couldn't believe the mess she'd gotten herself into. The whole time she thought she was coming to meet a decent man, only to find a snake. Well, he wasn't going to get away with this.

"I'm going to see the colonel," Brandy said.

"That's a good idea. We will both go," Sam said as they walked down the hill to the fort.

Once they were in Colonel Moonlight's office, Brandy explained what had happened.

"You did accept money from Sam?" Moonlight asked.

"Yes. But his ad said marriage," Brandy explained.

"She owes me a great deal of money, and I expect payment, Colonel," Sam demanded.

"I've known you a long time, Sam. You run a pretty decent place that helps my men out with their, er, needs. When I met Miss Brown, I figured she was fresh blood for your place, but she has children with her and a wagon master who will be checking back in on her, so you can't force her into the house. However, she does owe you a great deal of money that will have to be paid. Or you could marry her."

Sam came to his feet. "Marriage is out of the question. I run a business. I need her working."

"We can all work to pay off our debts, but not with our bodies," Brandy told them.

Sam glared at her. "You'll have to work a long time to pay what you owe me." He rubbed the back of his neck. This wasn't going the way he planned. Here was a beautiful woman who could make him a bundle. But those damn brothers and sisters presented a problem. However, once she was at his place, he could always bend her to his will, so maybe he should be agreeable at first. "Maybe having a few extra hands around the place wouldn't be bad. I have cows and chickens that need tending. Cooking for the girls that live there. And they don't clean house, either."

"We are perfectly capable of doing odd jobs," Brandy informed him.

"Good. It's decided," the colonel said and walked them to the door. "I'll be out to see you shortly, Sam. Tell Molly I said hello."

When they were walking back to the wagon, Sam said, "You'll have to live in that wagon, which you can park next to the barn. I'll not provide you with anything more including food until your debt is paid off."

Brandy nodded as they reached the wagon.

Then he leaned closer to Brandy. "And if you don't live up to your end of the deal," he said just low enough for her to hear, "then I'll put your young, firm body to work until all the debt is paid." He ran a finger under her chin, and Brandy shuddered with revulsion.

Pandora's box had just been opened.

She slapped his hand away. "We will follow you to your home."

Once they had hitched the horses and were on their way with Sam riding ahead of them, Billy said, "Thanks for taking up for us."

"Yeah," Mary and Ellen said from the back of the wagon.

Brandy, who was sitting beside Billy, said, "We're a family. It's taken me a while to learn that, but we stick together no matter what." Now that she'd learned what Sam's true intentions were, she almost wished she could leave the children at the fort so they wouldn't be around such goings-on, but she wasn't sure she trusted the colonel any more than she did Sam.

"Father Brown would never believe that we're all getting along so well," Billy said.

"He's probably up there smiling down on us," Brandy said, then added, "I just wish he'd give us some answers as to what to do. Sam isn't what I expected. I don't want to live like this forever."

"Can you believe what he brought you out here to do?" Mary said from the back of the wagon. "He never intended to marry you."

"No, I can't," Brandy spoke with light bitterness. "I think he is very sneaky, so please be careful around him. I wonder how many other women he's tricked. First he gets the woman out here, and then she's alone and has no other way out." Brandy reasoned. "I'd probably be in that situation, too, if I didn't have the rest of you with me."

"See, we're good for something," Scott piped up from the back.

Brandy laughed. "Yes, you are."

"So what are we going to do?" Billy asked.

"Make the best of a bad situation, for the moment. We should be used to that by now. We've been living in this wagon for the past four months, so for now we'll have a roof over our heads. Or should I say canvas? Then maybe we'll hear from Nettie and Mac-Tavish, and we can travel to where they are. Do any of you have a better idea?" Brandy turned around to look at the girls.

"Nope," Billy said. "Maybe I can find something to do around the fort to earn extra money. The way I see it the faster we pay off the debt the sooner we can get on our own."

"It's going to take a lot of money to repay Sam," Mary said.

"Has anyone ever noticed that all our problems have something to do with money?" Ellen commented from the back of the wagon.

"That is very true, Ellen," Brandy said, then turned back to face the front.

"I wish Thunder were here," Scott commented in such a small voice that Brandy wasn't sure if he'd said it or she'd imagined it.

I do, too, Brandy thought. *I do, too.*

SEVENTEEN

The mountains came into view, and Thunder knew he was near his family summer campgrounds. A bald eagle flew overhead, looking for his next prey, his white head glistening in the sun from the water he had just risen above. He evidently had missed the fish he'd dove for.

Thunder followed a creek to the base of the mountains; he saw teepees camped along the edge of the stream.

Finally, he was home.

Nudging his horse forward, he started down the well-worn path and listened to the sound of rushing water cascading over rocks. He'd not ridden a hundred yards when he was knocked from his horse and landed hard on the ground.

Thunder cursed himself for his carelessness while he fought to catch his breath. It was a good way to get himself killed, he thought as he wrestled with the Indian brave who seemed to have appeared out of nowhere. He hadn't even thought about the lookout. His mind had gone soft on him.

Thunder struggled with the brave. He gained the upper hand and looked down at the surprised face of the young man who had jumped him.

"I am Rolling Thunder," he said in his native tongue. "Who are you?"

"I am Straight Arrow, son of Wounded Bear."

Thunder stood and extended a hand to the brave. "I am not your enemy. I have come home. Walk with me to camp."

Straight Arrow was quiet as he strolled beside Thunder. He knew the brave was ashamed that he'd been bested by a stranger, but the fact was that Thunder had more experience. The boy had been very young when Thunder had left.

As he walked through the village, he saw children playing. Women were scraping buffalo skins. Nothing seemed to have changed since he'd been away. There must have been a successful hunt because meat hung from poles drying in the sun.

Everyone from the camp had turned out to see what the commotion had been. They stepped aside, and those who recognized Thunder patted him on the back and welcomed his return. But he didn't stop until he reached Black Kettle's lodge.

Chief Black Kettle threw back the flap and stepped outside. His eyes narrowed as he focused on Thunder. A sudden glimmer of recognition lit in his dark brown eyes. "You have come home."

Black Kettle had aged since Thunder had last seen him, but he seemed as wise and strong as ever. As a chief, it was Black Kettle's duty to maintain harmony for his people. He was an exemplary man—calm, generous, kind, sympathetic, and, most of all, courageous.

Thunder embraced the chief. "It has been too many moons. Where is my mother and father's teepee?"

"She's there." Black Kettle pointed. "Go. We will speak later."

Thunder drew open the teepee flap and looked inside. He left it open when he realized how stuffy it was inside. His mother was lying on buffalo robes on the far side of the teepee. She didn't look at him when he entered, but she stared straight ahead as if she awaited death.

"Why are you in here alone?" Thunder asked, not bothering to speak Cheyenne because his mother had always spoken to him in English.

Slowly, she turned her head and gazed upon him. Her face was much too pale and her eyes dull. "My— my son." She held up a hand to him.

"Yes, Mother," Thunder said as he sat down cross-legged beside her. He took her hand in his.

"You've come home," she said as if a burden had been lifted from her.

"Only to find that you are very sick. Why is no one caring for you?"

"Help me to sit," she said. Thunder barely recognized her voice.

Gently he pulled her up until she could sit on her own. She opened her arms, and he held her, feeling the comfort that only a mother's embrace could bring. She was much too thin, and from what he saw in the tent she hadn't had enough nourishment.

"I love you, my son."

"I love you, too, Mother, but you are burning up with fever. Here, lie back and let me get wet rags to cool you. When is the last time you have eaten?"

She stared at him, her eyes not really focusing. It was as if her body were there, but her spirit gone. "I don't remember. After your father died, time just seemed to stop," she murmured as she stretched back out on the blankets.

"Well, time starts again as of this moment," Thunder said firmly. He shoved to his feet. "I am going to find food."

He went to the next teepee and was thankful to find Dancing Water, who had been a friend of his mother's for as long as he could remember.

"Thunder, you have changed. I now see a man standing before me," Dancing Water said. "There will be many young women who will be casting their eyes upon you, for you have grown strong and tall as the trees."

"Yes, but I am back now and find that my mother is not well. I must have some broth for her."

"Come." Dancing Water motioned for him to follow her from the lodge. She went over to a kettle that was suspended over the fire. "They killed buffalo yesterday, and I have just made this broth. Take this bowl to her, and here is some powder that should help her." She shoved it into his hand. "I have tried to get her to take it myself, but she refused. I believe she still mourns Crazy Arrow."

"I have not yet asked about my father, but I will once my mother is stronger."

"I am glad you have come home, Rolling Thunder. Maybe Little Woman will want to join the living again."

For the next week, Thunder stayed by his mother's side, feeding her and sponging her down with cool water. He left the teepee flap open to let in the cooler air. He knew there were squaws to do such work, but

Thunder insisted. He felt guilty that he'd not been here when his father died, and he decided he'd not let his mother go so easily.

It was well into the second week when he finally saw a change in his mother. She sat up on her own for the first time.

"I feel like walking today. I have been cooped up much too long," his mother said in a voice that sounded more like the one he remembered. She started to rise, then sat back down. "I fear you will have to help my bones to get going."

Thunder got to his feet, then assisted his mother into a standing position. "Are you sure you are up to a walk?"

She smiled at him. "You have given me back my strength." She stepped from the enclosure out into the open air. "It has turned cooler since my illness. Come." She held her hand to Thunder, and he grasped her arm for support. "We need some fresh air."

They started slowly across the camp. Squaws rushed over to greet Little Woman, telling her they were glad that the gods had spared her life.

As they left the camp, heading toward the river, Little Woman said in a wistful sigh, "I'd forgotten how blue the sky is this time of year. It is amazing how sadness can rob one of the will to live."

Thunder nodded in agreement. "There have been times I have said the same thing. I missed the wide open sky when I was in Boston."

"Come, sit, and tell me about my parents. Are they well?"

"They called you Helen."

She smiled. "That is my Christian name. Do you not like it?"

Thunder looked at her and grinned. "You do not look like a Helen, and it sounded strange when I first heard it. My grandparents were shocked when I suddenly appeared," Thunder said with a smile. "As a matter of fact, Grandmother fainted upon laying eyes on me. I believe she thought I was going to take her scalp."

Helen smiled. "I never thought about that. I had hoped that word had gotten back to them that I was alive."

"No." Thunder shook his head. "They thought you were dead."

"My poor parents," Helen said sadly. "How I wish I could see them. It has been so long."

"They want to see you."

"And I want to see them," Helen said, then changed the subject. "Tell me, did you learn while you were in Boston?"

"Yes. I studied to become a lawyer and then the war broke out and I learned how the white man fights."

"I am glad I sent you home. There is so much more for you in that world, but I do admit to being happy that you are here now."

Thunder smiled at his mother. It was good. She was more herself. "Tell me what happened to my father," he said.

A sad look immediately replaced the faint smile that had been on her face only a moment ago. Thunder regretted that he'd asked.

"I loved Crazy Arrow very much. It is one of the reasons I could adapt to this way of life." She paused for a moment, then continued. "Crazy Arrow was killed in June. The Cheyenne were accused of rustling one hundred seventy-five cattle from a ranch on the Smoky Hill trail. The governor, John Evans, had four unsuspecting Cheyenne villages raided. Ours was not one of them, thank goodness, but Crazy Arrow had gone on a buffalo hunt and had stopped at one of the unfortunate villages after the hunt. He was shot along with Chief Lean Bear, who only wanted peace with the whites. Now the Cheyenne and Arapaho are on the warpath and have raided many ranches." She shook her head. "I don't know where all this will lead, but I have an uneasy feeling about it, my son." She sighed. "Have you spoken to Black Kettle since your return? He will tell you more than I have."

"Just briefly when I first arrived," Thunder told her. He slipped a long wheat straw into his mouth and chewed thoughtfully. "Now that you are better, I will go and speak with him. Maybe there is some way I can help."

Helen reached out and placed her hand on her son's and gave it a small squeeze. "I sense a sadness about you. Do you want to tell me what bothers you?"

"You could always read my mind." He chuckled. "I just feel strange being here. Everything is the same, yet different. Not like I remembered."

"Maybe it is you who has changed." She looked at him with knowing eyes. "You left a boy and returned a man. You have experienced many things that you couldn't have if you had stayed here. But tell me, what of your heart? Have you had a chance to experience love?"

Thunder looked at his mother's probing eyes. It was as if she could see all the way to his soul, but the subject was something he wasn't ready to speak of just yet. "That, Mother, I cannot say. I have experi-

enced feelings. Strong ones. But I do not know how
I feel."

"In time, you'll have your answers," Helen said to
her son. "Just give it time."

A month had gone by and Brandy was certain she'd
done a terrible job of taking care of the children.
Surely, Father Brown was frowning down on her. How
could she have gotten mixed up with a whorehouse?

The best she could do was just take one day at a
time until they could find a way out.

They now lived in the wagon beside a barn where
they had pitched the tent for the boys. Somehow, they
had made their own little compound so they were able
to stay away from the main house. Brandy especially
didn't like Scott or Ellen going to the big house and
when they did they had to go with one of the older
children.

Sam had claimed the horses as part of the payment
that Brandy owed him, and Billy and Scott had taken
the responsibility of feeding and caring for the animals. Billy would ride out and hunt for food when he
could slip away. He was becoming a very good shot.
If he hadn't provided their family with meat, they
might have starved.

The girls cooked, cleaned, and washed clothes for
the big house. And, of course, Sam kept trying to convince Brandy that she and Mary could earn much
more money working for him in the house. And he
didn't mean cleaning. Just the thought of what Sam
wanted made her skin crawl.

Three women lived in the house who worked for
Sam. Brandy had made friends with Molly, one of the

working girls, but she couldn't say the same for Sam. He might look nice on the outside, but Brandy sensed evil lurking just underneath the surface. He liked to take advantage of people, and he wanted to use her just like he had everyone else.

Last week, when Sam threatened to put her body to work, Brandy started carrying the small gun Annie had given her in her pocket just in case she needed it.

The air was crisp this morning. The days were still warm, but at night Brandy and the children needed Annie's quilts to keep them warm. As they ate breakfast, Billy said, "I'm goin' to the fort and see if I can get work. Maybe we can pay the debt off faster and get out of here on the next wagon train coming through."

"That would be wonderful," Brandy said. "I'm not sure where we would go. But anywhere is better than here."

"Heard it's payday at the fort," Billy said as he wiped his mouth. "So you know what that means."

"I'm afraid I do," Brandy admitted with a frown. "Drunken soldiers will be pouring into the house. We better get everything cleaned up early," Brandy said, then looked at Mary and Ellen. They nodded in agreement. Brandy rose and slid her plate into the dishpan. "You be careful," she told Billy as she held out her hand for Billy's and Scott's plates. "Don't let Sam catch you."

Billy got up. "I won't."

"What about me?" Scott asked. "I don't ever get to do anything but milk that stupid cow. Can I go?"

"Don't see what it will hurt," Billy answered with a smile. "You can ride with me. But we need to feed the animals first." Billy motioned for Scott to come on. "See you girls later."

"Wait a minute," Brandy said, then swallowed hard. "While we are all together, I want to tell you how sorry I am that I ever got us into this mess."

"Whoa," Billy said and held up his hand. "This ain't what we expected, I'll admit, but if we'd stayed in Independence, we'd be homeless and starvin'. At least, here we have a wagon and food, and look at what we've learnt."

"That's true," Mary agreed. "We didn't know what to do a few months ago. But, I'd rather have learned to care for myself some other way."

"We'll get out of this mess sooner or later, I promise," Brandy said, feeling much better that they were not blaming her. A few months ago she probably wouldn't have cared what they thought, but now she did. And they cared about her, too.

The three of them went to the house to clean. Molly, Sally, and Nell were the doves, as Sam called them, and they usually slept until way past noon.

"I'll clean up the parlor while you get the kitchen," Brandy said.

"You always did hate to work in the kitchen," Mary said as Brandy continued on to the parlor.

The furniture of the house was shabby but clean. At least Sam took care of his possessions. The parlor consisted of three battered chairs, one green and two brown, one very old, blue couch, and old wall calendars for decorations.

Brandy picked up empty glasses and trash. She'd just grabbed the last shot glass when Molly came downstairs. She was a tall, slender woman with large hazel eyes. Her eyes appeared extremely red this morning.

"You're up early," Brandy said.

"I'm feeling a bit under the weather. Couldn't sleep. This damned headache is driving me crazy!" Molly rubbed her temples. "I thought I'd get some laudanum from the kitchen," she said as she shuffled by Brandy.

"Maybe you can take the night off," Brandy suggested as she set the glasses down on the sideboard by the kitchen.

"Not likely," Molly grumbled. She went into the kitchen. In a minute she'd returned with a brown bottle of laudanum and a glass of water. She plopped down in a chair, throwing her leg over one of the arms. Her faded pink robe rode up high on her leg, revealing smooth skin, but it didn't seem to faze Molly at all. Her modesty had left her a long time ago. She was the oldest of the girls and still attractive, but the rough life had obviously aged her.

"Have you ever thought about quitting?" Brandy asked the question she'd been thinking.

"Yes, sweetie." Molly nodded slowly. "I've thought about it a lot. But where would I go? I don't have any money."

Brandy drew in a long breath, surprised Molly had been here so long yet she still didn't have any money. "Surely you earn money here."

"Yeah, but somehow it seems to all go to Sam, and we never get to touch the stuff."

"I see." Brandy started to dust the furniture. Sam would always have these girls under his thumb, and they didn't have any hope of escaping. What an evil man he was. "If you don't mind me asking, how did you get into this business?"

Molly took a swig of laudanum, then chased it down with water. "Let me see, honey. Been so long ago." She rolled her eyes as she thought and then focused on Brandy. "I was a young thing like you about five years ago." Molly paused to take another swig of laudanum.

Brandy tried not to gasp. She'd thought Molly was a good ten to fifteen years older than herself.

"Let me see, where was—oh, yeah, I came out on a wagon train. I was supposed to marry Frank Green. We were going to have a little house with a picket fence, a family." She sighed with a faraway look of another time and another place.

Brandy had stopped her dusting and was now sitting across from Molly. "So what happened?"

"Well, sweetie, life has a funny way of going wrong."

"I know what you mean."

"I arrived at the fort to meet Frank when he was a soldier stationed there. Anyway, when I arrived, I found out he'd been killed two weeks earlier while out on patrol. I was stranded. I had no place to live, no money. Nothing." Her eyes were cold and her face hard. "Then I met Sam. He happened to be in the room when I was talking to the colonel. He offered to give me a place to stay until I could find something else. And I guess you know the rest."

Neither of them had heard the front door open. "Is this how you pay your debt, Brandy? Or have you finally come to your senses and decided to join Molly and the other doves?" Sam reached down and grasped Brandy's chin in his hand. "You'd make a good piece."

Brandy jerked her face away and stood her ground. "Don't touch me." She moved around him and started to dust.

"Molly, you look like hell," Sam informed her. "Now get upstairs and fix yourself up before the men start coming in. They pay good money for you to look nice. And give me that bottle before you get drunk." He jerked the brown bottle from her hand.

"I've got a headache," Molly complained as she stumbled to her feet.

Sam slapped her hard enough to knock her back a step. "If you don't get up those stairs, more than your head is going to hurt."

Molly began to cry but she said nothing else as she stumbled up the stairs.

Sam whirled on Brandy. "And you better get busy, too. You still owe me quite a bit of money."

"Go to hell," Brandy said before she thought it through.

Sam reached back as if he was going to slap her, and Brandy stepped quickly out of his reach.

"If you hit me, I will kill you," she promised.

"You need to be brought down a notch or two, sweetheart," Sam snarled. "And you think those kids protect you?" He gave her an ugly laugh. "I do admit they are a problem that I hadn't expected, but there are ways they could disappear." He spoke in a low, sinister voice.

Momentary panic sprang up her back. "You leave them alone or I'll go to the fort for protection."

Sam gave her a sick smile. "You are a naive thing. I think I'm going to enjoy showing you how a man should treat a woman. But I have better things to do now." He came closer and grabbed her chin. "Rest assured, your day is coming very soon."

When he was gone, Brandy let out her breath. She would have to warn the children to always stay together and not get off by themselves. Somehow, some way, they had to get away from here before something terrible happened to one of them.

"Thunder, if you can hear me, please come back for us," she said as she shut her eyes and tilted her head toward Heaven.

Was Thunder thinking about her? Or had he forgotten all about them? She ached to be held in his arms. She could only pray that he felt the same way.

She sent the silent plea: *We need you.*

EIGHTEEN

The sun was just coming up over the horizon, giving the sky a purplish hue before it brightened the day. Autumn had arrived, bringing the crisp nip, reminding Thunder that winter wasn't far behind and summer was a fading memory. The leaves still clung to the branches and provided an array of oranges, yellows, and reds.

But what held his attention this morning was the purplish horizon. He sat on a hill, watching the sun as it tried to burst from the earth, but what he really saw was a pair of sultry amethyst eyes holding him spellbound. Many unanswered questions lurked in their debts.

He wondered how Brandy was doing. Had she married the man who had paid her passage? Was she happy? Did she love him? His jaw tightened at the thought. For some strange reason, he didn't want to think of her in another man's arms. But a part of Brandy belonged to him.

What had happened when her fiancé found out she wasn't a virgin? Had he grown angry? Thunder didn't want to think of that possibility. He knew the only way he'd find answers was to return and see for himself. But first he had other obligations. His mother was finally well, but the tribe was still unsettled.

"What has you frowning so much, my son?" His mother sat down beside him with a light blanket draped around her shoulders to ward off the chill.

"Nothing." Thunder shrugged, then added, "It is good to see you out more."

"And it is good to smell the morning's breath, but do not change the subject. I am not blind to what I see. I think it is time that you told me what causes the frown I have seen so many times when you didn't think I was looking. Now that I am much better, I know you no longer worry about my health which leads me to believe that something else is bothering you. Do I assume that your heart is elsewhere, my son?"

Thunder turned his head and smiled at her. "My heart is always with you."

"I know that." She smiled and reached over and patted him on the leg. "But there is another. I can see it in your eyes."

"Mother, you have always been wise," Thunder said with a sigh. "There *is* something bothering me. I thought when I returned to the village I would be at peace once again, but I have not found that which I look for. And now I'm not so sure what it is I seek." Thunder thumped his chest with his fist. "I still have this restless animal that paces within me. When I am with the white man I long to be here, and when I am here I think of the white man."

"Or is it a white woman?"

Thunder smiled. "Yes. There was one that still fills my mind even though I try to shove her from my head."

"And your heart?"

"Of that, I am not sure. But I do miss her and the children."

"She was married?"

"No." Thunder shook his head. "She was taking care of five children from an orphanage."

"I see," Helen said as she pulled her blanket closer. "Does she love you?

"I don't know," he said honestly. "She was engaged to marry another which was the reason she traveled on the wagon train."

His mother was quiet for a few minutes before she asked the next question, "Did she know this man?"

"No."

Helen pulled a piece of grass from the ground and rolled it between her fingers. "Did you see her married before you left?"

"You are full of questions this morning," Thunder said with a smile. "When I arrived at Ft. Laramie, Little Big Bear told me you were sick so I left immediately to come to you," he explained. But for some strange reason, he wanted to make her understand Brandy. "The woman is different. She didn't look at me as a half-breed as some whites do."

"Then she is a wise woman because you are not Cheyenne, my son," Helen said softly.

Thunder's head snapped around to gape at his mother. "Do you want to explain?"

"No one else knows but myself. You see, I was pregnant with you when I was taken hostage, but it was early and I did not show that I was with child. When I married Crazy Arrow, he always thought you were his child, and I never told him differently." His mother's face clouded with uneasiness. "Your father was killed when our wagon train was attacked."

"White man," Thunder said the words tentatively as if testing the idea. "I do not know what to say. Who was my father and what was he like?"

"He looked very much like you do. Tall. Strong. We were only married a few months when he heard of the gold strikes and he wanted to go west, but he didn't want to leave me. So we packed our few things and boarded a wagon train. When we were attacked, I didn't expect to live, but I knew I was with child and I would have done anything to protect you," she said with a smile. "Everyone was killed on the wagon train but me. Why I was the lucky one, I'll never know. But when Crazy Arrow found me, I didn't fear him like the rest. We married fairly quickly so it was easy for him to believe that you were his son. I feared if he knew the truth that he or someone else might try and kill you." She reached out and touched Thunder's hand. "Crazy Arrow was a good man also and a good father to you.

"The Cheyenne teach a simple way of life, but we don't belong as we once did. The Cheyenne believe man's life is a complete circle, and man, trees, rocks, and clouds are all a part of nature and each other. Since Crazy Arrow has died I have felt this same restlessness that you speak of. I know that Black Kettle has arranged for a meeting with the Governor. He still hopes for peace, and he wants you to go with him for the meeting."

Thunder nodded. "He has already asked me."

Helen slowly stood. "I have given this much thought. Once our tribe is settled and safe, I think we should leave. I am ready to go to my other home and see my parents before they die. They have no other family besides the two of us, and they have suffered long enough. I knew I could never leave Crazy Arrow, not after everything he had done. And he would never have agreed to go to Boston. But now I have no one here. Will you come with me?"

"Yes, Mother, I will take you to Boston." Thunder got to his feet. "But now I must meet with Black Kettle."

Together they walked back to camp, where Black Kettle had already mounted his spotted pony. The chief looked very old and tired, yet he still had that regal bearing that demanded respect. His face had many wrinkles and lines, which showed he had worried over his people and their fate. Thunder knew Black Kettle would fight for his people.

White Antelope rode up with Thunder's horse. "Come," he said as he handed over the reins. "It is time for us to go."

Thunder did not hug his mother as he wanted to, but mounted instead and together the three men rode off. It was hard for Thunder to believe he wasn't Cheyenne. Yet he didn't have time to think about what his mother had confessed because Black Kettle approached him.

"Have you been to Camp Weld?" Black Kettle asked.

"No. I have seen many forts. They are all the same."

"Governor Evans is nervous," White Antelope said. "I have been told that there is near-famine in the city due to our many raids."

Black Kettle grunted. "We would not have raided had not Chivington shot Chief Lean Bear."

"Why did he shoot the chief?" Thunder asked.

"First they accused us of stealing their cattle,"

Black Kettle said. "Did you see cattle in our camp or fat bellies from the beef?"

Thunder shook his head.

"Well, Colonel Chivington believed the tale. Chief Lean Bear was peaceful. He always wore the medal the Great Father in Washington gave to him. He was proud of his medal. He thought that it meant something.

"When Chivington rode into camp with his soldiers, Chief Lean Bear tried to wave the colonel away. He wanted Chivington to understand that Lean Bear and his people wanted peace but one of the pony soldiers shot him without ever speaking the first word."

"What do you think we'll find when we arrive?" White Antelope asked.

A thoughtful look came upon the chief's face. "I hope it is peace. I grow weary of war." Black Kettle sighed. "Major Wynkoop has arranged this meeting. There are not many white men that I trust, but I do trust Wynkoop. He does not speak with a forked tongue. I believe him to be a good man."

On September twenty-eight at Fort Weld, Governor Evans spoke to Colonel Chivington, commander of the District of Colorado, before the meeting with Chief Black Kettle was to take place. Because of the threat to Denver, the governor had called for help, and the war department had responded by authorizing one hundred men to train with the military so that Denver would be protected.

"It appears that we will have peace. Therefore, I see no need for the 'Hundred Dazers,'" Governor Evans said before he put a cigar back in his mouth.

"My men have trained hard. They are volunteers who have trained to fight the Indians, and that is what they want to do. They are fine men. Well trained. After all, the war department authorized the special regiment," Colonel Chivington protested.

"If we reach a peace agreement today, then we will have no need, Colonel. It's best if you don't attend the meeting. The chiefs seem to trust Wynkoop. Now, if you will excuse me," Governor Evans said, dismissing the man as he walked away from the red-faced Chivington.

Black Kettle was impressed when they rode into the fort. He'd asked for the meeting to be held outside around a campfire so everyone could see the talks take place. Governor Evans and Major Wynkoop stood by the fire, waiting for the chief. Governor Evans extended his hand, and the chief shook it before he took his place on one side of the fire with Thunder to his right and White Antelope to his left. The governor and Wynkoop sat across from them with Chivington standing in the background.

"I'm glad you have come," Governor Evans addressed the chief.

Black Kettle's gaze settled on the governor. "Major Wynkoop received my letter offering to end the hostilities on both sides. He is in agreement with me." Black Kettle looked at Wynkoop for acknowledgement, then back to the governor. "What do you have to say?"

"How do we know that this is not just talk?" Governor Evans asked.

Major Wynkoop spoke before the chief could say

more. "Black Kettle is an honorable man. When I visited him earlier to discuss peace, he released four prisoners to me as a sign of good faith. He has also come to the fort today as I requested. So I guess you could say that Chief Black Kettle has tried to do everything we have asked him to do."

The governor nodded, then looked at the chief. "Will the others follow you?" Evans asked.

"The Cheyenne and Arapaho will follow. However, there are some younger warriors who I do not have the ability to control."

The governor bowed his head and thought for a moment. "I will make a suggestion. You have just conceded your inability to control some of the younger warriors?"

The chief nodded with a frown.

"Then bring your tribes to settle at Fort Lyon, where you will be protected by Major Wynkoop. It's not far from here. You can move your village about forty miles northeast to a place called Sand Creek. There you will be able to hunt and make camp. The army will protect you as long as there is peace. Do you agree?"

Thunder thought it sounded good. Almost too good. But he, too, liked Major Wynkoop, and he knew him to be honest. So when Black Kettle glanced at Thunder and then White Antelope, they both nodded their approval. Thunder remembered his mother's words but his heart would always be part Cheyenne.

"We will accept this agreement. And hope to bring peace to this land once more," Black Kettle said as the meeting was concluded.

In the background, Colonel Chivington was livid. He swung around and went to his office, where he sent a letter to General Curtis falsifying the nature of Wynkoop's conciliatory policy and asking for a replacement as soon as possible.

His men had trained hard. They deserved to see some kind of action.

Every day Sam was becoming more difficult to deal with, due to his consumption of liquor. Brandy tried to avoid him as much as possible.

She couldn't see that they were any closer to getting out of Sam's grip, and she didn't know what to do about their situation. She just prayed a letter would come from MacTavish or, perhaps, Thunder would return. But it had been months and he hadn't come, so she willed herself to stop thinking about him.

The weather was just as gloomy as her mood, she thought as she stared out the back of the wagon. The dark clouds had opened up and a steady rain had fallen all morning. She wished she'd kept that ugly black dress she'd had in Independence. Now that the days were much cooler, it would be comfortable, and it would reflect her despair. She wrapped a small blanket over her head, climbed down from the wagon, and ran for the house.

She darted around to the front of the house because it had a porch where she could shake off the water. Entering, she brushed the water from her clothing, then glanced up just as Molly paused before going upstairs. Her hand rested on the rail as she turned to look at Brandy.

Brandy gasped. Molly's eye was puffy, and her lip was split and swollen.

"He's in one of his moods today," Molly warned

Brandy. "Been drinking since last night. So be careful 'round him, honey."

Brandy didn't have to ask who. "What put him in such a mood?" She strolled further into the room.

"Remember those soldiers that got into a fight last night?"

Brandy nodded. "We could hear it from the wagon."

"The colonel put the hog house off limits for six weeks, so it ain't gonna get any better."

"At least you'll have some time off," Brandy said, trying to find a bright side.

"I'd rather be working than put up with Sam and his foul temper." Molly sighed. "Better go up and put something cool on my lip."

As Brandy watched Molly climb the stairs, she had an uneasy feeling. If Sam started beating on his doves and that didn't satisfy him he just might turn on the rest of them, too, she thought as she reached for the cloth she used for dusting. She looked around at what was left of the furniture.

Two or three pieces had been busted up in the fight last night. She and the children had heard the commotion from the wagon. However, they knew better than to investigate and had stayed safely away.

Brandy could see the next six weeks as a living nightmare with Sam taking out his reduced profits on anyone who came near. She'd better warn Mary and Ellen to stay clear of Sam.

Upon entering the kitchen, Brandy saw Mary washing dishes. Mary turned at the sound of the door. "You can't be finished already."

"No. I came to tell you and Ellen something." Brandy looked around. "Where is she?"

"I made some extra biscuits. Ellen carried them out to the wagon so we can have them for supper. Then she was going to get some milk since she'd promised Scott that she'd do his chores while he was gone. Remember, he went hunting with Billy."

"That's right." Brandy shook her head and drew in a deep breath. "They both will probably be sick in all this rain. Have you seen Sam?"

"No, thank goodness," Mary said and rolled her eyes. "Saw Molly, though."

"Then you know what Sam is capable of doing?"

"Yeah." Mary nodded. "I remember men like him when I was growing up. One of the ladies who worked with my mother was cut up real bad with a straight razor."

Brandy made a face as she imagined the horror; then she went over to the kitchen door. "I'm glad, although I wouldn't have admitted that I was when you first came to the orphanage. I'm glad you got out of that situation." She smiled at Mary, then looked out the door. "Look at that rain. It's coming down harder and it's a cold rain."

"You know," Mary said, wiping her soapy hands in a towel, "Ellen's been gone a long time. Maybe she's had trouble with the cow."

"Throw me one of those cloths and I'll run out and check on her." Brandy wrapped the material around her head, jerked up her skirt, and dashed toward the barn, jumping two big puddles on the way.

Just as she entered the double doors, she heard Ellen screaming. Throwing the towel to the side, Brandy darted to the stall where the cow was kept. She saw a half-filled bucket of milk, but no Ellen. Had Brandy just imagined the scream?

She turned and looked back. A muffled whimper came from over her head in the loft. Brandy ran to the rough wooden ladder and climbed quickly to the top.

Over in the far corner, Sam had Ellen pinned down in the hay. He was holding her with one hand and undoing his trousers with the other.

Brandy dashed over and threw herself at Sam, knocking him away. "Leave her alone!"

Sam grabbed Brandy's wrist and jerked her back. She tried to escape his grasp. He rolled on her and held her down. "So, you want to take her place?"

His breath reeked of whiskey, and Brandy turned her head, trying to avoid the stench. She glimpsed Ellen, who had finally gotten to her feet and was straightening her skirt. She was sobbing uncontrollably.

"Run, Ellen," Brandy shouted before Sam got any bright ideas about grabbing the girl again.

Ellen just stood there like a frightened doe.

"Run, Ellen," Brandy repeated and finally saw it register on her face. Ellen bolted by Sam just as he lunged out to grab her. Brandy rolled away from him and tried to stand.

"Not so fast," Sam said, turning his attention back to Brandy. "Don't matter none," he said, grabbing and pushing her to the hay. "I still got a fine piece of ass under me." He bent down and his slobbering mouth caught Brandy's.

She struggled, pushing against his chest, but he was too strong for her. He didn't budge. She tried bucking him off, but even drunk he was too heavy and much stronger than she was. He pressed his mouth against hers, but Brandy refused to part her lips and twisted away.

He wrapped his hand in her hair and jerked her back. "There ain't no escaping me," he said before attacking again. Brandy still refused to open her mouth. With his other hand he began to unbutton her blouse. She tried shoving him, but it didn't do any good.

Before she knew it, he'd slid his hand into her blouse and caught her nipple, pinching it. She gasped with pain, and he took advantage and plunged his disgusting tongue into her mouth.

The whisky tasted awful and she wanted to vomit. Instead, she bit down on his tongue, and he immediately jerked away.

"You bitch!" He wiped his mouth. His eyes blazed with anger as he backhanded her across the face and tightened his grip in her hair.

Pain shot from the roots of her hair to the end of her toes. And before she knew what he was doing, his mouth was fastened on her breast, and she couldn't move him. Panic surged through Brandy. *Remain calm,* she warned herself, and then she remembered the gun in her skirt pocket. If she could just reach it.

She squirmed, and he finally rose, but only for a moment. He leaned down again, but Brandy threw a forearm across his throat. They struggled.

"Damn it," he swore and knocked her arm away. He grasped her throat and shook her. "You are going to learn to obey, one way or the other. Even if I have to choke the life out of you."

Fear ran rampant through her body. She couldn't breathe. Was this the way it was going to end for her?

Death in an unknown land by a man she couldn't stand? Frantic, she tried to yank his hands away.

They wouldn't budge.

Blackness swept in quickly.

"Get your hands off her!"

Suddenly the pressure eased, and she gasped for air. She took several deep breaths until the dizziness cleared. What was the commotion? Brandy pushed herself up.

Mary and Ellen had jumped on Sam and they were hitting him with their fists. Finally, Sam straightened, and he had the upper hand as he cuffed Ellen. She screamed.

Brandy dug her heels into the straw and pushed away from them so she had some distance between them. Jerking at her skirt, she felt the cold steel of the gun and she yanked it free.

Sam was just getting ready to strike Mary, who had managed to give him a swollen eye. He drew his arm back.

"Let her go," Brandy demanded. "Or I'll shoot you."

Sam jerked around, his left hand still holding Mary's arm. "Hell, that pea shooter won't stop no one." He shoved Mary away from him. "Give that thing to me." He held his hand out.

Brandy pushed herself up, keeping her aim on Sam's chest. "You're not getting the gun. And I will use it if I have to. I suggest you get out of here while you can."

"It's my barn, girl. I ain't going nowhere but on top of you," he snarled as he lunged for Brandy.

Mary and Ellen screamed.

The bullet exploded from the gun just as his body landed on Brandy, knocking the breath from her.

"You bitch!" He reared up, blood rapidly staining the front of his shirt.

Brandy gasped for air until she finally got her breath back.

"I'll kill you," he swore and reached for her neck.

Brandy wasn't sure she had the strength to fight off this man again. But as he reached out, he collapsed on her, his eyes wide open and staring at her in death. My God, she was the last thing he saw before he died!

Someone was screaming.

She was screaming.

And she couldn't seem to stop.

Finally the girls managed to pull Sam off her. Brandy sat up and looked down at her dress. It was soaked with blood, and her hands were shaking.

"He's dead," Mary said as she shoved him over.

"You killed him," Ellen said in a tearful voice.

Brandy looked down at her hand. It was still shaking and still clutching the bloody derringer. "Yes, I did," she said in a small voice. She threw the gun away from her into the hay.

"What are you going to do?" Mary said as she sat down on the straw next to Brandy.

"I wish to heaven I knew."

Ellen took Brandy's hand. "Will you go to jail?"

Brandy glanced at Ellen. The thought had never occurred to her. Jail? They would lock her up. They could hang her.

Someone was coming.

The three girls huddled together. Now what were they going to do?

Whoever it was, was climbing the ladder.
Brandy reached for the empty gun.
They held their breath and waited.

NINETEEN

"Was that a shot I heard?" Molly said as she poked her head up through the hole in the loft, a rifle grasped in her hand. "Oh, my God! You killed him." Molly looked down, then nudged the body with her foot. "Yep, he's dead all right." She looked at Brandy and a slow smile spread across her face. After a long moment of silence, she said, "Good shot. I wish I'd had the nerve to do that a long time ago."

The three of them just stared at her.

"Don't worry." Molly looked at the three stunned faces. "When it quits raining, we'll simply bury him. And he really doesn't even deserve that much."

Finally, Brandy managed to say, "We've got to tell the colonel."

"No, we don't." Molly shook her head. "They'll hang you, sweetie. Better do it my way."

"But it was self-defense. Look at my neck." Brandy swept her hair back. "He was trying to choke me."

"I see the red marks. But you know how men are. They don't think much of women around here, so I'm not sure how good your word would be."

"But burying him isn't honest. And I don't want to be running and looking over my shoulder for the rest of my life. One day I want a normal life. If there is such a thing."

"Where the hell is everybody?" Billy shouted from down below, his voice muffled by the distance, but his concern evident.

"Billy?" Mary seemed unable to connect his voice with the young man below.

"Whatcha doing up there?"

"Ah—there's been an accident." Mary tried to sound casual, but she was way off the mark.

"Did anybody get hurt?" Scott's voice joined Billy's.

"You could say that," Molly replied. "Just a minute, we're coming down." She turned to Brandy. "We don't need the kid coming up and seeing this."

Mary went down first, followed by Ellen, Molly, and finally Brandy.

"What are all of you doing? Having a party up there?" Billy joked, but his smile faded at the solemn expressions on their faces.

Brandy turned from the ladder, and Billy's eyes widened at the sight of her blood-splattered dress. "What the hell?"

"Are you hurt?" Scott asked, and moved toward her.

"I don't think so," Brandy said. "Careful." She held her hands out and made pushing gestures so Scott wouldn't get blood on him.

Billy folded his arms over his chest. "By the looks of that dress, somebody's hurt . . . real bad. You want to tell me what's goin' on?"

"Sam is dead," Brandy said in a dull voice, still not believing she'd pulled the trigger.

Ellen began to weep. "It's all my fault."

"No. It isn't," Brandy assured Ellen. "You were just the one that he chose to pick on."

"Look, sweetie," Molly said to Brandy, "I'm going to the house to let the other girls know what's happened." Molly put her hand on Brandy's shoulder. "I'd think long and hard about what I said up there." Molly nodded toward the loft, then gave Brandy a smile and shuffled off toward the house.

"So what did happen?" Billy asked again.

Brandy sighed. "Let me get out of this dress." She frowned as she looked at the hideous red stain—the last of Sam's life. The dress that would never be the same again. Every time she saw the blood, she felt a wave of nausea. "Then I'll tell you everything."

"Where's the body?"

"Up in the loft," Brandy said as she prepared to dart out into the rain.

After Brandy had dressed, she talked to Ellen and tried to reassure her that although Sam was an evil man, all men were not that way. Brandy was relieved that Sam had not molested Ellen, although that had been his intent. Thank God, Brandy had arrived in time. Ellen finally managed a smile, then ran to the house where Mary had gone.

When Brandy was by herself, she prayed that, somehow, some way, she would be able get out of this mess, but she couldn't help wondering if God was listening. She'd just committed the worst sin of all . . . she had taken a life, even if it was to protect her own.

Brandy covered her face with her hands and wept. How would she ever get out of this one?

* * *

"What's the use of all this training if we ain't going to shoot Indians?" Corporal Dare complained to Colonel Chivington.

"Just keep shooting at the target, Corporal. Things are going to change," Colonel Chivington assured him. Then he jerked around to see who was riding across the field at Fort Lyon. "And maybe sooner than we think," he said over his shoulder as he hurried to meet the rider.

The rider dismounted, then brushed the dust from his blue uniform. He motioned for the fifteen men who had accompanied him to dismount.

The major saluted Colonel Chivington.

"I am Major Scott Anthony, reporting for duty."

Colonel Chivington smiled. The general had listened. "I am Colonel Chivington. Welcome to Fort Lyon," he said with a smile.

Major Anthony did not return the smile. "I must see Major Wynkoop."

"Corporal Dare," Chivington called.

"Yes, sir."

"Take Major Anthony to see Major Wynkoop."

"Yes, sir. Follow me, Major," Dare said.

They walked briskly across the parade field to headquarters. Corporal Dare knocked on Major Wynkoop's office door. "Major Scott Anthony here to see you, sir."

Wynkoop placed the quill down on the desk, then stood. "And to what do I owe the pleasure of your visit?"

Major Anthony glanced at the corporal. "If you'll excuse us . . ."

Corporal Dare hesitated. He wanted to stay and find out why the major had arrived, so he could report back to the colonel. But there was no way that he could, so he left. However, he was careful not to shut the door completely. Quickly, he looked around. The other men were outside on detail, so if he were very quiet, maybe he could hear what they were saying.

"Major Wynkoop, I am here to replace you as head of Fort Lyon. You are to report to Ft. Sheridan immediately," Major Anthony said in a curt voice.

"Why wasn't I informed of this change?" Wynkoop snapped.

"That I do not know, sir. Only that General Curtis has received word of your conciliatory policy and is concerned."

There was a moment of silence before Wynkoop spoke. "We have taken many steps to ensure peace between the Indians and the white man. I have promised the Cheyenne and the Arapaho that we will protect them as long as they remain peaceful."

"I understand. I will assure them of the fort's protection."

"Good," Major Wynkoop said. A chair scraped across the floor. "The chief you need to speak with is Black Kettle." A moment of silence followed, then the desk drawer was being pulled open. "Give me a minute to clean out my desk, and I will turn the fort over to you and wish you and your staff the best of luck, sir."

Dare scrambled away from the door before he got caught eavesdropping. He hurried back to Colonel Chivington and reported what he'd overhead.

"Good job, Corporal," Colonel Chivington said. His smile was as wide as a river when he walked back to the men.

Evidently, his letter had paid off, Chivington thought. With a new officer, things were surely looking up.

Thunder and his mother had accompanied the tribe to Sand Creek, where they set up their village along the dry creek bed. A month had passed, and so far everything remained peaceful.

One day his mother said, "I believe I am ready to leave now, my son."

Thunder nodded. "I have told Black Kettle of our plans, and he gives his blessing for a safe journey. He also told me there is a new major at the fort."

"Who?"

"Major Anthony. I do not know much about him, but he has promised to protect the two tribes. I will help you gather your things, and we shall leave tomorrow. However, there is one thing I must do before we return to Boston."

"What is that?"

"I must return to Ft. Laramie and see if Brandy and her family are safe and happy."

"So her name is Brandy?" Helen smiled. "I will look forward to meeting this woman."

Thunder frowned at the way his mother sounded. "It is only a visit."

"I see," she said, trying to conceal her smile as she left him.

On a frosty morning in November, Colonel Chivington and his hundred-day soldiers approached Black Kettle's camp.

The peaceful scene of the sleeping village spread out before them. But that wouldn't last long, Chivington thought with a slow smile.

Lieutenant Lee rode up beside him. "Sir, we have promised the Indians protection," he protested. "They are at peace."

Chivington turned and glared at Lee, watching as the lieutenant squirmed in the saddle. "I have come to kill Indians, Lieutenant," Chivington raged. "When I give an order, I expect you to obey, or I'll shoot you myself. Have I made myself perfectly clear?"

The lieutenant swallowed hard and finally nodded before wheeling his horse away.

Chivington jerked his horse around to face the troops. "Kill and scalp all. Big, little, it makes no difference," he said in a stern voice with no vestige of sympathy. Taking a deep breath, he held his sword up, then shouted, "Charge!"

Screams cracked the air.

Thunder jerked awake.

Something was wrong. The screaming seemed to be coming from everywhere, he thought as a knot formed in his stomach.

"Get up, Mother! We are being attacked!" He grabbed his rifle and shoved another toward his mother.

She took the weapon and grabbed the bag she'd packed. She reminded him softly, "But we are at peace."

When Thunder stepped out of the teepee, he couldn't believe what he saw. The village was being attacked by the cavalry—the very ones who had prom-

ised them protection and had put them in this godfor-
saken place.

All Thunder could see was blue shirts as he
crouched just outside the teepee to figure out the best
course of action. Then he realized there was no time
to do anything but run. Soldiers were killing women
and children before their very eyes.

"Come, Mother!" Thunder shouted and pulled her
from the tent. "We must find shelter in the sandy
creek bed. There are too many to fight. This is a
slaughter."

Thunder's first concern had to be for his mother's
safety. She was all he had. Keeping their heads low,
they darted between the teepees, dodging everyone
fleeing in panic ahead of them. Out of the corner of
his eye, he saw Black Kettle. He had raised the American flag and then the white one. There seemed to be
a dazed look on his face.

But the killing went on.

"Go ahead, Mother. I'm going back for Black Kettle."

"Be careful, son," Helen said as she darted for
cover.

Thunder skirted around the edge of camp to Black
Kettle, but stopped cold when he spotted a soldier
aiming a rifle at a three-year-old. Without pausing,
Thunder swung his rifle to his shoulder and put a stop
to the madness. Then he scooped up the child and
handed him back to his weeping mother.

When Thunder reached him, Black Kettle looked
confused. "We must run for safety!"

"I do not understand." Black Kettle shook his head.
"We were promised protection."

"Once again the white man gives you false hope.

We need to get you to safety so that you may lead your people another day."

Black Kettle nodded. "Come, Slow River." Black Kettle motioned to his wife, who took off running toward the creek bed.

Thunder provided covering fire as they made their escape; then he turned to run after them, but he didn't get far when he heard singing. Turning, Thunder spotted Chief White Antelope. He was singing his death song. Thunder started for him, but the chief saw Thunder and shook his head. Thunder stopped. The warrior was ready to die.

Thunder nodded, and respected White Antelope's wishes. Thunder could still hear the chief's sad song as he left camp. He would hear it in his heart for the rest of his life.

"Nothing lives long . . . except the earth and the mountains."

Thunder wanted to stay and fight the soldiers who murdered at will. They murdered the women, the children, and the helpless. But the Cheyenne were outnumbered, and Thunder knew the troops wouldn't stop until everyone was dead.

Thunder found his mother and Black Kettle in a dug-out space in the side of the riverbank. "We are not safe. We must run."

"Slow River has been shot," Black Kettle said.

"Nine times," his mother confirmed, "but she still lives."

"I will carry her," Thunder said. "If we stay, we will all be killed."

Black Kettle nodded in agreement. "I will carry my wife," he said, putting her carefully over his shoulder. She moaned, but they didn't stop as they headed out.

Skirting around the banks of the dry river, they used the bank for cover. The troops were still in camp and hadn't made it this far yet. But they would. They were not men anymore, but animals in a killing frenzy.

When Thunder and his party had gone several miles, Thunder spotted his horse. He whistled, and Lightning trotted over to him.

"Good boy," Thunder praised, patting his mount's neck. Thunder grabbed a handful of mane and mounted the animal. "I will go get three more horses. Stay here," he told the others.

When Thunder had rounded up the horses, he brought them back. "We need some rope."

Helen turned around and got the bag she'd grabbed when she'd fled camp. Rummaging though the bag, she pulled out a blanket. "We can tear this into strips and braid it for rope."

Thunder smiled. His mother always had the answers to his problems. Quickly, the three of them tore and braided until they had lead ropes to go on the horse's halters. Slow River was holding her own. Evidently, the bullet wounds had only been flesh wounds, and for that they could be thankful. But she was very pale and had lost consciousness several times.

"This is where we say goodbye," Black Kettle said.

"Do you want us to go with you to the next camp?"

"No. You were leaving. You should go. We will find another camp where I can nurse Slow River back to health." Black Kettle sighed, looking much older today than yesterday. "I am growing old," he said sadly, hanging his head. Then he snapped it up like the proud chief he was. "I had hoped to see peace among our people before I die. Now the possibilities seem dim."

"The white men have lied many times."

"You speak the truth. But perhaps with men such as yourself on the other side they will see that we can all live in harmony with nature."

Thunder looked affectionately upon the elderly chief. "You speak with great wisdom. I hope you find the peace that you seek."

Black Kettle seated his wife in front of him on the horse, then looked at Helen. "You have been welcome among our people for many moons. Go and find your family. But do not forget us."

Helen smiled and touched Black Kettle's shoulder, then squeezed Slow River's hand. "I will never forget my days with you."

Thunder watched the old chief ride away. With him went a way of life that Thunder would never forget. It had been a carefree life, but it was rapidly changing, and he realized that he belonged in his mother's world. Yet, he would fight for the peace that Black Kettle hoped for.

TWENTY

Thunder and his mother were both tired as they arrived at Ft. Laramie mid-morning. He had seen his mother nod a couple of times, but she hadn't complained about their pace.

Instead of going to the fort, they went directly to the Indian camp by the river to see if someone might know of Brandy's whereabouts.

Little Big Bear stood outside his tent. He smiled when he recognized them.

"You come back," Little Big Bear said with a grin, then added, "I see you reached Little Woman." He turned to Helen. "It is good to see you well and on your feet again."

"Thank you for sending my son to me," Helen said with a smile. "I am feeling much better."

"Why have you returned to the fort?" Little Big Bear asked, looking at Thunder. "Would it be because of the woman?"

Thunder didn't like the way Little Big Bear said that, but he swallowed his irritation and gave a curt nod. "Has she married?"

"No."

Thunder hid his surprise. That wasn't the answer he'd expected, but before he could say anything else his friend added, "Things are not good."

"What do you mean? Is Brandy sick?"

"No. The woman with fire hair shot the keeper of the hog farm."

"Hog farm?"

Little Big Bear leaned over and whispered to Thunder, explaining what the hog farm was used for.

Thunder frowned. How in the world had Brandy gotten mixed up with such people? Was it his fault that he'd left her, knowing how naïve she was? Of course, he'd figured her future husband would take care of her. What had happened to the man?

"I will go and see her," Thunder finally said.

Little Big Bear shook his head. "It is too late. They took her to Denver a week ago."

Thunder rubbed his chin. "And her family?"

"I hear they are still at the farm." Little Big Bear took Thunder's arms and pulled. "Come, you must eat before moving on. We leave tomorrow for winter camp, so I will not see you for many moons."

Stomachs filled, but with questions unanswered, Thunder and Helen arrived at the house known as the hog farm a couple of hours later. He immediately saw the familiar covered wagon, and he nudged his horse toward the barn. He couldn't quite explain the surge of happiness that ran through him.

"Thunder!" Scott squealed. He jumped up and down, clapping his hands. Then the other children started to appear one by one, each grinning their welcome.

Thunder dismounted and held his arms open for Scott to run and jump into them.

"I've missed you," Scott told him as he gave Thunder a big hug. "I kept telling Billy that you'd come back. I just knew you would," Scott said with a serious expression. Then he peered around Thunder and his eyes widened, "Who's that?"

Thunder set Scott back down on his feet. "This is my mother. Mother, I would like you to meet Scott, Ellen, Mary, and Billy." Thunder pointed out each child as he called their names.

"It is nice to meet all of you. I have heard so many wonderful things about each of you," Helen said.

"What do we call you?" Ellen asked.

"My name is Helen," she said with a nod. "I hope we will all be good friends," she told them. Then she went over and introduced herself to the girls.

Billy propped his foot against the wall and stood beside Thunder, who was leaning up against the side of the barn. "Have you heard about Brandy?"

Thunder nodded with a frown. "Some. How did she get mixed up in such a place?"

"Her so-called fiancé only brought her out here to work as a whore in that house." Billy jerked his head toward the house. "The only thing he didn't count on was Brandy bringing a family with her. So he was making all of us work off her debt by cleaning and cooking." Billy scuffed the dirt with the toe of his boot. "Truth is, he was real ornery and deserved to die. I just hate that Brandy was the one who killed him."

"Then she didn't—? Only cook?" Thunder couldn't bring himself to actually say it.

"Of course not. Sam did threaten to force her a couple of times."

Thunder let out his breath. "I was told that they had taken Brandy to Denver."

"Yeah, the circuit judge is supposed to come through and try her."

Thunder glanced at Billy. "Why have you not gone there?"

Billy looked embarrassed, then hung his head. "Didn't know what to do," he admitted and shrugged his shoulders. "Thought making decisions would be easy, but when it comes down to it, it's dang hard. 'Sides, don't know rightly were Denver is," Billy said. "I know one thing. If Brandy doesn't get a good lawyer, don't know how much of a chance she'll have."

It sounded like Brandy had really gotten herself in a mess this time, Thunder thought. "She has a good lawyer."

"She does?"

"Me."

Billy's mouth dropped open, then he caught himself. "You're a lawyer?" He couldn't keep the surprise from his voice.

Thunder chuckled. "I am a man of many talents." He pushed away from the barn. "How soon can you be ready to leave?"

"About an hour."

"Good. I'm going to take a bath in the river and change clothes," Thunder said as he saw Mary come toward them. "Is there one of Brandy's dresses that my mother can change into?" he asked the girl.

"We'll find her something. Your mother is very nice," Mary said, then asked, "Can you save Brandy?"

"I'm not sure," Thunder admitted. An unwelcome tension wrapped around his body, making him very tired . . . but determined. "But I'll try."

* * *

They were having an Indian summer day, so the water wasn't too bad, Thunder thought as he gazed up at the darkening sky. The sunset was red, and he knew the cold air would soon be upon them.

After Thunder had bathed, he had his mother cut his hair. Now it barely reached his collar. When she'd finished, he stood and brushed off his shoulders before turning to face her. "What do you think?"

Helen smiled and cocked her head to the side. "You look like my son, the lawyer."

"I thought I'd be better received if I looked like a lawyer. There is more than one way to skin an animal."

"It is time that you discovered your heritage. And time for me to return as well. How do you like my dress?"

"You look very pretty and different," Thunder told her. "It is surprising how different clothes can make a person look and feel."

"That is true. But no matter what clothing we don, we are always the same inside. Let us go and find this woman of yours. I want to meet her."

Brandy stared at the steel bars, the same ones she'd been staring out of for the last two weeks. Time dragged by, and the longer she stayed in this dark, dank place, the more uncertain her future looked.

The only information that the sheriff had told her was that they were waiting on the circuit judge to arrive to try her. This morning when he'd brought breakfast to her consisting of a dry biscuit and coffee, the sheriff said the judge would be in town tomorrow.

She pulled a blanket around her and drew her knees

up on the cot. It was dark and cold in her cell. The heat from the potbellied stove in the front office didn't quite reach to the cells in the back.

What would happen to her when she stood up in court without a lawyer?

Would they hang her?

Or leave her in prison until she was a shriveled up hag?

She lay down on the cot and threw her arm over her eyes. Her tears had dried up a long time ago. Now misery was her only company. Could she even remember back to Independence when life was simple?

She was so tired.

Tired of making decisions.

Just tired of life in general, she thought as she drifted off to sleep.

Father Brown's kind, weathered face became vivid in her dreams. Brandy was leaning over his sick bed as he watched her through half-closed eyelids.

"Where are the other children?" he asked.

Brandy sighed. "I've let you down, Father."

"No, my child, you have not," he said in a scratchy voice. "As a matter of fact, I'm very proud of you. You have kept the family together and made a home for them."

"Some home," Brandy muttered, then frowned. "It's a wagon. And worse, we lived near a—a house of ill repute."

Father Brown gave her a slow smile. "I'll bet you'd like to see that wagon right about now."

She nodded.

"You see, that simple wagon has come to mean something to you. A home isn't necessarily boards and nails. It is where you feel the most comfortable."

"I guess you're right, Father," Brandy murmured. Weariness enveloped her as she tried to feel positive, but it was getting harder by the minute. "But look where I am now. What am I going to do?"

"Come sit on the bed beside me." Father Brown patted the covers to indicate the spot.

She did as instructed, picking up his parchment-brown hand, which felt smooth and warm just as she remembered. And though he appeared frail, Brandy could feel the strength in his hand. And God knows she needed some of his strength. All of his strength.

"I wish I had the answers that you need, my child. But life is not always simple. You will go into the courtroom and tell the truth, and I will pray that the judge is wise and realize that the other man was evil."

"I'm scared," she admitted as the tears slipped slowly down her face. She pulled his hand up to her lips and kissed the back of it. "Please don't leave me. I'm so lonely."

"Dry your tears, my child." Father Brown patted her hand. "Always remember . . . even though you won't see my body anymore . . . I will be with each and every one of you in spirit. Every step you take, I will take with you. And when you fall down, I will be there to pick you up."

She closed her eyes, remembering the same words she'd heard at the graveyard. "This is one of the times I need you to pick me up, Father."

When she opened her eyes he was gone, and she was back, alone in the empty cell.

But ever so faintly she heard his voice, *"I will be there . . . I'll always be there."*

Keys rattling on the other side of the door drew her from her memories. The wooden door which led to the cells opened and two men walked through. Maybe it was time to eat again, she thought. It was one of the few reasons that the door opened. It was hard to tell time since she'd been shut away.

She sat up and wiped away her tears with the heels of her hands.

The guard approached and inserted the key into the lock. "Your lawyer is here," the man said.

"Lawyer?" Brandy rose and tried to see the other man. Had Father Brown indeed worked a miracle and sent her a lawyer?

"You can leave us now," the other man said as he entered the cell. His hat was pulled down, casting shadows on his face, but that voice, it sounded so familiar. But she didn't know anybody here.

The gentleman removed his hat.

"Thunder?" she whispered, then her knees gave way.

Quickly, Thunder caught her.

The guard turned around. "She going to be all right?"

"Yes, she's just a little stunned. I'll call you when I'm ready to leave," Thunder said as he moved Brandy over to the cot.

He wasn't sure what he expected, but fainting hadn't figured into his plan. He set her down on the bunk and bent her over her knees until she started to struggle.

"It seems to me that we've been in this position before," he said as he held her back up.

Brandy blinked a couple of times. "Is it really you?" She reached up and touched his face. "Your hair. You look so different."

"Thomas Bradley at your service," he said, then

added, "I thought if I was going to defend you, I should look the part."

"But you're not a lawyer."

"Yes, I am. If you remember, I went to Boston to study, and law is what I studied. I assure you I'm a very capable lawyer," Thunder told her confidently.

So many emotions filtered across her face that Thunder wanted to scoop her up in his arms and tell her everything would be all right. But if he did, the guard would surely burst through the door, and Thunder didn't want to damage Brandy's reputation further. It was bad enough she'd been living at a house of ill repute.

Why wasn't he holding her? Brandy wondered. Had he not missed her? Seeing him now and feeling her heart ache, she knew how much she loved him. Slowly, she placed her hand on his and said, "I've missed you."

"I have missed you, too," Thunder said in a husky voice. His eyes held her with the desire she saw in their depths. She could tell he felt something for her. But did he love her?

"How did you know where to find me?" Brandy finally asked.

He leaned back against the wall. "I went back to Ft. Laramie to see how you were doing."

Her heart did a small flip. "You actually came back to see me?"

"Yes. Only to find that they had taken you to jail."

"Did you see the children? Is someone taking care of them?"

"They are here with me."

"Good." She breathed a sigh of relief. "I've been worried about them."

"The children are fine, but will be happy when you are released. The trial will be held tomorrow at noon." Thunder sat beside her on the bunk and managed a businesslike expression. "Keeping with your luck, I understand he is the hanging judge," Thunder told her. "Tell me exactly what happened."

"I seem to have gotten myself in a mess," she said with a frown. Her eyes widened. "You don't think they will hang me?"

"Not if I can help it. Now start at the beginning and tell me everything."

As Brandy retold the events, Thunder's stomach tightened. He would have liked to kill Sam himself. It was probably a good thing that Brandy had beaten him to the deed. Then pride began to take the place of his anger as he realized how Brandy had taken up for herself and the children. At the beginning of their journey, he hadn't been too sure that any of the children would ever take up for the others. Yet, he always knew that one day Brandy would see just what the children meant to her . . . The priest had been wise, even in death.

Slowly, Thunder got to his feet. "I must go and prepare my case."

She rose also and gazed up at him. He could see the shimmer of tears in Brandy's eyes. She appeared frightened and he felt helpless to ease her fears.

"Please hold me," she finally asked in a breathless whisper.

That was his undoing. His back was to the outside door as he took her hands in his and leaned down and whispered, "I would love nothing more than to take you in my arms and kiss you." He held her hands to his lips and brushed a soft kiss on her knuckles. "But we don't want the sheriff to get the wrong idea about you. We are supposed to be strangers."

The outside door opened, and Thunder immediately dropped her hands and gave her a faint smile.

"Are you ready, Mr. Bradley?" the sheriff asked, then spat in the bucket by the door.

Thunder turned and nodded to the sheriff as he opened the cell door. "I'll see you in court tomorrow, Miss Brown. If you think of anything else that you haven't told me, please ask the sheriff to contact me."

"Thank you for coming, Mr. Bradley," Brandy said.

With a nod, Thunder was gone.

Brandy stared at the closed door, and for just a moment, she wondered if she had dreamt the whole thing.

TWENTY-ONE

It was just after ten o'clock when Brandy and Marshal Shelton left the jailhouse and started down the sidewalk toward the courthouse. The marshal had handcuffed Brandy to him so she wouldn't escape, so she had to walk fast to keep up with him.

They moved past the hotel; the smell of ham coming from inside made her stomach rumble because she'd been so nervous that she hadn't been able to eat this morning. However, at the moment, food was the least of her worries. What would happen to the children if she were found guilty?

A young woman with a child in tow came toward them. When she looked up and saw Brandy, the lady averted her eyes and took the child's hand and stepped completely off the sidewalk to avoid contact. Now Brandy truly felt like a criminal.

The weathered, wooden courthouse was located at the end of Main Street. Worrying about her fate, Brandy entered the building, still handcuffed to the marshal. He led her to the main courtroom and down the center aisle. A large desk sat high up on a platform at the end of the aisle, which provided a good view for the judge who sat behind the desk. He was dressed in a dark suit, a gavel in his right hand. Something cold and fearful gripped Brandy; she would have turned and run if not for the handcuffs.

Bare wooden seats were located on both sides of the aisle, but they were only half-filled with people, none of whom she looked at as she passed them.

When they reached the front row, the marshal nudged her to the left. Another trial was in progress, so they would have to wait their turn. Couldn't they just get it over with? She glanced at the judge. He did not look very friendly.

When Brandy started down the row, she noticed Thunder seated on the long wooden seat. He looked so good to her as he lounged indifferently on the bench that she wanted to fling herself into his arms. His long legs were stretched out in front of him, crossed at the ankles. He might look indifferent, but she could see how tightly his jaw was clenched and she knew he was ready to do battle.

He was neat and clean and dressed all in black. His new hairstyle definitely complimented him, and those vivid silver-blue eyes were as beautiful as she remembered.

She sat down beside Thunder, and Marshal Shelton took a seat to her right. Shelton pulled a set of keys out of his pocket and unlocked the handcuffs, then slipped them in his pocket.

Thunder leaned over and whispered, "Are you all right?"

She nodded as she crossed her legs at the ankles and spread out her skirt. Her left hand rested on the seat beside her, and suddenly she felt warm fingers lacing through hers. She smiled, feeling somehow a little safer with Thunder next to her.

The judge hit the table with his gavel and drew her

attention away from Thunder. He turned to the defendant. "What do you have to say for yourself, Mr. Allison?"

"It was self-defense, Your Honor," Allison replied.

"Tell the court what happened," the judge instructed.

"It started with a horse race, Your Honor. I was upset that Chuck Clifton's horse beat mine. We agreed to mount our horses and face each other at a distance of one hundred yards. Then, at a signal, we were to run our horses toward each other, firing until one of us dropped to the ground."

"Is that what happened?" the judge asked.

"No. We went back to Clifton House, where Chuck suggested that we eat first so that one of us would go to hell with a full stomach."

The few in the courtroom laughed, and the judge banged the gavel on the desk again. "Silence in the courtroom!"

"Continue, Mr. Allison," the judge instructed, a stern look on his face.

"We took our places at opposite ends of the table, our six-shooters drawn and resting on our laps. During the meal, Chuck casually dropped one hand below the table and grabbed his pistol, but in lifting the pistol the barrel struck the edge of the table and when he fired he missed me. I had no choice but to fire immediately."

"So you killed him?"

"Yes, Your Honor. Shot him right above the eye, and he fell straight forward into his stew. But it was kill or be killed."

"Step down," the judge said. For a few minutes everything was quiet while the judge pondered. Finally he looked up and said, "I find the defendant not guilty." He banged his gavel. "Next case."

And then it was over. The bailiff escorted the man from the court as murmuring started all around them.

The next thing Brandy knew, the marshal was tugging on her arm, and she had to move up to a table on the other side of the rail. Thunder held the chair for her to sit; then he took the chair beside her.

Rap, rap, rap, the gavel sounded against the pine board which composed the judge's desk. "Bailiff," the judge called. "What is our next case?"

"Murder, your honor. A Miss Brandy Brown shot and killed one Sam Owens near Ft. Laramie."

"Who represents Miss Brown?" the judge asked.

"I do, Your Honor," Thunder said. "Thomas Bradley."

The judge adjusted his glasses as he peered at Thunder. "I don't remember seeing you around here before, Mr. Bradley."

"That's because I'm from back east, Your Honor. I'm new in town."

"I see," the judge said and folded his hands in front of him. "How does the defendant plead?"

"Not guilty."

"Do you have any witnesses?"

"Yes, I would like to call Miss Molly Tobin to the stand."

Brandy watched in awe as Thunder questioned Molly as she told what it was like to be in Sam's house and how he'd tricked all the girls into coming to him. Thunder was so professional, Brandy almost wondered if she'd imagined him being an Indian. He still moved with the grace of a warrior, but he appeared as civilized as any lawyer would as he walked back and forth, firing question after question to the witness.

Next he called Ellen, and Brandy was surprised. She hadn't seen Ellen when she'd first entered. She turned around and saw that Mary was also in the courtroom. Brandy managed a smile, and Mary waved at her.

"Ellen, can you tell us what happened?" Thunder asked in a gentle but firm voice. She looked as if she were going to cry, but she sat a little straighter and composed herself.

"Sam attacked me while I was milking the cow."

"What exactly did he do?" Thunder questioned further.

"He hit me. Then dragged me up the stairs to the hayloft."

"Then what?"

"He shoved me down in—in the hay and pulled my—my skirt up," Ellen said in a quivering voice.

"That's enough," Brandy said as she came to her feet. "I can tell you the rest. Ellen is only a child."

"I won't tolerate any outbursts in my courtroom, Miss Brown. Sit down."

Frowning, Brandy reluctantly sank back to her seat.

When Brandy was seated, the judge snapped, "Proceed, Mr. Bradley."

"That is enough for Ellen, Your Honor. I want to call Miss Brandy Brown to the stand."

Brandy marched to the stand and took her seat. She held one hand up and placed the other on the Bible and swore to tell the truth. Then she started from the beginning and didn't hold anything back as she told the judge how she'd been tricked into coming out west. She told him that she had agreed to pay the money back. Then she explained what had happened that morning in the hayloft. When she'd finished, she felt completely exhausted, as if she'd relived the whole thing again.

The judge excused himself and retired to his chambers for a few minutes. There was nothing to do but wait.

"What does that mean?" Brandy asked.

"I'm not sure," Thunder admitted. "Let's hope that it's good. I'm accustomed to having a jury back east, but they don't always do things the same out here."

Finally, the judge returned. He rapped on the desk again to bring quiet to the courtroom. "Miss Brown, will you stand and face the bench," he instructed.

She pushed the chair back and rose.

"After reviewing all the evidence, I find—" The judge started coughing and Brandy thought she'd collapse in anticipation while he grabbed a glass of water and drank. "Excuse me." He cleared his throat. "After reviewing all the evidence I find the defendant not guilty."

Brandy grasped the table to steady herself. Relief swept through her.

"But," the judge continued, "I am not sure you can properly care for children without an income. Therefore, the court will take custody of the children and place them in homes."

"No!" Brandy screamed. "I can take care of them."

The judge leaned over his desk. "I'm not so sure about that, but I will give you five days to show me you can provide for them before they are taken away."

"Thank you, Your Honor," Thunder said and grasped Brandy's elbow, squeezing it tight so she wouldn't say anything else and land them all in trouble.

When they were out of the courtroom, the girls ran over to Brandy and hugged her.

They started walking to the stable to get their horses. "The judge can't take us, can he, Brandy?" Ellen asked, her expression tight with strain.

"I hope not," Brandy said and looked at Thunder.

"I think I have an idea," Thunder said. "But first we need to go and get the others."

"I sure hope it's a good idea," Brandy said when they reached the horses.

As they rode away from Denver, she asked, "Where are we going?"

"Billy, Scott, and my mother are camped outside of town by a small stream."

"Your mother is with you?"

"Yes, she is going back to Boston."

Brandy wondered if this meant that Thunder would be going with her. They rode to the top of a grassy knoll and then the road straightened out. She wanted to ask, but didn't want the answer. "Thank you for coming to my rescue."

He glanced at her as they rode. "I remember a time when you defended me." He looked at her and grinned. "Of course, you did have an ulterior motive."

Brandy laughed. "I was desperate."

"Well, let's say I, too, was desperate this time."

Brandy looked at him, puzzled. "You were? Why?"

"I was afraid of losing you," he said simply, then added, "I want to talk to you later. Privately."

Brandy felt her cheeks warm as she shyly looked at him and smiled. He'd never spoken to her like this before, and she wasn't sure what he meant.

He'd said he wanted to talk to her. But what about? Was he merely going to tell her goodbye and leave them again?

They were quiet as they rode away from town, and she began to think. What would happen to her and the children? They were on their own with no place to live other than the wagon, and they had no money. The judge was right, but he couldn't take the children and separate them after coming this far. She would think of something.

Brandy sighed. Their problems always began and ended with money.

Sunset was fast approaching when they reached the wagon beneath a group of trees.

As soon as she dismounted, Billy and Scott ran over to her. Scott hugged her waist.

"Are you free? Or do we have to pack up and run?" Billy asked dryly.

"I am free, thanks to Thunder." Brandy grinned.

A woman climbed from the back of the wagon and started toward them. Thunder's mother looked so much like him with her long, black hair and blue eyes that Brandy would have known who she was even if she hadn't expected to see the woman.

"So you are Brandy?" Helen said. She came closer, then gasped, "I can't believe it."

"What?" Thunder asked, concerned.

Helen grabbed both of Brandy's arms. "You are the spitting image of Bonnie. She was my childhood friend from Boston. We both married at the same time."

Hope surged through Brandy. Could this woman actually have known her mother? "My mother was from Boston."

"I can't be sure because Bonnie didn't have any children the last time I saw her. Thunder told me that you were in an orphanage."

"My mother left me at the parsonage when I was five," Brandy said.

"If she did, she had a good reason. Not many mothers would leave their children, unless it was for the child's safety. If you were Bonnie's child, I remember how much she talked about wanting children, especially a girl." Helen smiled. "We'll talk later—I know that you must be very tired."

Brandy nodded. "Let's do talk later. I would like to learn more about my mother. If she is my mother." Brandy squeezed Helen's hands, then said, "Thunder has spoken of you. I can see where he gets his blue eyes."

"Thank you. Come, you probably would like to get into some clean clothes," Helen suggested.

"Even though it is cold, I need to wash."

Helen smiled and then turned to Mary and Ellen. "I have started dinner. If you both will finish cooking, I will assist Brandy."

Brandy almost smiled at how much at home Thunder's mother seemed to be—and she had definitely taken charge. Brandy was glad to turn over some responsibility because she was very tired. All those days in jail, she had barely dared to relax much less sleep. And she wanted to hear more about this woman who Helen thought could be her mother. There would probably never be any way that they could be sure who Brandy's mother was, but it would be nice to imagine the possibility. Right now her main concern was getting clean and washing her dirty hair.

"Something sure smells good," Ellen said.

"Billy brought home a chicken and a rabbit," Helen told them.

Brandy and Helen walked away from the group down to the small creek. "Over there is a deep place where you can bathe and wash your hair," Helen said.

"I can't wait," Brandy said as she unbuttoned her blouse. She shivered as the cool wind touched her body. "I can't remember when I last bathed. I know that water is freezing but I'm so dirty I really don't care."

"Here is a bar of lye soap and a sheet to dry yourself with. I will go back and get some warm water to help take the chill out of your body once you bathe."

When Brandy was by herself, she finished undressing and slipped into the water so cold it immediately took her breath away. She wasted little time diving under the water to stop the slow torture of inching her way in. Quickly, she lathered her hands and scrubbed her body and hair and then rinsed all the soap away. Her teeth were chattering as she emerged from the water and wrapped the towel around her.

Helen appeared with a big pot of warm water. "Here, let me pour this over you. It's warm and will take the bite from the cold."

Brandy threw the towel to the side and stood still while the water ran over her head and down her body. When she opened her eyes, Helen had wrapped the sheet around her and it was amazing that Brandy did feel a little warmer.

When she was dressed, Helen took Brandy to be near the fire. Brandy sat on a blanket that had been warmed by hot stones placed beneath the blanket, and Helen began drying Brandy's hair. A peaceful feeling of contentment settled over Brandy as her hair was dried. Brandy had never had a mother to do these things for her. She realized that a mother's touch was a special thing that she had never experienced. It was a wonderful feeling.

"What did Bonnie look like?" Brandy asked.

"Exactly like you," Helen told her. "Bonnie's hair was the color of yours except it was more of a dark brown, but the man she married had red hair, so that would explain your reddish color. Her eyes were exactly like yours. I've never seen such a rare color. You have been blessed with beautiful eyes."

"Thank you," Brandy replied to the compliment. "What else can you tell me?"

"Let's see," Helen said as she continued to brush Brandy's hair. "Bonnie was shorter than you are, and she was very sweet and rarely raised her voice."

"Well, that's where we are different. I don't think the children would say that I'm sweet." Brandy chuckled.

"I think you are too hard on yourself," Helen leaned down and whispered in Brandy's ear. "When I left to come west, Bonnie had started teaching school, and she had absolutely no desire to go west. That is the one thing that bothers me—how she ended up in Independence.

"I guess we will never know for sure, but thank you for sharing the information with me. I have been so long without a mother that I grew to accept what fate had in store for me."

When her hair was dry, Brandy thanked Helen. "Were you surprised to see Thunder?"

Helen nodded. "I was," she said with a smile. "But after a while, I could see that he was not happy."

"I'm surprised to hear you say that. All he talked about was returning home."

"That is because he expected things to be the same as when he left. He did not take into account that he'd changed. He left a young brave and returned a man. Things are not as we always remember. But he had to go home to realize that he had changed." Helen looked at Brandy for a long moment before adding, "I think he longs for something more, perhaps a thing he really isn't sure of."

Brandy really didn't know what his mother meant. "He tells me that he is taking you home."

Helen smiled at her in a funny way. "I have asked him, but I'm in no hurry."

They all gathered for dinner, and Brandy soon discovered that Helen was a wonderful cook, almost as good as Annie. While they ate, Thunder and the girls told Billy and Scott what had happened at the trial. When they got to the part about the children leaving, everyone grew quiet.

"What are you going to do?" Billy asked.

"I don't know, but I have five days to find out. Besides, Thunder said he had a plan." Brandy looked at Thunder.

"What's that?" Billy persisted.

"I will tell you later," Thunder said. "Let's finish our meal. We can worry about problems tomorrow."

Scott licked his fingers. "You know what I miss?"

"What?" Ellen asked.

"MacTavish's stories," Scott told her with a sigh.

"Who is MacTavish?" Helen asked. All the children jumped into the conversation, explaining about the wonderful stories that MacTavish used to weave for them.

Helen nodded slowly as she put down her plate. "How about if I tell you a story? I'm pretty good, or so the children of our village told me."

"My mother is a great storyteller," Thunder said as he stood. "But if you'll excuse me, Mother, I need to speak with Brandy while you keep everyone entertained." He motioned for Brandy to come with him.

She grabbed a blanket and wrapped it around her as they headed away from camp. They strolled down to the river where a huge water oak towered over the bank. The full moon filtered in through the bare branches, making it easy to see Thunder in the dark.

Leaning against the tree, she dreaded what he was about to say. She just knew he was leaving. First, he'd tell them how to solve their problems, but then he'd leave. Could she let him walk out of her life again?

Could she stop him?

Thunder stood gazing out at the water. The moonlight made his hair look so black that it shone with blue highlights. After several minutes, he turned to face her. "I thought I knew exactly what I wanted to say, but now I'm not sure."

He was leaving her. She just knew it.

But she couldn't bear to hear those words just yet. She looked at him with all the love she had. "Did you miss me?" she finally whispered, breaking the silence.

Thunder wondered if he really knew what he was about to do. This was the point he'd gotten to once before when Elaina had turned on him. He sensed that Brandy was different. He was getting ready to make the biggest decision of his life, and he'd come up with all kinds of reasons why he shouldn't marry Brandy, but in the end his heart had won out over his head. And though he might not be good at expressing his feelings, he hoped maybe his actions might speak louder than mere words.

He turned and braced his arm on the tree as he gazed down at her. He brought his right hand up and gently touched her face. "Did I miss you?" he repeated to himself as if he didn't know the answer to the question and had to think it over.

"I missed your lips," he said softly tracing her bottom lip with this thumb. Then he picked up a lock of hair that rested on her breast. "I missed your beautiful hair, too." Next he looked into her eyes. "Most of all, I missed your bewitching eyes. Every morning when the sun rose and tried to match their color with the sky, I thought of you even though I tried very hard not to," he said as he lowered his head.

He was so close to her mouth, she could feel his breath, yet he still hadn't touched her. "Did you miss my kisses?" she whispered.

His mouth melted into hers as he gathered her into his arms. He moved his mouth over hers, devouring its softness. The pressure of his mouth pushed her back against the tree.

The shock of being in his arms made her tremble. She kissed him with unrestrained ardor, her arms going around him. His kisses were as warm as she remembered. They were teasing and tormenting as waves of passion flowed through her.

Suddenly, he pulled away and the cold air swept between them, causing her to open her eyes.

"I didn't miss you at all," he said with a twinkle in his eyes.

Her feelings would have been hurt if he hadn't been

smiling. The harder she tried to ignore the truth, the more it persisted. She loved this man, and she couldn't let him walk out of her life again. She just couldn't. She had to make him want her enough to stay. "Then maybe we should try the kiss again. We probably didn't do it as well as we could have."

"I have something to say to you first."

"You're leaving?"

"No."

"But I thought you were taking your mother back—"

He placed a finger over her mouth to silence her. "That will wait. Let me finish. We have been together for a long time and I have grown fond of you."

Brandy laughed. "Fond?"

He nodded. "I do not have much to offer, but together I think we could brave anything."

Brandy's heart leaped in her throat. She wasn't exactly sure what Thunder was trying to say. He definitely hadn't said he loved her. "You want a business partner?"

"I want you to marry me."

"Why?"

"Because that is what men and women do."

"Not unless they are in love with each other," she pressed. She reached out and grabbed both his arms. "How do you feel about me? I need to hear the words."

"When I was away from you things were not the same. I thought of you. I thought how much I wanted you in my arms. I tried to forget about you. God knows, I tried, but I couldn't."

Brandy wanted to leap into his arms, but she was

cautious after the last time. "What about the children?"

"I want them, too."

A slow smile touched Brandy's lips. "It would help if you loved me."

He swept her into his arms. "I do love you—you should know that," he said as he nuzzled the side of her neck.

"Sometimes you have to hear things to believe them," she said with a smile and a light kiss on the lips. "I accept your proposal on my behalf, but we'll have to ask the children."

Thunder hugged her so close, she melted in his embrace. "We don't have much money. Are you sure you won't be sorry you married me?"

"Money seems to be something I hear about but have never really had, so that won't make any difference to me. And I won't be sorry that I married you, but . . . you might be sorry to be saddled with me and the kids," she whispered.

Thunder didn't disagree. He simply sealed his promise with an earth-shattering kiss.

The next morning after breakfast, Thunder got to his feet and said, "I am supposed to ask your permission to marry Brandy." Thunder looked at the four stunned faces and wanted to laugh. He couldn't remember them all being quiet at one time. Certainly not Scott. Of course, Thunder's mother was smiling.

"Does this mean I have your approval?"

"What about us?" Scott asked.

"You are part of Brandy's family, so we will all be one big family. And this time, for good," Thunder said.

"In that case," Billy said, "it's about dang time you two realized you couldn't live without each other. I want to be best man."

"I wouldn't have it any other way," Thunder said, grinning.

They all gathered around and congratulated them. Thunder looked at his mother. Her smile was brilliant, and her eyes twinkled so he knew she was happy. And so was he.

"We don't have much money," Thunder said. "We will have to rely on the things around us."

Billy chuckled. "We're used to that by now."

"I did have enough money to buy a small piece of land outside of town. As soon as we eat breakfast, we can start for our new home."

Mary looked at Brandy. "Does this mean the judge will not separate us?"

"If we can prove we have a home, I don't think the judge will have a reason to," Brandy said with a smile.

"You also have one more thing that you didn't have before," Helen said and they all looked at her. "You now have a mother who will look after you. I've always wanted a big family. Now I have one."

Brandy hugged Helen. "Thank you for everything," she said, tears filling her eyes. "Especially Thunder."

TWENTY-TWO

The place Thunder had bought was beautiful . . .
Well, the land was beautiful . . .

The house—the house was standing. Brandy smiled at her first impression of the small house in need of repair. No matter what kind of shape it was in, it was home.

The house had a lovely wraparound porch that was only collapsed on one end, and there were beautiful trees all around the house which was set on a small rise, so that you could see in every direction. And there was a river below that would provide them with plenty of water.

Billy pulled the wagon to a halt and everyone tumbled out. As Billy and Thunder unhitched the team, Billy yelled, "Scott, put the rocks under the wagon wheels so it won't roll backwards."

Before Scott could get the rocks, a small brown-and-white puppy with big floppy ears ran out of the house. "Look, a puppy," Scott said as he ran for the bundle of fur.

Thunder and Billy were not paying attention to Scott and his distraction. As they released the horses, the wagon started to roll backwards. Shouting for help, they ran to grab the wagon's tongue but they were not strong enough to stop the wagon, and Scott and the puppy were directly in the wagon's path. "Get out of the way, Scott."

But the child didn't move. He seemed frozen to the spot.

Brandy heard the shout and swung around. Her heart lodged in her throat as she run toward Scott.

She was the closest.

She had to make it before it was too late.

"You have to move, Scott! The wagon!" Brandy screamed.

Scott looked at her and then bent over to pick up the puppy, who was whimpering.

But there wasn't time to get the puppy!

The wagon bore down on Scott. A loud crash sounded as the wagon's wheel hit a large rock, stopping its backward movement. The impact dislodged some of the contents of the wagon, sending them spilling to the ground.

"Nooooo," Brandy screamed as she reached the wagon and frantically searched for Scott. By now, everyone had reached the wagon, and for a moment the stricken look on everyone's face confirmed Brandy's worst fears.

"I'll look behind the wagon," Thunder said in a solemn voice.

Tears streamed down everyone's face, especially Brandy's. Scott was just a child. She should have given him more attention instead of treating him like an adult. Reaching out, she placed her hand on the side of the wagon to brace herself. This had started out to be the happiest day of Brandy's life, and now it was the worst day. She would never forgive herself.

Helen came up and put her arm around Brandy. "It wasn't your fault. It was an accident."

"But I was responsible," Brandy cried. Something tugged at her skirt and she couldn't move. She must have caught her dress on a piece of wood, she thought as she looked down.

There, staring up at her, were two big brown eyes and two small brown eyes. "Is it safe to come out now?" Scott said, the puppy still clutched to his chest.

Brandy half-laughed, half-cried as she pulled the child out from under the wagon and hugged him. The puppy licked her face.

"I'm sorry. I forgot the rocks," Scott said as the puppy squirmed in his arms.

"I'm so glad you are not hurt," Brandy admitted and hugged him again. "I thought the wagon had crushed you."

"Nope, I just ducked between the wheels" He grinned. "It pays to be small sometimes."

"What is all that wood?" Billy asked from behind the wagon.

Thunder bent over and started brushing the wood away. "I'm afraid it is what is left of your trunk, Brandy," he said, looking up at her.

Scott puckered up and started to cry. "I'm sorry, Brandy. I didn't mean to."

Brandy knelt down and looked at the child and the puppy. "I can see how you could have been distracted." She rubbed the puppy's head. "You mean more to me than any old chest, Scott," she said. Reaching up, she wiped the tears from his cheeks while the puppy licked his chin. "What are you going to name your new friend?"

Scott grinned. "How about Buddy?"

"I like that," Brandy said. "He'll be your buddy."

"Brandy. Thunder. You better come see this," Billy said in an odd-sounding voice.

They both moved closer to where the remains of the trunk and a few other things were strewn. Billy was holding up the end of one of Brandy's dresses as he looked at something beneath it.

Brandy stooped over to see what had gotten Billy's interest, and there, shining up at them, were six gold bars. "Gold," Brandy whispered. "Where did it come from?"

Helen had moved over behind them. "I saw some gold bars like those in Boston one time. I had a wealthy friend who liked to show everyone his money."

Thunder picked up a gold bar and handed it to Brandy. Her hands immediately sagged toward the ground from the weight.

"Do you remember how heavy that chest was?"

Brandy nodded.

"Evidently, the gold bars were hidden in a false bottom. This could also be the reason that your parents were killed." Thunder looked at his mother.

Helen added, "That could also be the reason your mother left you at the parsonage. She feared for your safety."

"And all this time, I thought it was because she didn't love me," Brandy whispered as she experienced a gamut of perplexing emotions.

The unspoken pain in Brandy's eyes touched Helen, and she was about to comfort the young woman when she spotted a blue-and-white blanket that had a "B" embroidered in the middle. She picked it up and ran her hand over the "B."

"That was in my trunk," Brandy explained. "I think my mother made it for me."

"No, Brandy. I recognize this," she said with a note of incredulity in her voice. "I made this blanket for your mother and stitched her initial in the middle," Helen said in a choked voice. "The 'B' stands for Bonnie." Helen gave Brandy a smile. "Now I know that my friend and your mother are the same. Somehow, she has made it possible for us to find one another," Helen told her with tears in her eyes as she hugged Brandy. "I think things are going to start looking up for us," Helen finally said as she wiped away her tears and started picking up some of the things that were on the ground.

"This means we don't have to worry about money no more," Billy said with a grin.

"We can have a big ranch." Brandy smiled. "Now I know what Mother meant when she said to keep the chest with me always."

Helen smiled as she straightened. "She is still taking care of you even though she isn't here."

With tears in her eyes, Brandy nodded.

"The funny part is you've had this money all along," Billy laughed. "We wouldn't have had to go without any of this."

Brandy thought for a moment. "No, but we would still be fussing and fighting with each other, so I'm glad we didn't know."

"Yeah, when you put it like that, so am I," Billy agreed. "We may never have gotten to see Mary's other side." He chuckled.

"Oh, shut up," Mary said, her hands full of clothes.

"Does this mean we're rich?" Scott asked as he put the squirming puppy back on the ground.

"Yes, it does," Brandy said.

"Can we get one of those servants that MacTavish talked about?"

"Now why would we need a servant?" Brandy asked Scott with hands on her hips. "We don't have a decent house yet."

"So I don't have to milk that blamed cow no more," Scott said, frowning.

They all laughed as they pitched in and started to carry things to their new home. The house would take a lot of work, but they had finally found a home, and they wouldn't have to worry about money or anyone kicking them out again.

And they were together. As a matter of fact, their family had grown. Most of all, Brandy had grown.

She would love to know that she had turned into the woman that Father Brown had hoped she would become. She smiled up to Heaven. The wind started to blow, and in the wind she could hear Father Brown's voice as if it danced on the breeze.

"You have done well, my child. But then I always knew you would."

That night after dinner, Brandy and Thunder stood outside looking at their new home.

"Can you believe that its ours?" Brandy asked.

"Not yet. Everything has happened so quickly," Thunder said. "I thought I wanted one thing, and when I got it, it wasn't what I wanted at all. I had what I really wanted near me all the time." His eyes swept Brandy's body in one long caress.

"I knew what I wanted," she said, taking his hand

in hers. "Just had a hard time convincing him," she said tenderly.

He stepped forward and clasped her in his arms. "You're rich now. Are you sure you still want me?"

His breath was warm and moist against her face, and her heart raced as she gave him a saucy little smile. "I want you more than money."

He had the oddest expression when he said, "We should go to town first thing tomorrow."

"Why?"

The silver shone in his eyes as he gazed at her. "So I can make you my wife before you change your mind."

She looked at him with all the love she had. "I won't change my mind," she assured him.

He lowered his head and his mouth moved over hers hungrily. "It's been a long time since we made love," he whispered huskily.

She melted into his embrace and clung to him, never wanting this moment to end. She desperately wanted more of him, and now she would have a lifetime of loving him.

When the kiss finally ended, Thunder whispered in her ear. "Are you happy, Brandy?"

Her long fingers traveled up to the nape of his neck, and she smiled. "When I'm in your arms, I feel like I could dance on the wind. My happiness is you."

AUTHOR'S NOTE

I hope you enjoyed Brandy and the children's story as they struggled to become a family. I knew I was hooked on these characters when Brandy had to tell Ward and MacTavish goodbye, and I cried. It was tough typing with one hand as I held Kleenex in the other.

Thank you for all the cards and letters. I really enjoy hearing from you. One of my favorite notes sits beside my computer. It says, "Thanks for giving me a reason to smile." That note was great. I realized that I had achieved the goal I set when I started writing—to take a reader away from the everyday world and make her smile, relax, and get lost in my make-believe world.

My contest was so successful that I want to offer another one. Please check my Web sites to see what the big prize is. But as always, the first fan who writes a letter about this book will get a special gift from me, and the first five will receive an autographed cover.

Keep those cards and letters coming. I do answer all fan letters. A SASE is appreciated.

May all your dreams come true,

Brenda K. Jernigan
80 Pine Street W
Lillington, NC 27546
Bkj1608@juno.com—e-mail
http://www.bkjbooks.com
http://www.members.tripod.com/brendajernigan